COLD
COURAGE

1914 IMPERIAL TRANS-ANTARCTIC EXPEDITION

COLD COURAGE

Extraordinary Times

WILLY MITCHELL

COLD COURAGE
EXTRAORDINARY TIMES

Author Credits: Favaloro LLC

iUniverse books may be ordered through booksellers or by contacting:

iUniverse
1663 Liberty Drive
Bloomington, IN 47403
www.iuniverse.com
1-800-Authors (1-800-288-4677)

ISBN: 978-1-5320-9032-5 (sc)
ISBN: 978-1-5320-9031-8 (hc)
ISBN: 978-1-5320-9030-1 (e)

Library of Congress Control Number: 2019920215

Print information available on the last page.

iUniverse rev. date: 12/11/2019

We are the Pilgrims, master; we shall go
Always a little further: it may be
Beyond the last blue mountain barred with snow,
Across the angry or that glimmering sea,
White on a throne or guarded in a cave
There lives a prophet who can understand
Why men were born: but surely, we are brave,
Who make the Golden Journey to Samarkand.

—James Elroy Flecker, "The Golden
Journey to Samarkand"

We leave our pleasant homelands,
For the roaring south east winds,
All words of love and friendship,
For yearning hearts and minds,
For clasps of loving fingers,
Dreams must alone.

—Sir Ernest Shackleton, 1902

We sail atop the big white crests.
We set about our exploring quests.
The north to the South we do go.
Heads of stone, hearts of steel.
All the men and all the crew,
When others watch, the exploring we do.

Seeking new lands where no one has been,
Sighting the mountains that no person has seen,

Sailing the oceans and trekking the land
For the next discovery of humankind.

Following the footsteps of no one before,
We travel the ocean looking for more.

What point do we do this for?
Always wanting to open a door.
New places to discover and to roam.
All of us signed up to a long way back home.

If ever we return, it will be with applause.
And maybe just that is what we are doing this for.

—From *Dramming*, a book of previously unseen poetry

Imperial Trans-Antarctic Expedition 1914 - The Journey of The Endurance

London

Plymouth

The Endurance
On Foot
The James Caird
The Yelcho

Madeira

North Athlantic ocean

South Athlantic ocean

Buenos Aires

Stromness
King Haakon Sound
Grytviken
South Georgia

Punta Arenas

Elephant Island

Weddell Sea

Vahsel Bay

Antarctica

Imperial Trans-Antarctic Expedition 1914 –
The Aurora and The Ross Sea Party

Australia

Sydney

OOOOO Vahsel Bay Party Route
XXXXX Ross Sea Party Route
------ The Aurora
↓↓↓↓ Aurora Drift

Hobart

New Zealand

Wellington

Antarctica

South pole

McMurdo SOund

Ross sea

Vahsel bay

Elephant
Island

CONTENTS

Part IV Cold Calm

ACKNOWLEDGMENTS

COLD COURAGE **IS THE THIRD** book by Willy Mitchell, after *Operation Argus* and *Bikini Bravo*. Brave men and women converge as all of these stories unfold, no less so than in this novel, *Cold Courage: Extraordinary Times*.

Thanks to all those whose stories inspired these books, including everyone who has sacrificed for liberty, freedom, good, and right.

Although *Cold Courage* is a novel, it is based on true events.

www.willymitchell.com

Thanks to my wife, my daughter, and those who have encouraged me through my writing journey. Thanks also to Charles and Jay, who have been kind enough to beta-read my books. To Gary, my lifelong friend and partner in crime. To Jimmy, who provided great support, including his black-and-white photography, and to Jeffry for his inspiration, Prentiss for being a great inspirational leader, and Hans for just being a wonderful person. Thank you, all my friends.

And thanks to all my readers and supporters, including, my uncle Billy; my cousin John; and my friends Claire K., Liddle Jo, and Jeff Z.; the amazing adventurer Georgina; the inspiring triathlete Laura; my school friend Jo; Randy, the awesome photographer and inspiring entrepreneur; the very cool Eric D.; and of course the darling Kathy.

And finally, thank you for your reviews and support: Andrew Hemmings BA (Hons) FCILT, author and researcher; Alta Wehmeyer, writing teacher passionate about tales of the Antarctic; and Stephen Scott-Fawcett, a graduate of polar studies, fellow of the Royal Geographical Society, committee member of the James Caird Society, founder of the Facebook group Sir Ernest H. Shackleton Appreciation Society, and author.

Thank you to all I have mentioned and to all I have missed!

PART I

CLASSIFIEDS

PROLOGUE

1929
Port Wellington, New Zealand

MY GRANDAD WALTER BEATTIE MITCHELL left Glasgow to see the world decades back. His travels took him far, and he enjoyed, or barely lived through, numerous adventures. He regaled me with some of his stories when I was a boy. We used to work together in his garden long after he returned home for the last time.

"Did I ever tell you about when I was in New Zealand in 1929, and I happened upon a homeless man in the port of Wellington?" he asked as he planted another sunflower. He looked over at me and grinned, almost like an imp or Scottish leprechaun, if ever such an abomination existed in reality or legend. He knew I didn't know the story. He told many tall tales, and even as a boy, I'd come to ignore most of them as the fanciful ramblings of an old man who had seen much, done much, and had plenty to say, especially after a fair share of pints in his favorite pub. But he hadn't told me about what happened in New Zealand in 1929, and I was curious—quite curious indeed.

I said I didn't think he'd shared that particular adventure. He beamed at me and jumped right into the tale. I still remember it well all these years later.

Walter introduced himself to the homeless man and invited him to join him for a plateful of grub and a pint or two. He figured it was the least he could do for a fellow Scotsman who was down on his luck. The homeless man, whose name was Harry McNish, said that he'd love to have something to eat. He said he was hungry, and Walter believed him. Harry accompanied Walter as they walked the short distance to the Thistle Inn, opened sixty years earlier, on the corner of Mulgrave Street, across from the port originally known as Port Nicholson.

The Thistle was dressed all in white with the distinctive thistle above the wooden double doors leading in to the wooden interior with a floor and seating area. The pair sat in the corner by the fire. Walter felt quite at home, and he saw that Harry noticeably relaxed in the cozy environs. Walter knew that the man before him was a person of interest. He knew that Harry had a story to tell. He knew that he wanted to spend some time and listen in exchange for a beer or two, some nice warm food, and some good company.

My grandfather had been on this journey alone for a while, and it was obvious by looking at this homeless man before him that he had been too. As the two had walked from the port, many people had nodded, winked, and tossed a coin to my grandfather's newfound friend Harry McNish.

"Quite the celebrity round here, aren't yer?" Walter said.

"Aye, son. I guess you're right, sure enough." He smiled and winked as they each took a sip of their first beers.

Walter was dressed in his Stewart Christie & Co. Magee Tweed three-piece suit, Church's shoes, and flatcap, carrying the deck pocket watch that his father had given him. This was the suit he had worn for his wedding ten years earlier to his wee rose Margaret Watson, now Maggie Mitchell.

Walter was considered by Maggie's father, a fruiterer, to be beneath their social ranking, as on Walter's return from France, after the war, he'd found himself a job on the *Clyde* in the dockyards with steel-toe boots and flatcaps. The couple managed to get over their social differences and married at the Gorbals Parish Church in fine glory. One bairn later and another on the way, Walter wanted to get out and find a new life for them and himself.

Harry McNish was dressed in what looked like a British Royal Navy–issue peacoat with sailor pants, a scarf, and a woolen hat pulled over his white hair above his weathered face. He had the face of a sailor, an adventurer, an explorer.

"To Mrs. Chippy," Harry announced as he raised his glass and took a sip of beer.

"Mrs. Chippy," Walter echoed, somewhat bemused. "Uh, but who's Mrs. Chippy?"

"An old friend of mine, son. An old friend."

The Thistle had a group of a dozen sailors, seemingly just arrived from Australia with their Aussie drawl and their loud beer songs, catching the ear and the amusement of Harry as he listened, watched, and smiled with a faint glint in his eye.

"Are you an ex-sailor yourself, Harry?"

"Aye, you could say that, son. A sailor of sorts in times lang gan."

"What's your story?" asked Harry.

"Trying to find a new hame, a new job, family at hame and all," he answered, pointing to the *Wellington Evening Post* stuffed in his suit pocket.

"Aye, lad, it's worth a try getting out of that hellhole Glasgee."

The waitress arrived at the table with the list of Thistle delights, and they both opted for mince and tatties—an old Glasgow favorite—and two more pints of Hancock's Bitter.

"I'm looking for work and a place to live."

"I escaped in '14. What sort of work?"

"Worked on the *Clyde* for a while after I came back from France."

"The shipyards?"

"Aye."

"I was like you, looking for an escape. Got a newspaper, the *London Times*, and answered one of those ads."

"What, like a job ad?"

"Aye, of sorts. Low pay, high danger, no guarantees of return. That sort of thing."

Walter looked puzzled. "What sort of *job* was it?"

Harry paused for a moment, took a sip of his beer, and looked Walter in the eye.

"Which yard did yer work in?"

"Denny's. You?"

"Fairfield."

"Ha! Know it well," Harry said.

Walter took another sip of beer, leaned back in his chair, and said, "Okay, so tell me. What sort of job did you apply for?"

The waitress arrived with the mince and tatties: stewed minced beef and onions, overpeppered with white pepper to add bite, and fluffy mashed potatoes dolloped on the side. She brought them each a fork, a spoon, and a round of white buttered bread. Perfect.

An apparently local patron walked in looking as if he'd come straight from work—from the port, Walter assumed—and doffed his merchant seaman's hat in the direction of Harry. Moments later, two more Hancock's appeared before the pair.

Harry looked up and raised his glass. "Cheers, Archie," he shouted to the other end of the bar. "To Mrs. Chippy."

"Mrs. Chippy" came the response from Archie.

"So, who the hell is Mrs. Chippy?" asked Walter.

Harry McNish looked at him with a frown. Walter looked back and wondered what error he had made.

"Son, there is no need to curse. The English language has plenty of room for maneuver to avoid the hells and the buggers and the bollocks."

Walter looked at Harry and nodded. He agreed and was amused by his interesting choice of words to describe his apparent dislike for cursing.

"My cat." Harry looked at Walter as though he had asked the dumbest question.

"Oh, okay." Walter took a forkful of the meat and potatoes before him. "So, where's the cat now?" Walter asked, figuring

Harry would get around to starting his story when he was good and ready.

Harry looked at him again. "He's dead."

Walter felt that somehow he should have known that answer. For the life of him, though, he didn't know why.

"He?"

"Och, well, that's a different story altogether." Harry laughed to himself. "Yer see, we thought she was a she until we found out that she was a he! And by that time, it was too late, at least according to Shacks."

They continued to enjoy their food.

"It were a bit like that stowaway boy, young Blackborow, yer know." They carried on eating. McNish let out a big, approving belch and continued speaking: "By the time the boss discovered him, it were too late. What was he going to do, throw him overboard?" He'd asked the question expecting Walter to answer.

Walter didn't really understand the question, so instead he asked, "So, what about this job?"

"What?"

"Well, what was it?"

Harry took a moment to properly swallow his last forkful, taking in his newfound friend, who disliked belching as much as McNish clearly disliked cursing.

"Sailing to the South Pole."

Walter looked at him in awe. He had remembered the legends and the heroes of the Antarctic expeditions, Captain Scott, William Bruce, Amundson, and Shackleton, and the race to the South Pole. At that point he made the connection and reference to Shacks.

"So, what happened to Mrs. Chippy?"

Harry looked at Walter once more. His eyes lit up like saucers. He seemed frantic, like a madman, for a moment. "He shot my bloody cat!" he announced at the top of his voice for all the bar to hear.

Walter sat back suddenly and inched his chair backward, not quite knowing what to do. The place went silent. The folks in the bar looked around as Harry calmed down as quickly as he had reacted. The humming of conversation restarted, and the moment was over.

Harry took another mouthful; he was obviously hungry. It was clear this was a very sore point for him, and Walter wouldn't mention it again, unless Harry did, of course. Apart from his toasts, he never did bring it up again.

The pair sat together and talked some more. After they had finished eating and were full of Hancock's Bitter, the landlord sent over a bottle of Balblair whisky, a favorite of Harry's. Apparently the distillery had closed back in 1911, but the Thistle still had a fair stock left. The story was that the owner had bartered a dozen barrels in exchange for an errant crew's unpaid bill. It was a shrewd deal on behalf of the landlord, another Scotsman, apparently named Hamish, Hamish Mackay.

Harry pulled out his pipe and lit up, puffing from the corner of his mouth and blowing rings of smoke like wisps in the air as a wizard would, or so Walter imagined—television came much later, along with the ability for people to visualize stories from the script and not on the silver screen. In addition to long journeys and often solitude, people like

Walter took to reading for learning, for education, and for the imagination. Robbie Burns was one of Walter's favorites.

Walter looked at his deck watch. The time was four. He looked at Harry, who was slurring and starting to fall asleep in front of the fire.

"Come on, Harry, let's get yer hame," offered Walter.

"Aye, lad. I canny take me whisky like I used to."

Harry seemed to take an age to stand up. As he fully stretched out, his wood chair tipped backward, making a loud bang on the floor. No one seemed to pay any attention, as they had obviously seen a lot worse in the Thistle, which resembled many a bar back in Glasgow, Walter thought.

He helped Harry out. As they walked to his shelter, which seemed comfortable enough, he mused that there were surely better options for a man like this.

"Och, dun nay mind," protested Harry. "If you only knew the places I've slept—this, this is like the Ritz!" Shooing Walter away, he sat on a makeshift stool and rattled around in a bin with the clink of empty bottles. He pulled out a half bottle of Balblair, pulled the cork with his teeth, took a swig, and raised the bottle to Walter.

"Slainte!" (Cheers!)

Walter looked down at him and said, "Do dheagh slainte." (Your very good health.) Then he walked back to the Thistle, to his lodgings and bed.

Having first visited Australia, arriving in Perth and then going on to Sydney, Walter had drawn a blank on his dream, and Wellington was his last chance. The economic downturn had hit his dreams, and he had decided to return home, taking the nine-week voyage via Cape Town, South Africa, on to Plymouth, and eventually back to Glasgow.

Over the next week, he would meet Harry each day, taking him to the Thistle for a long lunch, including beer and whisky, and letting his story unfold.

McNish spoke of Burlington Road, the *Endurance*, Shackleton, Worsley, and Wild. He spoke of the two young soldiers, Jimmy Smith and Richie Blundell, he'd met at the interviews. He told the tale of Winston Churchill's orders to proceed and how he had crafted a box of the finest mahogany for the king's flag. He talked about Buenos Aires, the stowaway from Wales, and Shackleton's reaction. He talked about the brawl in Grytviken and the journey back.

Harry made it sound like it was some sort of fun excursion, and Walter recognized the traits similar to an old soldier, similar to his own experiences after France and the Great War. He knew that as time passed, the mind only wanted to remember the good times, the happy times, and not the terrors, the dangers, or the sadness. Walter reflected on his own sadness for a time.

"Yer knaw, I have a lot of respect for them men, yer knaw?" Harry looked over at Walter amid one of their lunchtime sessions. "That big Kiwi Worsley, hell o' a man. How on earth he managed to navigate the *Caird*. Eight hundred and fifty miles, yer knaw? Amazing." Walter nodded, understanding the enormity of the apparent feat.

"Then big Tom Crean, Wild, even Shackleton himsen." Walter looked at McNish quizzically. "Well, yer knaw, he never took to me, and then the Mrs. Chippy incident an all. But yer knaw, Walter, the boss was a good man, and I have"—he corrected himself—"had a lot of respect fer 'im." Walter nodded.

"Poor feller. Heard he had a heart attack and dropped dead. In South Georgia of all places." McNish was intently nodding his head in approval. "That was his second hame. That was the right place fer 'im to be laid to rest," he said, concluding his point. "Even though we didnay see eye to eye, he was a good man.

"But that Franky Wild, he was a good en. He and I used to get on better. Ol' Franky is in South Africa nowadays. I heard yer should pop in an see 'im on yer way past." He looked at Walter, and the look on his face revealed, as the penny dropped, how he thought that was a really good idea.

"How do yer knaw all this stuff, Harry?" Walter was confused about his new friend's knowledge of all the different things going on around the world.

Harry pointed out the window at the port across the way. "Och, man. I live on the portside with ships coming in from all around the world ev'ry day. I get news all the time. Dint yer knaw that the likes of Shacks, Worsley, and Wild are legends? Everyone knows who they are, and news travels fast when yer that famous."

Walter nodded his head and realized that he had witnessed the same. He also realized that Harry McNish was also one of those legends but probably didn't quite realize to the extent that he was.

The night before Walter was to sail out from Wellington, he took Harry back to his temporary home one last time. Harry kneeled and was ferreting around and came out with a packet wrapped in what looked like leather with a piece of old twine around it.

"Hey, Walter, I want yee to take this," he said, passing up the package with two hands as if it were something sacred.

Walter looked down at Harry, who he noticed had the glimmer of a tear in his eye. He knew this was something special to McNish.

"What is it, Harry? It looks pretty old."

"It's me book," he responded, looking Walter in the eye with a tear welling up. "I want yer to take it to Franky Wild on yer way past Cape Town."

Walter was again confused that Harry thought it was that easy just to pop by another continent and bump into someone. But, Walter realized, this is what these men were like: no matter how big the world, they made it feel small in how they looked at it. After all, spanning the Antarctic from one side to the other was a fantastically crazy idea in the first place, wasn't it? So how big was the world, really?

Walter accepted the packet and the instruction, and he agreed to do as Harry asked.

"Och, I knay where he is working, some diamond mine doon there or something. Send 'im a telegram to let him knay, and I am sure he'd be glad to meet up with yer. He's a very good man, Franky Wild—*the right-hand man* they used to call 'im, yer knay."

Walter unwrapped the book. As he opened it, McNish announced, "It's time to take it out of wraps, young Wally Mitchell."

"It's my book of poems. I wrote it. Never showed anyone before noo." He looked up at Walter with sad eyes. "I want yer to take it, Walter. I want yer to take it to show Franky, then I want yer to take it hame to Glasgee and see if yer can get it published, maybe alongside Rabbie," he said with a toothless smile, referring to the Scottish poet laureate Robert Burns.

Walter had a quick but careful flick through the leather-bound notebook with handwritten notes, hand-sketched maps, comments, and what he assumed were poems. He looked at the title page at the front:

Dramming
A Book of Poetry
by
Harry McNish

"The baird and his cat!" McNish took a swig of whisky and sounded like a pirate, laughing hysterically with a mad look in his eye,

"I shouldnay take this, Harry. It's too important to yer." In an attempt to avoid the big responsibility he was being given, Walter was shaking his head.

"Aye, you will. I want yer to. I'm serious. There's some bloody good poems in there, and I really want yer to try and get it published for me."

Walter paused, a long pause, as he thought about the size of the request.

"Well, I suppose I could ask me father-in-law. He might know someone for sure." Walter tried to look as hopeful as he could.

"If yer get any money for it, be sure to send it down here. I want to share it with the crew and their widows. Keep 20 percent for yersen. You promise me, Wally. You promise me! You'll keep yer promise, won't yer, Wally?"

"Aye, Harry, you have my word."

"Now off with yer, Walter. No bloody long goodbyes. Away with yer. Get back to yer sweetheart and give her a kiss for me."

"Who? Maggie?" Walter looked confused.

"Nay, man, Scotland. Glasgee!"

After taking another swig of whisky, Harry passed out.

Walter rewrapped the package and realized that the leather was too soft, too thin, and too delicate for leather. Some alternative sort of animal hide, he assumed.

Walter made Harry as comfortable as comfortable could be, and then he made his way into the evening and back to the Thistle Inn for what would be his last night in New Zealand.

The next day, Walter's ship was departing. Harry McNish came to the port side to wave off his newfound friend and now confidante. As the ship sailed out of the harbor, Harry raised a half-empty bottle of Balblair whisky. "To Mrs. Chippy!"

Walter found his hip flask fully filled with Balblair, courtesy of Hamish. He took a wee nip and shouted back, "To Mrs. Chippy, my friend. To Mrs. Chippy and Mr. Harry McNish."

"May you sail with a fair wind." Harry waved from the port side. "And dinnay forget yer promise."

I
LONDON CALLING

Glasgow, Sixteen Years Earlier
September 15, 1913

HARRY MCNISH KNEW ABOUT THE strange goings-on in the heavens that were predicted for the coming evening. He'd heard chattering about the total lunar eclipse all day long. Frankly, he didn't see why people were making such a fuss, but then again, he didn't see why people fussed in general about every this, that, and other thing. People fussed all the time, and he didn't see the point. But he did see how it was possible for some to get excited about a celestial event that had not occurred, supposedly, since 1797.

On his way home, Harry picked up a copy of the *London Times* to see if that gave any more detail on the eclipse and if they would see anything in Glasgow that night. He would stop off for a pint at the Anchor on his way home and have a read.

There was a mass exodus of men from the shipyards and the associated industries in their flatcaps and hobnail boots, walking on the cobbles, marching to a beat. They were heading home from whatever industrial slavery they had been doing that day, heading home to food on the table, to wives, to kids, and then to the pub later—a Glaswegian tradition to have the priority of spending of their hard-earned wages, even if that meant tobacco, beer, and whisky.

The crunching on the cobbles sounded like an army marching, and an army maybe it was. There were horses pulling carts full of loads on the way to the shipyards from factories unseen for the next day of production. The smell of rain on the cobbles mixed with the oil, the sweat, and the aromas of hard graft.

As McNish got closer to home, the crowd had thinned as the men had made their way to their tenement homes in the sea of red brick. Each house had one room and a kitchen downstairs and two rooms upstairs. If you were lucky and you could afford it, then you had two rooms downstairs and three up, with each room being just big enough to swing a cat.

That thought amused Harry as he pictured his cat, Mrs. Chippy. She was a tortoiseshell, his companion. Although a bit dainty, she was as big as a dog, and sometimes Harry thought that she was a dog.

Harry had always been fascinated with words. He had always been interested in the origins of words and especially naval sayings.

He was partial to *shipshape* and *Bristol fashion*, referring to the most prosperous British port on the west coast, which had a very high tidal range, as much as forty feet, the second highest in the world. McNish remembered stowing everything away neatly, or tied down, in anticipation of the tide and how the ships moored would be aground with the keels falling to one side.

He also liked the phrases "shot across the bows," "high and dry," and "dead in the water," and many references to the ship's cat. Cats had been on ships since the beginning of maritime excursions, a natural way to reduce the growth of vermin while at sea. There was also a reference to the cat-o'-nine-tails, the infamous whip used to punish errant sailors, from whence came the phrases "not enough room to swing a cat" and "as mad as a ship's cat."

He had been married to Lizzie, Lizzie Littlejohn, six years already. His first two wives had died by that time, so this was technically his longest marriage. It was fine. It was tough. Making ends meet made little time for romancing. In the morning, he'd go to the yard then go for a pint. He'd go home for dinner and head back out for a quick nightcap before bed. Repeat that six days a week; that was life in Glasgow at that time.

He knew it was a life of misery, an existence at best. If he could only get out. But part of him also knew that as soon as he left, he would miss it. Harry was like that, a voluntary stoic who almost thrived on the misery of his endurance. It's what fueled his cynicism, a condition that had driven away all his ambition, hopes, and dreams. But maybe it wasn't too late, he pondered.

He thought of Lizzie and her strange ways, and he applied the old saying in its more common interpretation: "As mad

3

as a ship's cat," he muttered to himself, laughing and shaking his head as he pictured his idiosyncratic bride probably sitting at home and muttering to herself as she often did.

He liked the *London Times*, as it gave him a broader view of what was going on in the world, at least from the perspective of the sassenachs south of the border.

Glasgow and the shipyards weren't doing it for him, were not fulfilling his wanderlust. After all, Scotsmen like him had been traveling the globe for centuries, fighting wars on behalf of their paymasters and then the British, and in more recent times seeking their fortunes on the high seas or in some mining town in godforsaken lands such as Australia, the United States, and Africa.

Harry walked into the Anchor, which was crowded as usual at this time of night, with the boys from the yards swearing, cussing, drinking, and fighting. He didn't care for the cussing; in fact he despised it. He belonged to the United Free Church of Scotland. He detested bad language.

At thirty-nine, Harry needed his last adventure. Lizzie was home. She would be cooking dinner on the stove right now. He would have a couple of pints and then head home later. Of course she would have something to say when he was late, but they would work it out. She didn't really care too much. That's how it was between them.

Given his years, Harry had a level of seniority in the yards. He went to his quiet corner at the bar, sat on his stool, and ordered a pint of Belhaven Bitter.

A couple of moments later, the strong brown brew was handed over the bar just as Harry had unfolded his newspaper. He took a sip as he started reading, glancing over the headlines of the day, of socialist strikes in London and tensions in Europe. A story caught his eye. It was about the apparently famous French aviator Adolphe Pégoud, the first man to loop the loop in an aircraft.

"Whatever next!" He pointed out the article to the barman, Eddie.

"Aye. Those wonderful men in their flying machines, eh?"

Harry lit his pipe and kept on browsing. He came to the classifieds section, and an advertisement popped out from the page:

London Times, September 15, 1913

MEN WANTED: For hazardous journey, small wages, bitter cold, long months of complete darkness, and constant danger. Safe return doubtful. Honor and recognition in case of success. Sir Ernest Shackleton.

Harry squinted his eyes, ordered another Belhaven, and reread the advertisement several times as if it were an apparition.

"Well, I'm nay frightened of hazardous journeys. Not sure about the small wages, but it's got to be better than 'round here." He looked around the Anchor to prove his point.

"Constant danger. Safe return doubtful. Honor and recognition in case of success. Sounds just the ticket for me!" he proclaimed to the busy bar, though no one was listening.

"What did yer say, Harry?" asked Eddie.

"Och, I'll have another beer and a wee dram of that Bowmore."

"Are yer celebrating, Harry?"

"Aye, kinda," he answered as he glanced down at the advertisement again.

"Och, Lizzie would be fine with it," he convinced himself. "Eddie, give us another Bowmore, will yer?"

Framnæs Shipyard
Sandefjord, Norway

Lars Christensen didn't know what hit him. His operating partner, Adrien de Gerlache, was talking, but the words sounded garbled, almost unintelligible. Could it be that his partner had just informed him that he was pulling out of their joint venture? It seemed so, and for Christensen, the frank pronouncement amounted to nothing less than the end of his financial world.

"For God's sake, man, you cannot pull out now. She's just a month from being finished." He stared at his partner, finding it hard not to leap up from his fancy mahogany desk to throttle the simpleton.

"Lars, I cannot continue. I have run out of money, and I owe the yard too much to bail her out."

"You could get financing and get her on the seas. Just like we had always planned, Adrien."

"I am afraid it is too late, my friend. I have already told the bank, or should I say the bank has already told me. It's simply too late."

Lars looked at his business partner, realizing that Adrien was now a former business partner and that he himself would have to find the £20,000 that the Framnæs Shipyard needed for her release.

The two had commissioned the ship to be built to pursue their venture of running polar cruises for tourist hunters. Lars was from a wealthy family. To him it was less about the money; de Gerlache was his operator. *What the hell am I to do with a boat built for a specific purpose and no operator?* Lars thought, frustrated.

Polaris was a barkentine—three masts, the foremast square-rigged. It was 144 feet long with a 25-foot beam and weighed 348 tons with a 350-horsepower coal-fired steam engine capable of very modest speeds up to ten knots—an ice-capable steam yacht with luxurious accommodations to attract wealthy tourist hunting parties. It had ten passenger cabins, a spacious dining saloon, a galley, a smoking room, a darkroom to allow passengers to develop their photographs, electric dynamo lighting, and bathrooms.

Then there was the construction, specifically for polar conditions. From the outside it was like any other ship of its size, but underneath it had maritime engineering with extra-thick solid oak keel members; twice as many frames as a normal ship of its time; and a bow with each timber made from a single oak tree.

Polaris was perhaps the strongest wooden ship ever built, but apart from hungry polar hunter tourists, who else would want her? She was too heavy and too slow for warmer waters. She was overequipped for commercial or expeditionary use in the polar regions.

As the conversation was clearly finished, Christensen walked around his desk and gave de Gerlache a big man hug. Lars knew that Adrien was in pain breaking this news to him. He knew that he wouldn't have done it unless he'd had to. He understood but was still frustrated at his lack of options and confused about his next steps.

"What will you do?" asked Adrien, trying to help.

"I don't know, Adrien. I really don't know," he said as he ran his fingers through his hair. "I will work something out, my friend," he said, completely unsure of what he would do next to avoid being thrown into a financial hole he couldn't climb out of. He was stuck with a ship he was quite sure nobody else would want and with a dream that had now been dashed to pieces against the rocks of a stormy lee shore.

They hugged again, then Adrien walked out of the room, went down the external steps, and walked onto the shipyard slipway back toward the main road.

"Farewell, my friend," Lars whispered. He remained leaning on the windowsill overlooking Framnæs Shipyard long after Adrien had disappeared from view.

Adrien de Gerlache was an explorer in his own right, having been a part of numerous expeditions to the South Pole. The son of a Belgian army officer, he knew from an early age that he was destined to a life at sea, joining an ocean liner and taking trips to the United States at the age of just seventeen. He'd made trips to San Francisco, South America, and the Antarctic. In 1897, he set sail on his ship with the crew of the *Belgica* only for it to be trapped by ice in the Bellingshausen Sea, returning to Antwerp two years later. Expeditions to Persia, Greenland, and back to the Antarctic followed.

At forty-six, his expedition days were over. The *Polaris* had been his latest dream, one that was now shattered.

Expeditions were an expensive business, and the need to find willing funders was a constant challenge, especially with so much competition to conquer the last undiscovered territories. The *Polaris* dream was intended to open that adventure to a wider, more discerning, and infinitely wealthier clientele.

Their idea was to replace explorers and scientists with paying tourists, but Adrien's financial past had caught up with him, and neither he nor his funders could support the *Polaris* project any longer.

Christensen, on the other hand, had been born into a wealthy Norwegian family, inheriting his family's whaling fleet after finishing school. He was an investor, a shipowner, an entrepreneur, and a philanthropist. He also had a deep interest in Antarctica and its wildlife. Where *Polaris* was de Gerlaches's dream, it was Christensen's vision, and his own money had gotten the project off the ground.

De Gerlaches's withdrawal was the factor that prompted Christensen to be done with the project and sell the vessel for the best possible price. The headache of what now to do with the *Polaris* was now firmly back in the hands of Lars Christensen.

2
BEGINNING

Sarajevo, Bosnia and Herzegovina
Sunday, June 28, 1914

THE WHEELS OF THE TRAIN clacked in a steady rhythm as Archduke Franz Ferdinand gazed listlessly out the window at the countryside. He had much on his mind. The politics of late had heated up, and he was worried that things might get out of hand. He turned and looked at his wife, Sophie, the duchess of Hohenberg. Her beauty momentarily distracted him. She was wearing a dress of light blue and gray, an embroidered jacket, and a wide-brimmed hat with white flowers. As always, she had her hair pinned up in a neat bun beneath her hat. The trip from Ilidža Spa to Sarajevo would be mercifully short, and for that the archduke was grateful.

The couple were tied with the rules as set down before them. It had been judged by Emperor Franz Joseph that although Sophie was from an aristocratic family, she was not considered to be of high enough pedigree to share the

11

rank of the archduke, and, therefore, she was not permitted to be beside Franz Ferdinand at formal occasions. Nor would any of their children ever take the throne. These were harsh rules placed on a couple who were in love with each other, often a rarity in a time when, and amid a class where, couples married for convenience and power.

Today was an exception to the harsh rules, and a loophole. Sophie's opportunity to walk with the archduke was freed when he was on military duties. Today he was visiting the military barracks, dressed in his military uniform. He was considered as being on military duty, and hence Sophie was able to accompany him, walking alongside.

The train pulled into Sarajevo train station, and there to meet them was Governor Oskar Potiorek. After exchanging limited small talk, the archduke and duchess walked to their car, a Gräf & Stift Double Phaeton black convertible. Five other vehicles were in the convoy. The chief of police and three officers were in car number one. In car number two were Franz Ferdinand, Sophie, the governor, and Lieutenant Colonel Count Franz von Harrach. First stop: the military barracks. The other cars held security personnel.

Under the 1878 Treaty of Berlin, Austria-Hungary received the mandate to occupy and administer Bosnia, while the Ottoman Empire retained its sovereignty. Under the same treaty, the great powers of Austria-Hungary, Great Britain, France, Germany, Italy, and the Russian Empire gave official recognition to Serbia as a fully sovereign state. That meant that the Austro-Hungarian force was occupying this land. There were a growing number of Serbians who objected to that, including the chief of Serbian military intelligence

Dragutin Dimitrijević, his right-hand man Major Vojislav Tankosić, and the spy Rade Malobabić.

The mood changed after the assassination of the king and queen of Serbia in 1903. The new Serbian dynasty was more nationalist, more aligned to Russia, and less friendly with the Austria-Hungary occupiers.

Security that day was light, as despite the local military commanders' recommendations for the military to line the route, the local officials objected, saying it would risk offending the local citizens. Hence only the local police were on duty today.

As the motorcade made its way through the streets, crowds lined the way as the archduke and his entourage headed to the barracks. Ferdinand saw out of the corner of his eye a man wearing a flatcap hat and lobbing an object in their general direction. Instinctively the archduke ducked and leaned over toward Sophie with a protective arm as a matter of instinct.

The projectile missed their car and hit the paved street with the sound of heavy metal on the cobbles. Ferdinand lost sight, then a loud explosion went off under one of the vehicles behind them, throwing the vehicle into the air. Men, women, and children in the crowd were suddenly transported from waving at the procession to screaming and running in terror.

After the initial shock of the moment, the explosion still ringing in their ears, the governor and Lieutenant Colonel Count Franz von Harrach ordered the driver to go, go, go and leave the scene. Ferdinand could barely hear the bellow of his big booming voice, the explosion still throbbing in his ears. "Go, go, go," the archduke mimicked as he realized that he and his wife were in serious danger.

The open-top Gräf & Stift Double Phaeton maneuvered around the other vehicles and sped away from the scene. Ferdinand looked back and could see the other cars were following with the one destroyed vehicle wallowing on its side with what looked like a broken back, a fatal injury. The police were busy running around, as were the crowd, but some lay still and motionless on the ground.

"What the hell just happened?" the archduke asked, knowing that the occupants of the car probably had as much idea as he did.

He leant over to Sophie and saw the scared look in her eyes. "Are you all right, my darling?" he inquired. She just looked at him with an unconvincing smile and nodded back, her loving but scared eyes telling him everything.

The barracks was a longer drive, and in the interests of their safety and to avoid any other incidents, Colonel Count Franz ordered the driver to head to the city hall and eliminate the risk of going to the barracks. The occupants of the car were all shaken up, including Franz Ferdinand himself. He held Sophie's hand, both of them shaking, suddenly feeling the chill in the air. The smell of the munitions lingered in the car.

As the motorcade arrived in front of the city hall, the party got out. The mayor commenced his welcome speech, perhaps somewhat prematurely. The archduke interrupted him with his big bellowing voice: "Mr. Mayor, I came here on a visit, and I am greeted with bombs. It's outrageous."

The archduke was shaking in both anger and fear for his life and that of his bride.

The crowd in the town hall fell silent, an awkward moment, looking at each other and their shoes. No one knew what to do or where to look.

Sophie whispered, "I think you should prompt the mayor to continue, my dear."

Franz Ferdinand looked around at the crowd, realizing that he had been rude. He cleared his voice and prompted the mayor to continue. "Go ahead, Mr. Mayor. Go ahead." He guffawed.

As the mayor continued his speech, one of the officers brought Ferdinand his written-out speech, which had been in the bombed car, ruffled and covered in spatters of blood, which reminded him how serious the incident could have been. Ferdinand glanced over at his wife, Sophie, seeing the color coming back to her already pale skin.

He added to his prepared speech and thanked Sarajevo for their cheers and celebrations that the assassination attempt had failed. The crowd applauded with smiles and joy.

With the formalities over, all the archduke could think about was getting back on the train and returning home. They boarded the Gräf & Stift and made their way away from the reception and through the cheering and waving crowd as they drove through the city.

The archduke knew something was very wrong as the vehicle stopped abruptly on Latin Bridge. He saw out of the corner of his eye a man with pistol in hand mounting the rear running board of the sports car. Then came the blast, and then the numbness. He could feel the blood as it started gushing from his neck. His immediate reaction was to plug the wound. He felt helpless as the assassin tuned the pistol on Sophie and shot her at point-blank range. The car sped away, tossing the assassin onto the road.

"Sophie, Sophie, don't die. Live for our children!" There came no response. She sat motionless with her head backward, looking toward the sky with her eyes wide open.

Despair surged through Ferdinand. He started choking on his own blood. He'd never felt such intense pain. The driver headed to the nearest hospital at top speed. Everything began to fade and flicker as if the light of the world was running low.

"I love you, my Sophie. I love you, my darling."

After the events of that day, the world would never be the same. Walter Mitchell sensed it as he read the headlines about the assassination of Archduke Ferdinand. He understood that there would likely be a call to arms based on the geopolitical implications and knew that he, as a young man of prime fighting age, would no doubt be sucked up into the vortex of war. As he read, he felt more and more resigned to the fact that he would have to serve and to the possibility that he might die doing it.

As the news stated in stark black ink on flimsy newsprint, the archduke's cavalcade left the train station and passed two would-be assassins armed with guns and bombs, neither of whom apparently had the nerve to go through with the planned attack.

The third would-be assassin was Nedeljko Čabrinovic. He threw his bomb at the archduke's vehicle, and it missed, bouncing under another of the cars, exploding, taking out twenty people, and leaving a crater in the road.

As the motorcade sped off and headed straight to the town hall, Čabrinovic took a cyanide pill and jumped into the river. Unfortunately for him, his suicide attempt failed. The cyanide pill was old and just made him sick, and the river was six inches deep because of the hot, dry summer that year.

The crowd grabbed Čabrinovic, beating him up before he was placed into the custody of the police.

At just nineteen years old, the leader of the team of assassins that day, Gavrilo Princip, had gotten wind of the two *bottled* would-be assassins and the failed attempt on the archduke's life, so he worked out where best to position himself to do the job himself—outside Schiller's Delicatessen near the Latin Bridge.

Once the car had pulled up and Princip waited, the car stopped, giving him the chance to step up on the running board and point his FN Model pistol at Franz Ferdinand's head, shooting him point-blank, but through the jugular, and then shooting his wife, Sophie.

Princip was immediately apprehended as the car sped off for its occupants to seek medical attention.

As the summer progressed, the entire political tightrope that had been in place for decades simply was cut neatly in two. Attempts on the life of Russia's Grigori Rasputin, an armed resistance against British rule in Ireland, and Austria-Hungary's declaring war on Serbia all followed in quick succession. By September 1914, Germany had declared war on Russia, France had declared war on Germany after German troops invaded Belgium, and Britain had declared war on Germany because of its treaty obligations and to stop the spread of lawless militarism throughout Europe.

Not too long after that, Walter found himself fighting in the trenches in Belgium and France as World War I exploded onto the global stage with staggering violence and political effects. Walter never forgot his experiences—the sounds, sights, smells, and the taste of mud, and the feel of the cold steel of his bayonet on a dark winter's night illuminated with the bright splash of flares over no-man's-land. He never forgot the horror of seeing his mates blown to bits during an artillery barrage or mown down under machine-gun fire like so many lemmings dashing to the sea based on the orders of officers who should have known better. When Walter met Harry in that bar in New Zealand, it was no surprise to him that he'd immediately befriended a man who had served with Ernest Shackleton on his ill-fated expedition to traverse the South Pole. Men of the world and men of war tend to be drawn together like moths to a bright porch light on a warm summer's eve.

3

RIGHT-HAND MAN

Train to Burton upon Trent
Burton upon Trent, Great Britain
1914, Three Months Earlier

FRANK WILD BOARDED THE TRAIN from Bedford on
the Midland Mainline Railway. He was on a special mission
of sorts, and the foray at hand excited him. Deep down he
knew that seeing his friend Ernest Shackleton would spur
him to action on yet another new adventure. If Wild was
right, he figured Shackleton was up to something new, and
he wanted to know what.

Hence, he boarded a train heading in the general direction
of his homeland of Yorkshire, but he stopped way short at
Burton upon Trent, ninety-five miles from London and a
one-stop train ride from Bedford via Derby. Shackleton was
doing a lecture there that night. Wild had heard it all before.
In fact, for the most part, he'd actually been there. He looked
forward to a catching up and to *the opportunity* as Shackleton

had put it. Wild always liked opportunities, especially when they were being offered by a man of Shackleton's stature.

It was a long, rickety ride, but Wild was used to long and bumpy rides. After all, he had already completed three polar missions. He had endured a life at sea. At sixteen, Wild had joined the mercantile marine, which would later become known as the merchant navy, rising to the rank of second officer before joining the Royal Navy at the age of twenty-six as an able seaman on HMS *Edinburgh*. With three polar expeditions under his belt now, at the age of forty-one, was he considering his fourth? That was surely the reason the boss had reached out to him and summoned him to Burton, he surmised.

Wild lit his pipe as he looked out the window, taking a puff then another puff. As the puffs accelerated in frequency—eight puffs—the pipe was glowing at the end amid the often-described romantic smell, but the toxicity of the tobacco was wafting through the carriage. He amused himself again. *Just like a steam train,* he thought, smiling to himself as he puffed on his pipe.

He watched the fields passing by on each side of the train, green, flat, lush. Not until later on in the journey, near to then past Burton, would the great forests of the north commence in true fashion. Between the fields there was an occasional village or a stop at a town. This was an express train to Derby and therefore only had a handful of stops along the way. After a quick turnaround in Derby and a hop onto the local train, Wild would be in Burton by 6:00 p.m., and then it was just a short walk over to the town hall.

He reflected and thought about the great lands of ice he had witnessed on the crews of the *Discovery* in 1901, and the Nimrod Expedition that left London in 1907, with the Ross Barrier and Beardmore Glacier. He looked outside the carriage at the mass and miles and miles of green fields and crops before him, and he transposed them into his polar image—and vice versa with the polar image before him. *The difference in survivability is unfathomable,* he thought.

The train rattled around in the wind as the rain fell on the iron rails below. Wild thought there was a romantic kind of rhythm listening to the sounds of the engine and the rotation of the wheels in symmetry. It was mesmerizing, like listening to the whirring of a ship's engines or the music on the winds of the wild.

Every now and then they would stop with folks getting off with their curiousness and possessions, to be replaced by more curiousness and more possessions as the train picked up new travelers on the way. This amused Wild to no end. People-observing was one of his pastimes. He would walk the cobbles of London for hours, or when in Paris for days he would observe the *wildlife* as they would call it in expeditionary terms.

Traveling in 1914 is full of peculiarities, Wild thought, amused.

Born in Skelton close to Marston, the birthplace of Captain James Cook, in the North Riding of Yorkshire, Frank Wild was an adventurer. His mother, Mary Wild, née Cook, was related to the great explorer. The local stories of Captain Cook's adventures inspired Frank as a child.

The family moved around the north as Frank's father, Benjamin, moved from one school to the next as a teacher in Lincolnshire, in Wheldrake near to York, and then eventually in Evesholt in Bedfordshire.

After serving in the navy, Wild joined Captain Robert Falcon Scott's crew as an able seaman on the *Discovery*. That was the first time they had met, he and Shackleton, the latter of whom was a sublieutenant on the same ship. Between 1908 and 1909, they met again on the Nimrod Expedition, breaking a record of 88°23' south.

Tonight, Shackleton would be talking about some of those adventures.

Wild managed to successfully traverse from the mainline platform in Derby and hop on the Burton train, which arrived at Burton upon Trent station fifty minutes later. Wild thought it amazing that in this age travel could be so efficient, traveling many miles in relatively few minutes, as compared with few miles in sometimes many days on the polar adventures he had endured.

After a short walk to King Edwards Place and Burton Town Hall, he could already see the crowds of people outside and the billboards with the picture of a familiar figure and the words "South: An Antarctic Adventure."

The boss would be busy preparing. With one hour to go, Wild went for a pint at the nearest pub, the Oak and Ivy. Shackleton was a national hero, so the pub was packed with men, and a handful of women, who were all going to listen to this man's adventures, look at the pictures, and fantasize about making their own trips to some distant land someday.

Wild ordered a pint of Cold Courage, a Worthington's East India pale ale, and thought it both ironic and amusing. He would have a couple of pints of courage before the lecture.

India pale ale had originated in Burton. Worthington was a pioneer, making the ale robust enough to travel to India and still be drinkable when it reached its destination. Beer was one of the many safer alternatives to drinking the local water. It was IPA for the boys and gin and tonics for the bosses, with tonic water's apparently mosquito-repelling qualities, in India and across the empire on which the sun never set. He raised a toast to himself: "The empire." Wild liked his liked toasts and had plenty of them to share, one for every occasion, he prided himself.

As he walked up Wellington Street, he could smell that familiar town hall smell. Why was it that town halls all smelled the same? He tried to analyze this as he had tried to do before, and the best that he could come up with was sweat, sawdust, mold, and dampness, a phenomenon that had always challenged him but to which he had grown accustomed during his time on the oceans, where a similar aroma was present.

Thing is, as a traveler, one spends a lot of time on one's own with only the mind to keep one amused with what one gathers from one's senses. In clear daylight, one has access to one's sense of sight, but at nighttime, or in the depths of a ship or a snow hole, where the sun doesn't shine for months, the senses of sound, smell, and touch take over and call upon the mind of musing, thought, and imagination. Add to that the lack of food and sleep, and the exhaustion, and that is when the mind and mental strength are so important. So very, very important. Especially in Wild's line of business.

Wild had spent a lot of time in such conditions. He was a Yorkshireman, and he'd been born with mental strength, a skill he had sharpened over the years.

The crowd was settling and sitting down, and then the man himself came from stage left and appeared to great applause. Standing ovation. Again, he was a national hero, and most of those here today would gladly march with him anywhere. He was a natural-born leader and he was Wild's boss, *the* boss.

"My name is Ernest Shackleton, and I'm here to talk about my expeditions to the South Pole." The room broke into loud and respectful applause, and he began his lecture.

Wild's and Shackleton's eyes connected in the crowd. Shackleton saluted and introduced the great and famous Mr. Frank Wild to the audience. Wild needed no introduction; the audience knew him as the right-hand man. They burst into a renewed wave of applause. Wild looked around sheepishly, nodded, and acknowledged the unwanted recognition and limelight. Frank Wild was not the type of man who sought accolades.

One and a half hours later, the crowd dispersed in awe of what they had just witnessed.

"Well done, boss. Good turnout tonight."

"Mr. Frank Wild. The one and only Mr. Frank Wild. Sir, great to see you. Thanks for coming. I really appreciate it. Come on, let's go for a pint!" Shackleton broke out into that big, cheeky, mischievous Irish grin that Wild knew so well.

The pair embraced as old friends who had been through much together, which of course they had.

Five minutes later, Wild, this time with Shackleton, was back in the Oak and Ivy. They had two pints of Cold Courage Bitter in front of them. Shackleton had insisted on a larger table with chairs as opposed to alternative smaller arrangements.

Frank was indeed a Yorkshireman through and through—calm, levelheaded, practical, and straight with the truth. He was a brave, courageous man and a rock of strength to Shackleton and the rest of the crews they had served with. The two had developed a mutual respect and trust for each other, and that would continue through their adventures together as they remained friends for a lifetime.

As soon as the pair settled and had exchanged some small talk, Shackleton pulled out a big roll of drawings from his trench coat and laid out what looked like shipwrights' drawings and an artist's impression of a ship, apparently *Polaris* judging by the title of the drawings.

"What do you think, my friend?" Shackleton asked with an excited buzz. "Isn't she beautiful?" he asked Wild.

"Yes, boss, she truly is *pretty*, but what would we want with a *poncy* boat like that?" Wild, using his no-nonsense Yorkshire style, was referring to all the luxuries included on the drawings.

"Ah yes, well spotted. We will be rid of them soon enough."

Shackleton went on to explain the uniqueness of the *Polaris* design, its superreinforced hull and bow, the attention to detail, the intent of its design to be a dedicated polar ship capable in all the most extreme polar and ice conditions.

"You make it sound like the *Titanic*, boss. Unsinkable-like. What's the plan?"

Shackleton went on to explain the issues that Wild already knew too well. Wild was both calm and patient by nature. He was a good listener, and besides, he had plenty of time. As his father had always told him, "One sure foot in front of the other, no matter how fast, but deliberate, and never, never, *ever* give up." That was Wild's mantra.

He recalled Captain Robert Falcon Scott's tragic Terra Nova Expedition where Scott and his polar party died after losing the race to the Norwegian Roald Amundsen, who'd beaten them to the much-coveted prize.

"The British public expect more. No, they deserve more, better, and this is pride. We need to go back there and walk to the South Pole and across to the other side, Frank."

"Well, when you say it like that, boss, it sounds really easy. When do we go?" Wild could see that the sarcasm wasn't lost on Shackleton. It was truly hard to be around the boss when he was so passionate. It was hard to say no to Ernest Shackleton. Not that it had even crossed Wild's mind, but he had to bring a level of Yorkshire sense to the enormity of the project and ground his friend in the reality of the task ahead.

"What are we going to do about this floating Ritz?" He tapped on the drawings on the table. "It's a tad fancy for a trip across the Weddell," Wild said, knowing that the boss would have a plan already.

The waitress came with two more pints of Cold Courage and two bowls of the Oak and Ivy's best beef stew and dumplings. Piping hot, it was a pot of scrumptious thick broth with carrots and potatoes and steamed dumplings on top with delicious morsels of beef hidden beneath.

"Can you smell that fine Irish beef, Franky Wild?" Shackleton winked and tucked in with his mischievous sense of humor, which he could only share with the closest of his colleagues, his men, his friends.

"Smells like good old Yorkshire beef to me, same as Irish but without the bull!" Wild winked at Shackleton as the old friend he was.

Now another phenomenon that Wild had learned of over the years was that large families of brothers and sailors alike maintained silence when at the dinner table. Not out of manners necessarily, although being likable and getting on with folks was advisable when spending many months or years together in close quarters. This silence was more about the necessity of the act of refueling, a critical element to the survival of the human being. It was not to be taken lightly, the treating of each meal like the last. And in their line of business, that could prove true at any time.

They finished their meals and slurped the last of their beers, and the barmaid immediately replaced them with two more. They were feeling full, satisfied, the fire blazing at the Oak and Ivy, the pub thinning of its customers. Shackleton went on to explain his plan to basically gut the *Polaris*, leave the galley, keep the darkroom for a ship's photographer, strip out most of the cabins, and convert them to bunks for the boys, a twenty-eight-man crew.

"Who are you thinking about?" Wild asked as a confirmation of his own thoughts.

"Crean for sure. The man's a bloody legend. I have heard some good things about Alfie Cheetham. Marston as expedition artist. Apparently Frank Hurley's work from Mawson's expedition is pretty impressive—a bloody good photographer ..."

"Apart from the fact that he's a bloody Australian," Wild quipped and smiled.

"Then there's me and you, and I put an advert in the *London Times* for crew."

"Any luck?"

"Oh yes, my man. We had plenty of applications. We are interviewing next week. I have an office on Burlington Road, and I was hoping you could join me.

"*Polaris* arrived in Millwall Dock two months ago. Work is almost completed; she is nearly finished. We are going to rename her the *Endurance!*"

They retired to the fire, ordered a bottle of Scotch whisky—Mackinlay's Rare Old Highland Malt—lit their pipes, settled in, and talked, reminiscing on their adventures so far and planning their adventures to come.

At midnight, the landlord closed the bar, the explorers being the last two customers. They said good night and agreed to meet at Millwall Dock and Burlington Road for the interviews.

Shackleton's Offices
Burlington Road, Southwest India Dock
London, Great Britain

Shackleton had rented the office not far from where the *Polaris* was being transformed into the *Endurance*. Frank Wild was full of beans that morning at the prospect of a new adventure brewing as they walked down Burlington Road.

Shackleton opened the door to the office, and in they walked to a sparse, timber-floored room with two desks, a meeting table and a row of chairs, and a desk in the reception area with that familiar smell that reminded Wild of town halls again.

Wild looked around and noticed a familiar poem that had been framed and put on the wall, an old favorite of Shackleton's: "I hold that a man should strive to the uttermost for his life's set prize," by Robert Browning.

He looked around some more, observing the accommodations. Typical Shackleton, nothing fancy, very practical, with an air of mystery and adventure, true to form for the by now legendary explorer.

Although Shackleton glimmered in the limelight, the boss, like Wild, was a man of basic needs. Although he aspired to glory and riches, his ventures thus far had been largely funded by others. They had become trials of survival. And he had yet to make a positive impact on his own riches, largely relying on the security and wealth of his wife Emily's family.

They passed their customary greetings, knowing full well that it was only a matter of courtesy. They had both been to hell and back on their various expeditions. A bed of leaves under the trees was a luxury, never mind a real meal, a bed, walls, and a roof. They were both explorers, survivors, and even in the worst conditions they never complained. Complaining was unproductive and about as much use as trying to solve an algebra equation by chewing tobacco—an old joke between the two of them.

Shackleton brewed a pot of tea, and when it was done, he poured them each a cup and sat down at a table. "Here," he said, unrolling a scale drawing of the ship's interior. "As you know, the ship, or, uh, *Polaris*, was meant for pleasure trips into the polar regions, but the two partners went belly-up before they finished the build."

"Bad for them. Good for us," Wild said.

"Indeed. Very good for us."

Shackleton explained that the two partners had had a hard time finding any interested buyers for the vessel, mostly because of its unique mission. He'd purchased *Polaris* for just £11,600, or 225,000 kronor. Then he'd sunk another £3,000 to refit her.

After they had talked through the various detailed plans to turn this luxury cruise boat into a serious expedition ship, and once they had finished the last mouthful of tea, Shackleton played the reveal. "Let's go and see her, Frank."

Wild, now keen to see the *Polaris*, replied, "I thought you'd never ask."

Wild followed Shackleton out of the office, matching his pace as they walked down to Millwall Dock. Shackleton briefed him on the interviews for the following day.

"Tom Crean is coming in first, so we can sign him up. Then we have Alfie Cheetham and Hurley, and then we have a bunch of men who responded coming over."

As they entered the dry dock, *Endurance* stood proud. A swarm of workers were busy with the final touches of transforming the ship from a tourist frivolity to a serious expedition ship. The three-masted barkentine was something to behold. Shackleton had renamed the ship based on his family crest's motto, *Fortitudine vincimus*, or "By endurance we conquer."

"She's a beauty," Wild said, his excitement increasing by the moment.

"She sure is, Frank. Well, at least now that we have made her seaworthy."

Shackleton beckoned Wild on to the plank and took him aboard. He went on to show Wild excitedly how they had modified her for the expedition.

Firstly, he'd had her painted black, from her previous white, to distinguish between her hull and the ice. He had also painted over the gilt scrollwork on the bow and the stern. "Very pretty but pointless."

Despite her name change, the five-pointed star on her stern, originally symbolizing the polestar, and the name *Polaris* remained.

After stripping out most of the luxurious accommodations and fittings and removing most of the passenger cabins to make room for stores and equipment, the former crew cabins on the lower deck had been removed and converted into a cargo hold. The reduced crew of sailors whom Shackleton needed would occupy their quarters in the forecastle.

He had kept the darkroom, as he knew too well that photography and film were an important part of his funding strategy both prior to and after the expedition.

The new equipment included four ships' boats: two twenty-one-foot rowing cutters, one larger twenty-two-foot double-ended whaleboat, a one smaller motorboat.

They went to inspect the construction of the kennels and then went on to the galley. Wild's confidence in the vessel grew as his friend continued the tour. He knew full well just how harsh the conditions could be in the polar regions, either north or south, and a stout ship was needed for an expedition to have any chance of success. It looked to Wild like his friend had found the right boat.

"Welcome to the Ritz," Shackleton said, clearly animated and as excited as Wild was. Wild smiled to himself. He shared his friend's love of adventure. That was one of the things that had brought them together. It was like watching a magician at a show with his big reveal, or seeing a pantomime prompting the audience. It was like a dannaaaagh moment, Wild thought, his Yorkshire humor coming out again.

"Damn fine, sir," Wild confirmed. "Just the job," he said with approval, thinking about their stew and dumplings two nights previously and the banter that would be had during those long days and nights at sea.

Inspection over, they went to speak to the foreman, a big Londoner, Cockney, by the name of Barry, to get the lowdown on the estimated completion date.

"She's no more than two weeks away, boss. The kennels are about the last thing, then we do a full cleanup in readiness for handover, as planned—on time, boss, and to the penny," he said.

Wild knew that Barry's completion bonus relied upon delivering *Endurance* back to Shackleton on budget and on time. Bonuses were a London thing. They certainly were not a Yorkshire thing. Frank didn't trust people who needed more incentive than just getting the job done. Completion bonuses were alien to him and his outlook.

Shackleton smiled. "Thanks, Barry. Great work. Look forward to picking her up and taking her for a sail."

Wild didn't think Barry could deliver on his promise of delivery in two weeks, but he didn't say so. Why bother messing up a congenial visit? The ship would be finished soon enough.

"We'll get her done for you, sir," Barry said.

Wild looked Barry up and down and he decided it wasn't just the bonus thing; he didn't care for Cockneys too much with all their rhyming slang nonsense and their cheeky, chappy way.

The clouds had come in, and the rain started to come down.

"Let's go for a celebration," Shackleton suggested.

"Sounds good to me," said Wild. "Never one to turn down a good drink, boss."

They went for a pint at the George.

4
INTERVIEWS

Shackleton's Office
Burlington Road, Millwall
London, Great Britain

THE NEXT MORNING, SHACKLETON AND Wild sat in the office on Burlington Road. Shackleton had the short-list roster of folks who were turning up for interviews that day. He and Wild would meet fifty today. Wild put on the kettle and made a pot of tea. It was going to be a long day, and a good cup of hot Yorkshire tea was called for, a Wild tradition during long days—in fact, any day.

Wild looked out the window and took out his pocket watch. It was just 9:30 a.m., and he reported that a pretty decent line was forming outside. He and Shackleton went through the list of names and applications and divided them up between them.

At 9:55 a.m., they went out the front door to a throng of what Wild estimated to be close to a hundred men of all ages in various states of attire, from young boys to old men, from what looked like street urchins to old sailors and salty dogs. And then there were the men dressed for the occasion in suits and ties. Some wore flatcaps, sailor's hats, or woolen beanies, and a couple even donned bowler hats. The audience was clearly a very broad array of both dress and experience. Wild recognized a couple of familiar faces in the crowd and acknowledged each with a nod.

He knew that it wasn't the attire they wore that was important; it was what was between their ears and in their hearts that meant the most. He remembered how his father would refer to some of his teaching colleagues from perhaps more comfortable backgrounds. Regarding one, a physics teacher with all the latest gadgets and paraphernalia, he remembered his father's words: "All the gear but no bloody idea." The memory made Frank Wild smile to himself.

Shackleton cleared his throat, ready to address the crowd before him. He welcomed them to the opportunity of joining the Imperial Trans-Antarctic Expedition. As he was wrapping up, he spotted the unmistakable Tom Crean and invited him in.

Crean strode up with the gait of a giant. He had a weathered face beneath his woolen cap, a pipe in his hand, a naval woolen jumper underneath his dark blue navy peacoat, and a pair of sturdy leather boots that looked like they had traversed the world, which they probably had, Wild observed.

The three met at the door and shook hands. "Good morning, boss," said Crean with his grating Irish brogue.

"Tom, it's bloody great to see you. Up for another trip?" Shackleton beamed.

"Sure am, boss. What's the plan?" Wild reached out his hand and met with Crean's huge bear claw. *This man is a true legend,* he said to himself.

In this tough business of tough men, Crean was one of the toughest. He was already in possession of a Polar Medal and had been presented the Albert Medal for his heroics on the tragic Terra Nova Expedition where Scott had lost his life.

Shackleton gave Crean a quick briefing. Conscious of the task he had ahead of him that day, he signed him up and arranged to meet the following day with other recruits to go meet the *Endurance* and be given a full briefing of Shackleton's plans.

Shackleton knew Crean well from the Discovery Expedition and also knew of his exploits on Scott's last expedition. Like Scott, Shackleton trusted Crean, and on adventures like this, you needed men you could trust. The feelings were mutual, and not just between those two. Wild's reputation went before him too. The three men sat together, splitting up the roster over a cup of tea stewed on the stove, and started getting to work.

The interviews with Shackleton were different from those of both Wild and Crean. The boss was as interested in experience as he was in character. He invited many of the candidates to sing to give him an understanding of their wherewithal, showing again Shackleton's sometimes unorthodox way of going about his business.

Alfred "Alfie" Buchanan Cheetham was born in Liverpool and then later, with his family, moved to Hull, from one maritime town to another, where he went to sea as a teenager working on the North Sea fishing fleets. Shackleton and Crean also knew him from the Discovery Expedition. With his Liverpudlian accent and sharp wit, Alfie was a popular and cheerful addition to their recruit list. Alfie was hired, Shackleton announced with great fanfare.

Shackleton reminded them that the selection of crew was more than just determining the qualifications of the individuals. As important, if not more so, were the dynamics of a group of men who could get along through extended periods at sea, often in cramped, uncomfortable quarters and also often in the face of adversity. Wild and Crean both knew this, of course, but it served as a great reminder as they conducted their own interviews.

Alfie Cheetham was a great addition for all those reasons.

Next up was a young Royal Navy matelot, Hubert Hudson, a navigator. Shackleton liked the look of him. After twenty minutes, the three agreed that he would be the appointed navigating officer for the expedition.

By lunchtime, they had added to their list Lewis Rickinson, chief engineer, and Alexander Kerr, an engineer. Kerr, a Londoner from East Ham, a Cockney, was a maritime engineer and another bright, cheerful, positive, and humorous force to complement the crew.

Tim McCarthy from Ireland, and Tom McLeod, another Scot, from Glasgow, all passed muster and were chosen to be on board.

Wild thought that Tom Orde-Lees was an interesting character indeed. Born in Prussia, the son of a former barrister and the chief constable of Northamptonshire, and educated at Marlborough College, he was a climber, a parachutist, a skier, and a general man of mystery with the benefit of skills and a legacy of a silver spoon. Again, based on Crean's and Wild's advice, Tom Orde-Lees also made the cut. He had been turned down for Scott's Terra Nova Expedition, and despite his prickly edges, Shackleton saw the advantage of taking Orde-Lees to the Antarctic.

Harry McNish from Glasgow, a career sailor and carpenter, turned up with his cat Mrs. Chippy. Wild saw Shackleton look him up and down and recognized in Shackleton a difference in temperature. He recognized that look.

The day before, Harry McNish had said goodbye to his wife, Lizzie Littlejohn, on the steps of his modern home in the Gorbals. Lizzie pecked him goodbye and slammed the door shut behind her. Harry knew she didn't want him to go. Indeed, she'd told him so. They'd argued. The departure was not one that pleased Harry. With just his kit bag and Mrs. Chippy, he'd marched off down the cobble streets to Glasgow Central Station and the train that would take him south through Carlisle and on to London.

It was a long journey. McNish sat on his kit bag in the guard's carriage with Mrs. Chippy on a short leash. He had packed some bread and cheese and a flask of water, which they shared on the rickety journey.

Harry had spent some of his final pay packet from the yards and invested in a journal, a pack of pencils, and a pencil sharpener. His plan was to keep a track of this last adventure. One day, who knew, just like some of the others, he would sell it and make his fortune.

He looked at Mrs. Chippy for a moment, then said to himself, "But who would want to know the writings of an old carpenter like me?" The cat just stared back at him but somehow made him feel better.

"Just like the auld baird himsen. If it's good enough for 'im, it's good enough fer me, Mrs. Chippy."

Decision made and self-doubt banished, McNish set about organizing his journal as he took a wee dram of the whisky in his kit bag and looked into the dimly lit guard's carriage, listening to the rhythmic rattle of the train. He thought for a moment, took another dram, and like Archimedes in a eureka moment, said, "Dramming! That's what I'll call her, Mrs. Chippy!"

And that was it; the book *Dramming* was born. After the title and his name were emblazoned on the front page, the first installment would be a poem and then a sketch of Mrs. Chippy.

McNish passed in and out of sleep while traveling overnight. The train pulled into Euston station at 7:00 the next morning. He took a bus and then walked to Burlington Road for his interview.

Harry had been to many of the industrial and maritime cities of Great Britain, from Aberdeen in the north, and of course Glasgow, down to Newcastle and Liverpool and across to Hull. In the southwest he'd been to Plymouth, Portsmouth, and Southampton. This was his first trip to London in years.

As he passed through the London streets and on to the Millwall Docks, he noticed a difference from last time he had been. It was a little cleaner, certainly with more optimism than his hometown, but still heavy industry everywhere darkening the skies and that familiar smell of salt and coal, smelting and sweat.

This is what this opportunity presented to Harry McNish. Despite the austerity of the advertisement, this was Harry's hope for a new adventure, a chance to get away from this apparent "progress." He wasn't sure to whom that term applied, but he was certain it wasn't for his benefit. Getting away from Glasgow and Lizzie Littlejohn, at least for a while, was a bonus.

"Men wanted," the advertisement had read. He was convinced: *Sir Ernest Shackleton, Harry McNish is yer man!*

Two young men from Bolton turned up at the offices on Burlington Road, only one of whom had an interview. Both were on leave from the army and their duties in Egypt. Jimmy and his friend Richie had escaped their own version of hell, the coal mines and steel mills of Bolton, for a better future in the army that hadn't tuned out to be all they hoped for. For Jimmy Smith, this opportunity was a chance to get away to something new, something exciting—and who knew, maybe it was a chance for achievement, even notoriety and fame. Apart from the latter two, these were hopes that Harry shared with the young private soldier.

According to Jimmy, four weeks prior his father, a steward at the steel mill he had worked at for twenty years, had spotted the advertisement in the *London Times*. Apparently quite a bit of a fuss and buzz about the sensational advertisement and the intriguing job went around the mill in Bolton as it did in many other places, including the shipyards of Glasgow.

Harry could picture the scene as Jimmy told his tale: "Son, you should check this out. Sounds bloody interesting to me, and got to be better than being in them bloody rifles," he had counseled Jimmy. "That Shackleton will look after you better than that tosspot Haigh, you know?"

Harry winced at the cursing but let it ride, at least this time.

Apparently, Jimmy and Richie had taken the train the day before from Manchester Piccadilly to London, sleeping on blankets in the station and heading to Burlington Road. They had been outside the office since 7:00 that morning.

Like Harry, Jimmy also had no idea what the job was, how much it paid, how dangerous it really was, or how much praise and recognition would be forthcoming in the case of success. But it sounded pretty bloody interesting to Jimmy. Harry obviously agreed.

As they got to 10:30 a.m., it was Jimmy's turn. He went in to meet not Shackleton but the equally legendary Frank Wild. Harry was summoned shortly afterward to meet the boss himself. There were a lot of very talented men who wanted to join Shackleton on his venture. Wild understood just how important it was to select the right ones. Bad chemistry aboard the ship could ruin the chances for success. In fact, bad chemistry could get them all killed. He knew that the officers and crew needed to work harmoniously as a single unit if his friend's goal of reaching the South Pole would ever be achieved.

As it stood, the candidates for senior officers came together rather nicely. Among them were James Wordie, a Scotsman and geologist; Lenny Hussey, a meteorologist, archaeologist, and medical doctor from Leytonstone; and Frank Hurley, the veteran Australian photographer who had just returned from Mawson's Australasian Antarctic Expedition. Shackleton was not a fan of Mawson, and vice versa, but having seen some of Hurley's work, Shackleton had a double reason for recruiting him. He hoped the photographic facilities of the *Endurance* might be enough to demonstrate his commitment to Hurley's craft.

Shackleton knew the power of photography and film and how that could help postexpedition revenue and potential future projects. Hurley was a hugely important part of his commercial plans for the expedition. The same was true of George Marston as expedition artist. The potential for commercialization from both Hurley and Marston was a big future bet.

Reginald James, a math prodigy and naturalist, and Robert Clark, another Scot, a marine biologist, were both serious candidates, and Shackleton wanted them on board.

Shackleton was very conscious that despite all these candidates, he did not have a solid candidate for captain, clearly a fundamental role. Lionel Greenstreet was a potential candidate, but at twenty-five, he was too young for the role of captain, although Shackleton recognized the talent for future expeditions. Greenstreet would probably fit in as first officer.

Shackleton had one eye on the clock and was thinking of the lunch he had planned for later in the day, but as the interviews progressed, no suitable candidate for captain had shown up. Then at around 11:00 that morning in walked a tall, almost dapper man dressed in his trousers, shirt, and a tie, yet with a long double-breasted trench coat and boots. He was wearing a hat, slightly cocked to the side, and exuding confidence and maybe just a touch of arrogance. But in certain people and certain roles, Shackleton didn't object to a heightened level of self-confidence, as long as it could be justified.

"Good morning, gentlemen," the tall man said, pausing briefly before continuing, "I am looking for Sir Ernest Shackleton."

Based on his accent, Wild assumed that the man was either Australian or more likely Kiwi.

"I think that you have found him," Shackleton said. "How can I help you, sir?"

"Frank Worsley, sir. I read your advertisement in the *Times*, and unless you have already filled that position, I am volunteering as your ship's captain, sir!"

Wild and Crean rolled their eyes. "Typical bloody officer material," Crean commented under his breath.

"Come on now, Mr. Worsley, tell me why you think that I should make you captain of my beloved *Endurance*."

Worsley went on to explain his roots—from New Zealand, Akaroa, his grandfather from Rugby, England, a great exporter of the beautiful game to the antipodes. He mentioned how, as a boy, he had learned his craft and sailed the Akaroa volcanic crater, navigating his way and honing his skills, which set him up for his career on the oceans.

Shackleton nodded in encouragement. Wild noted that his friend had not caught the reference to the game of rugby, the oval ball close to his own heart.

Worsley then went on to explain his maritime career from a young boy with the New Zealand Shipping Company and his rise through the ranks—third mate by 1891, fifth officer the following year, second mate on the *Tutanekai* around the Pacific Islands, then on the *Hinemoa* as chief officer.

Worsley then apparently had sat for his examination for his foreign master's certificate and was one of only two students commended for their effort. He was given his first command, of the *Countess of Ranfurly*, a three-masted schooner that sailed the South Pacific trade routes, mainly around the Cook Islands and Niue.

Shackleton looked puzzled and cut him off. "So tell me, Mr. Worsley, why exactly does that make you qualified to captain my ship to the South Pole?" he asked with an element of humor attached.

"Well, sir, let me explain my full and extensive career to leave you in no doubt that I am absolutely the right man to captain your ship, sir.

"In 1902, I went on to join the Royal Navy Reserve, where I was appointed sublieutenant. I joined HMS *Sparrow* as chief officer and then went on to captaincy of HMS *Psyche*, then HMS *Swiftsure* and HMS *New Zealand*. Sir, I have traveled the seven seas. I can find a needle in the vastness of any ocean. I have captained many ships, and let me reassure you here today, sir, that I am absolutely the right captain you need for your expedition." Worsley clicked his heels and doffed his hat toward Shackleton.

It was a long speech, but Wild could tell that Shackleton liked Worsley. Wild did too. He looked him up and down, checked him out, and smiled.

"Welcome aboard, Captain Worsley," Shackleton said, reaching out to shake his hand.

Shackleton's instincts were sharp, and when he liked the look of people and had a basis for trust, that was good enough for him. He liked Worsley, his boldness, his uniqueness, and his experience. Shackleton had a reputation for making quick, instinctive decisions, and that was part of his allure and status as being a swashbuckling national hero. None of that surprised Wild in the least.

"Come on, Captain, let's go for lunch and meet our other officers." They shook hands again. The deal was sealed.

5
ROLL CALL

Southwest India Dock
London, England

THE NEXT MORNING, SHACKLETON ASSEMBLED the crew and asked each man to sign the articles of the expedition. Shackleton was pleased with the progress, and although there were still some gaps in the twenty-eight vacancies, all but eight had been filled.

It had been a good recruitment drive, and the key players were on board. The rest were able seamen, a cook, and a steward. These men could be picked up at most ports, including in Buenos Aires, before the crew took their plunge south.

"Gentlemen, our opportunity is before us. Since we lost the race to the South Pole, the next remaining frontier is to cross from one side to the other, and that is the mission in front of us." Shackleton boomed and inspired at the same time, his audience both obedient and captivated. The new crew of the *Endurance* sat up and listened to every word that Shackleton uttered.

"Today we have formed the nucleus that will take us on this adventure head-on, and through some luck and a lot of courage, determination, and soul, we will, together, achieve our aims and make our empire proud once more for our efforts and achievements." He was conscious that these men came from various countries, but this was, after all, the Imperial Trans-Antarctic Expedition, and all his recruits were from countries of the British Empire in some shape or form.

This was heady stuff. Shackleton was a master speaker. His reading and his love for the written word shone through when he spoke. He was mostly a man of few words, but when he did speak, he made every word count. It was like he was on a stage and he considered his words important enough to write them down on paper and play them through his mind over and over again in preparation for these moments when he knew his duty as a leader was to inspire. He wanted to live up to his reputation as being an inspirational leader, a reputation that sometimes chased him like a pack of wild dogs. Although he wouldn't, couldn't, give up his chosen position and notoriety, Shackleton understood the personal sacrifices, and oftentimes the accompanying loneliness, required of being a leader.

Regardless, Shackleton continued: "Together we will conquer the last frontier known to humankind. Through darkness and light, through peril and trusty passage, we will, together, conquer the never before treaded lands and make the journey from one side to the other," he said, referring to the planned trip from one side of Antarctica to the other, the key objective of the expedition.

"Gentlemen, we will make the ultimate sacrifice and conquer this final frontier together."

The audience was transfixed. A couple of them gulped at times, hiding their mixed emotions of loyalty to king and empire, this opportunity to become national heroes, and maybe some level of fear of the unknown.

"I can guarantee you that the journey will be far from easy, that the rewards may be thin, and that the recognition may be great if we are to set forth and achieve our goals as one, together.

"I invite you gentlemen to come meet our ship, the *Endurance.*

"Welcome to this, the Imperial Trans-Antarctic Expedition. We have the opportunity before us to shape the world."

The audience sat silent, almost stunned for a moment. Worsley was the first to stand, followed by Wild, Crean, then Harry McNish. And like a set of dominoes, the rest of the audience rose. They left the room in silence, amid lots of nods, winks, and mutual acknowledgments, and headed to the dock and the *Endurance.*

As they walked, Shackleton was lost in thought, his mind reviewing all the important aspects of the Imperial Trans-Antarctic Expedition that was about to begin. The name of the expedition deliberately included all the people of the empire, not just those of Great Britain, thereby broadening the pool of overall support and his chances of raising funds for the adventure—and of earning money from it when they returned … if successful, of course.

The entire expedition would consist of the *Endurance*, which would be known as the Weddell Sea party, and the *Aurora*, which would be known as the Ross Sea party. The latter ship was a 165-foot steam yacht. She wasn't ideal for polar expeditions, but given Shackleton's limited funds, she was the best vessel he could get.

The *Endurance* would make its journey to the pole from South Georgia to Vahsel Bay, and the *Aurora* from Hobart to McMurdo Sound.

The *Endurance*, the Weddell Sea party, upon arrival in Vahsel Bay, would send fourteen men ashore, of which six, under the leadership of Shackleton himself, would form the transcontinental party. This group would be equipped with sixty-nine dogs and two motor sleds and would undertake the eighteen-hundred-mile journey, via the South Pole, to the Ross Sea on the *other side*.

The remaining eight men would conduct their scientific work, three going to Graham Land, another three to Enderby Land, and two remaining at the base camp.

The Ross Sea party would set up base in McMurdo Sound on the opposite side of the continent. After they landed, they would set up depots on the route of the transcontinental party as far as the Beardmore Glacier, meeting there and assisting the venture back to McMurdo Sound, then home.

Geological and scientific observations, in addition to photography, film, and art, would be the products of the expedition, in addition to the achievement of conquering the last frontier on this earth known to humankind.There were still pieces of the Antarctic puzzle unknown as nobody had traversed the in-between landscape, other than Amundsen and the now dead Robert Falcon Scott.

"You look like you're a million miles away," Wild said, glancing over at Shackleton as they approached the shipyard.

"I am," Shackleton said. "So many details. So much yet to do. I sometimes wonder if I haven't bitten off more than I can chew."

Wild laughed, and that gave Shackleton some comfort. Clearly his friend didn't believe he'd bitten off more than he could chew.

"Well, let's just get to the next step," Shackleton said, "and sign the men up in an official capacity."

And they did just that. They arrived at the ship. Shackleton gave them the grand tour, and then they all gathered in the main saloon to sign the articles of the expedition. The articles included the ownership of all rights to the expedition: the photography, the film, the art, and even the diaries and memoirs of the crew. Shackleton knew this wasn't completely fair, but he didn't care. He needed to leverage and monetize these assets postexpedition. Commercializing the story was a big part of Shackleton's business model.

6
BOILING POINT

Buckingham Palace
London, Great Britain
August 8, 1914

SHACKLETON ARRIVED AT BUCKINGHAM PALACE after taking an early train to London. As the Queen's Guard escorted him through the big iron gates across the courtyard and into the palace, he fought back the urge to turn around and return to the ship. It wasn't every day that a subject received a summons from the king of the realm, and Shackleton sensed the invitation could spell doom for his expedition to the South Pole.

Shackleton had earlier sent a note to the Admiralty, the first sea lord, Winston Churchill, offering both the *Endurance* and its crew to service and saying they would wait in Plymouth to receive their orders. It was now August 8, just several weeks after the assassination of the archduke Franz Ferdinand, and the world was sprinting toward all-out war.

The first seaworthy ship had just passed through the Panama Canal, and the United States declared that it would remain neutral regarding the burgeoning conflict. The matter, it seemed, was Europe's sole problem.

Wearing his favorite dark gray suit and his Polar Medal tie, Shackleton was dressed for the occasion. He had the rare ability to mix with men of rank and commission, businessmen, and kings and queens using his Irish wit and his credentials as an explorer and a man of the empire. He chose his words carefully and could navigate his way around not only the oceans but also the varied nuances, complexities, and etiquettes associated with these different interactions. Shackleton prided himself as a poet, a writer, and an orator and leaned on his strength of character, his reputation, his loyalty, and his Irish wit to help him through.

He had leveraged his great fame as an explorer to secure public notoriety and funding for the expedition so far, but it wasn't quite enough, and he knew that underfunded expeditions had a habit of going wrong. He understood the enormity of the task in front of them more than any other, and he was determined to garner the right level of visibility and support for this imperial cause he was about to undertake.

Among the many visitors to the *Endurance* as she was preparing for her expedition were the likes of Queen Alexandra, the queen mother, and Princess Maria Feodorovna, mother of the Russian czar Nicholas, to name but two. These were of sufficiently high profile that they caught the attention of the press and therefore gained the eyes of the public and potential funders for his cause. Shackleton recalled the flashes of the cameras, the photographers behind, and then the headlines in the morning newspapers the following day.

This meeting with the king would be a great boost to his fundraising efforts. As Shackleton had thought through and planned his talk track the night before and that morning, he knew that this was a potentially momentous meeting for the success of his mission.

The footman greeted him in the palace and led him to the king's secretary, who gave Shackleton a full briefing.

"Mr. Shackleton, the king has only thirty minutes prior to his next meeting, so please be conscious of that. You will join the king in his drawing room. I have had a fire lit. After the greeting, you will sit next to the fire, in the right-hand chair facing the fire. I will escort you in to meet the king and settle you down, and then I will leave, returning precisely thirty minutes later. Welcome to the palace. Do you have any questions?"

"No, sir. I am good. Thank you for the briefing," Shackleton responded.

Shackleton was not a nervous man. He was full of confidence. But this meeting was with the king of England, and with so much at stake, the king's blessing would surely seal the last remainder of the funding he needed for the expedition.

Shackleton took a swig of his favorite Mackinlay's whisky from his hip flask to calm his nerves as he paced back and forth until the king's secretary reappeared ten minutes later, escorted him in, greeted the king with a salute, and sat him down in the chair to the right of King George V, facing the fire as instructed.

Between the two was a table. One of the stewards poured the tea. The two men exchanged brief greetings, and the king got down to business. He said he'd been fully briefed on Shackleton's adventure and, like Shackleton, he shared the great sadness at the loss of Captain Scott and over the fact that the Norwegians had beaten Britain to the prize of conquering the South Pole just a couple of years earlier. He was also well briefed on Shackleton's need for final funding. He knew that his endorsement of the expedition would put the wind behind the sails of the *Endurance* and help send her to Antarctica.

"Well, Mr. Shackleton," he announced, "the reason for my bringing you here today is to discuss your forthcoming expedition."

Shackleton smiled, a million things going through his head. "Yes, Your Majesty, we were due to set sail this week, but with recent events abroad, that has come into question."

"Yes, yes. I understand. The situation in Europe isn't positive with all the posturing going on. Our friends at the foreign office predict it could be a bit of a nasty affair."

"Your Majesty, I am very happy to put the *Endurance* and its crew at your disposal, sir," offered Shackleton.

"No, no, Shackleton, I don't think that will be necessary. The race to traverse the continent is important to maintain our standing in this world, Shackleton. It is an important venture and one that I fully support."

Shackleton breathed a silent sigh of relief and hoped that this message would get back to Churchill.

"Thank you, Your Majesty. I appreciate your generous words and your support in the name of the British Empire."

"Yes, yes, of course. Now I have something here for you, and I ask you one thing." As the king gestured to Shackleton, he was seeking over-the-top overtures for his backing. He wanted to get on with the important point of their meeting today.

"Yes, Your Majesty. Of course. How can I be of service?"

"Shackleton—may I call you Ernest?"

"Of course, sir."

"Ernest, you are one of the great leaders of this nation and this empire. You are already a knight bachelor, commander of the Victorian Order, and have your Polar Medal. Ernest Shackleton, you are one of the great men of the British Empire, and I thank you for that. This expedition is important, and I ask a favor of you as you cross the pole."

The king reached over to his left side and held a silk Union Jack flag folded neatly and tied with silk ribbon.

"When you are passing by the place where Scott and his men perished, I want you to salute them and make sure there is a monument to commemorate that place."

"Yes, Your Majesty."

"So that place is memorialized in history and their poor souls know that they didn't die in vain but with the gratitude of their king and all the people of Great Britain and its empire."

"Yes, Your Majesty."

"Then as you pass the South Pole, I want you to plant this flag of the empire to mark our crossing of the ice cap and your achievement of the last great challenge before humankind on this earth."

Shackleton looked at the king with his smiling Irish eyes and couldn't help wondering about the extent to which he realized the responsibility he was putting on his shoulders. He felt like gulping hard, but he resisted the reflex.

"Yes, Your Majesty, of course, Your Majesty," Shackleton said.

The king passed the flag carefully as if it were the crown jewels or as if it would shatter if dropped. Shackleton very carefully took the flag.

"Thank you, Your Majesty," he said as the king's secretary walked in, reminding them that their thirty minutes was up.

"No, thank you, Sir Ernest Shackleton. Thank you for your loyalty and service to the Crown and our people."

With the flag in his left hand, Shackleton saluted with his right.

"Fair winds and safe travels, Sir Ernest Shackleton."

The king strolled off, heading back to the depths of the palace. Shackleton turned around. Ten minutes later he was back at the gates of Buckingham Palace. The king's endorsement would make Shackleton's final fundraising goal a certainty. He would finalize the funding and meet the *Endurance* in Buenos Aires.

Today was a very good day, a very good day indeed.

Shackleton hastened to the *Endurance*. As he and the crew sat in Plymouth, waiting to go, Shackleton received a note from Churchill, a typical one-liner from one great man to another: *"Proceed."*

Shackleton breathed a sigh of relief, silently thanking the king for his endorsement and giving his blessing to the Admiralty. The next day, Lord Kitchener's poster "We Need

You" was launched—the same day that the *Endurance* set sail from Plymouth.

We Are Sailing

See her standing all pretty and proud.
Below, the water humbly cowed.
This blessed ship before you stands.
Bagpipes thrill loud, off to her distant lands.

She departs for oceans far south and across.
Six men for the circle that they shall cross.
Never done by any man
Until that Sir Ernest Shackleton.

Into cold waters of the south,
Passing through Buenos Aires and beyond.
To South Georgia and Grytviken too,
And then to the Weddell, and the bergs will be a few.

We sail this day from Plymouth Sound
With the clouds of war building all around.
We sit upon this pretty ship,
Waving goodbye to Old Blighty for a snip.

I will be back before too long
To grace your shores, where I belong.
Farewell for a while, my bonnie lass,
For in our hearts that time will quickly pass.

That time will go by, and we will be reunited,
And although never forgotten, our love will be reignited.
We know it is so strong and never to fade,
Back on the same footing as we are here today.

So fair art thou, my bonnie lass.
I will miss you for a while,
But I'll be back with my heart,
And it will feel like we were never apart.

Shackleton, despite his notoriety, his buccaneering, his clear leadership skills, and his mercurial status, was a man troubled by coming in second, a track record of financial failures, and a string of extramarital affairs. Maybe this was time for him to go for several reasons.

As the *Endurance* sailed out of Plymouth, Shackleton stood on the port side, watching her majestically navigate. She was on her way to Buenos Aires. He would stay in England for a few weeks more, tidy up some loose ends, finalize some additional funding, and head south to meet Worsley and the crew in Buenos Aires on one of the quicker mail clippers heading that way.

The storm clouds gathered, and it began to rain, an August storm. It would soon pass, not like this war, Shackleton surmised.

He thought of the race ahead, of conquests past, and of the opportunity to be the first to cross from one side of Antarctica to the other. The *Endurance* would hit land from the Weddell Sea with the *Aurora* at the other side at McMurdo Sound, the Ross Sea, laying food and supply depots. Then he and a small troop of six men would meet the *Aurora* and the Ross Sea party at the South Pole and take advantage of the depots for a successful crossing of Antarctica for the first time, regaining the empire's crown for polar exploration.

The race was a passion, an obsession, and now a way of life for Shackleton and men like him. It was a lonely life with often months or years away from loved ones, from home, from comforts.

He would make sure to stow as many of his luxuries as he could, including an extensive library. Shackleton liked to read—novels, journals, scientific papers, reference books, and encyclopedias. Learning was a constant quest, as was his love for exploration and pioneering.

Shackleton watched as the *Endurance* left Plymouth and quietly sailed on her way, listening to the Highlands notes from the two pipers he had arranged to serenade her as she departed. They would soon do the same for the soldiers on the fields of Europe.

The bagpipes had for centuries inspired hearts and instilled hope with a tinge of "Up yer Donald," reflecting invincibility and a sense of going at it dead or alive no matter the outcome. The bagpipes echoed the soundtrack of battles past, the rows of kilts baring their behinds at the English, the stories of Robert the Bruce and his spider in King's Cave, and "If at first you don't succeed, then try, try again." The bagpipes represented defiance to all the world and toward all the Lord could throw, defiance for survival, defiance for victory, and standing proud.

Shackleton stood for ten minutes longer puffing on his pipe, watching the *Endurance* disappear into the distance. Then as she took her turn southeast, he walked back to the Plymouth town and took the train back to London.

Onward! he thought, as he often did at times of success, hardship, sadness, and pain. That was his way, always onward no matter the adversity.

> It is in our nature to explore, to reach out into the unknown. The only true failure would be not to explore at all.
>
> —Sir Ernest Shackleton

PART II

TO SEA

7
SAILING

Day 1
The *Endurance*
Plymouth, Great Britain

FRANK WILD STOOD ON THE deck with Tom Crean, pipes in hand, as they sent their salutes and silent good lucks to Shackleton on the quay. They liked their gestures; words got in the way sometimes. They noted the distinctive figure of Captain Frank Worsley at the helm as they pulled away from the dock into the harbor, the crew watching their last sight of land for a while.

"See you in Argentina, boss," Wild shouted out loud to the dockside.

Crean agreed: "Aye, see yer in Buenos Aires, boss."

"Safe travels, boys," came the bellowing voice of Shackleton from the port side to the deck. "Look after her," he added, referring to the *Endurance*.

The rain came down, an August shower. Tom Crean went belowdecks to get a cup of tea and settle in. Frank Wild went to the helm.

Under steam, the *Endurance*, with its three-hundred-fifty-horsepower coal-fired steam engine, was capable of ten knots. Once they had gotten just out of port, they would hoist the sails and head down past the Canaries, then from there make the long haul across the Atlantic and on to Buenos Aires.

Worsley was at the helm with the ship's wheel in hand and his pipe out of the side of his mouth. The big New Zealander from Akaroa was clearly at home. This was his place at the helm of a ship in open seas, heading on an adventure. This was his chosen profession, his life, something that he had chosen as a boy at the age of sixteen.

He wore his sturdy eight-hole boots, woolen navy trousers, and a light knit cream jumper underneath his dark blue navy peacoat with his signature wool knit cream-colored balaclava revealing his full face but covering his neck and his ears. Worsley wasn't just a ship's captain; he was now an explorer too.

Although Wild wasn't sure at first, he had quickly grown to like and admire Worsley, who was a rugby man, a no-nonsense Kiwi with a dry sense of humor, much like Wild himself. Over a few beers in Plymouth, Wild had declared him an honorary Yorkshireman.

As the *Endurance* headed out of Cawsand Bay and rounded Rame Head, she sailed past the old Saint Michael's Chapel on the hill and tracked the southern coast of England toward Lizard Point, sailing on to the Celtic Sea and southward.

Wild and Worsley stood in silence as they watched on, excited but also apprehensive of their long journey ahead. Shackleton still had to come through with securing sufficient funding. They had to get the crew into shape between here and Argentina, then complete their full complement of crew when they arrived. Then of course there was the specter of the dark skies of war brewing to contend with, although no one really quite knew what that would entail if the conflict continued to develop as it had been doing since June.

Wild could see that the men around him were equally pensive, though practically trembling with anticipation. That would wear off. Of that, Wild was certain. He glanced around at the people on deck, well aware that every man he saw was thinking pretty much the same thing, namely, would they ever return?

Greenstreet and Hudson, first officer and navigator, respectively, stood in silence, the rain whipping across the gray sea, the ship rolling to the first of the ocean swells. Third Officer Alfie Cheetham brought the five officers on the quarterdeck mugs of freshly brewed tea. Wild fished out a bottle of rum to add to the tea, a small celebration of their momentous voyage. He poured a splash in each of the mugs and then handed them out one by one.

"Cheers." Wild led the salute as they crashed their mugs together and took in the aroma of the tea and the sweet rum combined.

"Cheers, Frank," Worsley reiterated. "Here's to the Imperial Trans-Antarctic Expedition!"

"The Imperial Trans-Antarctic Expedition."

Belowdecks, the crew were settling into their new quarters.

Wild and Crean were already all set, bunking together. They had earlier laid out their beds and belongings. They were old hands and didn't need much in the way of luxuries.

Crean had already developed a compassion for the dogs on board, especially Sally. He would name the dogs as they had pups along the way, names like Bummer, Chips, Hercules, Judge, Roy, Samson, Satan, Shakespeare, Slippery Neck, Steamer, Stumps, Surly, Swanker, Upton, and Wallaby.

The galley was a luxurious affair and one that they had not seen before. For the most part the *Endurance* was originally built for high-paying polar tourists, not low-paid explorers.

"This is a cracking galley, boys," Wild stated to the kitchen crew after coming below to get out of the rain.

"Aye, like lords and ladies down here, boys," Crean added.

"Like the *fricking* Ritz," added Vincent, the boatswain from Birmingham, in his thick brummy accent.

"C'mon boys, do you really have to swear?" asked Harry McNish.

"Aw, *fuck off*, old man," said Vincent.

"Come on, boys, we've only just left port. Now c'mon now, behave," Wild said, his voice firm and authoritative. He glanced at Vincent, trying to weigh him up, and noted that his quick reaction was maybe an indication of his Royal Marine background. He was probably more used to spending time on campaigns of the land instead of long journeys in closed quarters at sea.

"You'll need to behave better than that, Vincent, if you want the men to help yer when you most need it," Wild said, shooting a friendly but serious warning.

"Aye, when yer swimming in them cold waters and yer want someone to fish yer out, yer better make sure yer have a friend who wants to save yer skin," added Crean.

Wild knew he had experience in that regard.

"Aye, and a little less of yer cussing," McNish said.

Vincent said nothing, just rolled his eyes.

Wild and the other experienced men knew and understood the importance of having a crew who got along in such tight quarters on long and often arduous voyages. In such conditions, it was easy to fall out. Despite their toughness as men, learning to tolerate each other, keep their words to themselves, and get along was of paramount importance to any successful expedition.

Vincent was a Royal Marine, a wrestler, and a boxer. He was short and stocky and, Wild assessed, probably a bit of a handful to tackle. Frank would need to keep a close eye on Vincent.

"The Ritz it is," Crean stated, defusing the situation as he poured a splash of rum in each of the mugs of tea before him. "Here's to the Ritz and all who eat in her," he toasted.

"To the Ritz," the crew of the *Endurance* echoed as they swigged the tea laced with rum.

Wild and Crean got out a pack of cards. Vincent and Tim McCarthy joined them, and they started to play twenty-ones while the others continued to make themselves comfortable.

Willy Mitchell

Ode to the Ritz

Oh my, you little beauty,
My sweetheart, you little cutie
With pretty adornments
And yer luring aromas,
Yer padded seating and plumped-out bosom.
It's hard to imagine life without yer.

You tempt me into your warm abode.
It's hard to leave you for the terrible cold.
We sit in silence together.
You tempt me in with delights in all types of weather.
You soothe, you serenade, you sing.
Oh, you are such a beautiful thing.

What will I do without you once you are gone?
What will I do for comfort and song?
Who will treat me like you do
And set the table for a few and us two?
I will miss thy breakfast, lunch, supper, and tea.
Yer all a man ever needs when stuck at sea.

8
EMILY

Day 32
Mail Boat Uragayo
September 26, 1914

SHACKLETON LEFT FROM LIVERPOOL ON the mail
boat *Uragayo* to catch up with the *Endurance* and meet her
and his crew in Buenos Aires. It had been a frantic time since
he had said goodbye to the *Endurance* in Plymouth after his
meeting with the king and the flurry of investment meetings
he'd had as a result.

His expedition was all but fully funded now thanks
greatly to King George V's in effect public endorsement.
However, it was made more difficult by the timing of fate
and the outbreak of the turmoil and war spreading like
cancer across Europe.

Shackleton settled on the *Uragayo* in his cabin. He would
have a month to collect his thoughts, think through the
trip, and adjust any plans. The speed of the mail boat would

outpace the more pedestrian speed of the *Endurance*, although the latter was built not for speed but, as her name suggested, for endurance.

It so happened that the two were scheduled to arrive within a day or two of each other. There was plenty of time for Shackleton to think between now and then.

In the hold, he had brought additional tools, equipment, and luxuries, including final additions to his library. He was also well equipped with writing materials. As the hours passed into days and then weeks, he took his time to record his thoughts and start a book, large letters on the front of the leather-bound cover reading, South.

He had also stowed a supply of Mackinlay's to keep him company on the journey and to help him through the long days, the long nights, and his solitude. He had no official duties on the ship—he was just a passenger—and therefore kept to himself apart from the occasional conversation with the handful of passengers or a crew member in the galley.

It was with a stoic heart that Shackleton had said goodbye to Emily and the children at their family home in Eastbourne. Then he'd taken a car to the train station and headed on his journey.

The evening before, they had sat down at the dinner table, just the two of them. The children, Raymond, Cecily, and Edward, had all gone to bed with the governess presiding over bedtime stories and sleep.

They all knew that this might be the last time they would be together for some time. It had by now become part of their lives. The children accepted it as the norm. Emily realized that she had little or no say in the matter.

Ernest and Emily had sat across the dressed table from each other. Shackleton was in a suit, his jacket off, wearing his waistcoat and long shirt sleeves with his pocket watch. Emily was in a navy-blue dress with cream trim and a set of simple pearls around her neck. There was a candelabra between them with the candles flickering as the evening drew to a close.

Emily broke the silence between them. "What is it you see that I cannot, Ernest?" she asked. "What is it that you want that I cannot give you?" she added. "When will you come home?" She meant more than after this latest trip.

Shackleton didn't answer apart from the look of compassion in his eyes, which mirrored the deep appreciation he held for the mother of his children and the single constant in his life.

They exchanged small talk over the meal before them, discussing the children's progress at school and projects around the house, the church, and the community.

"How was the meeting with the king?" She looked at him like a mother looks at her son, with immense pride that her husband kept that sort of company.

Shackleton related the details of his meeting. Emily listened intently.

"How long will you be gone for this time, Ernest?"

"Hopefully, with a fair wind and a bit or luck, we'll be down, across, and back within twelve months," was his optimistic response. Emily looked skeptical.

"Have you secured all the funding you need?" Emily asked.

"The king's flag has certainly helped with that, Emily." He smiled with his eyes, understanding the genesis of her question.

He was well aware of the financial strain he had created and was hopeful that this expedition would turn around their fortune. It was not as though they were destitute—far from it. Her family's inheritance took care of that, but he didn't have much in reserves, and without sufficient funding, he would be heading to Antarctica with little or no safety net. Fortunately, the finances were coming together.

Emily sighed, dabbed at her mouth with her napkin, and gazed across the dinner table on this, their last night together before Shackleton sailed. She couldn't help but feel excited for him, despite her sadness at being apart again for so long. He certainly did have a bad case of wanderlust. Always had. She'd been attracted to him in large part because of his adventurous spirit, his courage, and his brilliance.

But her husband did have his faults. Emily had no desire to probe into the rumors of her husband and his dalliances. Even if they were true, she wasn't interested in unearthing them. She wasn't interested in the scandal, the gossip, or the humiliation, not just for her but also for the children and her other family and friends.

"I know you'll be careful, but I have had a series of dreams—no, nightmares—that involved you and this expedition," she said. "I fear there may be trouble ahead."

Shackleton leaned back in his chair and asked, "What sort of dreams?"

"I can't remember exactly," she said. "I think it's more just a feeling that something is going to go terribly wrong. I don't know what. But that's the gist of the dreams. I didn't want to tell you. I didn't want to jinx the expedition."

Shackleton laughed. "You shouldn't let your imagination get the best of you. Everything'll be fine. You'll see. When we accomplish our goal, we'll come back to England as heroes of the empire. Our fortunes will turn around. Then I won't have to depend so much on your inheritance."

"My family's money isn't the issue," she said, resigning herself to the fact that he would set sail in the morning no matter what she said. "Your staying alive and returning to us is the issue. I don't know what I'd do if something happened to you, if you didn't come—"

"Nothing is going to go wrong."

"You don't know that. Nobody can know that. Who do you think you are, God? Honestly, Ernest, sometimes I don't know what to do with you."

Shackleton poured himself some more wine. "Sometimes, my love, I don't know what to do with you either."

As the mail boat swiftly steamed southward, Shackleton fell into a basic shipboard routine. He ate in the officers' mess, strolled the length of the vessel to stretch his legs, and then headed to the small main saloon to read and reflect. As the days passed, he found himself thinking a lot about his past, a lot about his wife. He dearly missed Emily, and he felt a little guilty about leaving her and the children yet again. Still, what was a man to do? He had to follow his dreams. He had to follow his destiny.

"Ah, my sweet Emily," he whispered later as he lingered at the bow, the stiff breeze generated by the ship's forward momentum tousling his hair and making his eyes water. Emily ... Emily ... Emily.

Emily Dorman was the daughter of the wealthy and respected London solicitor Charles Dorman and a friend of one of Shackleton's eight sisters. From their very first meeting, Shackleton was smitten, but he quickly realized that neither Emily's father nor Emily was so certain, and probably for good reason, Shackleton reflected.

Shackleton wasn't known for his academic prowess at Dulwich College. He'd had from an early age clear career aspirations to be a man of the sea, which caused concern for Emily and her father.

Emily was the draw that caused Shackleton to leave his family home in Sydenham, South London, and live in Eastbourne, as they had courted on the south coast of England.

Before moving to England, Shackleton's father had given up his life as a landowner in Ireland to study medicine at Trinity College, Dublin, his Anglo-Irish ancestry making Ireland a dangerous place for him and his family to be following the assassination by Irish nationalists of Lord Frederick Cavendish, the British secretary to Ireland, in 1882.

Through the age of eleven, Shackleton had a governess for his education, until he progressed to Fir Lodge Preparatory School in West Hill, Dulwich, and then, at thirteen, Dulwich College.

School bored Shackleton, and instead he developed an interest in reading, particularly poetry, which was about his only academic ambition. Despite his lack of interest and enthusiasm, he still came in fifth place out of thirty-one in his final term, demonstrating his natural talent to excel and just get things done.

Emily's father, a keen horticulturist, invited Shackleton to the family farm in the Tidebrook Valley in the parish of Wadhurst, East Sussex. Shackleton was also invited to their family's summer house so that Emily's father could observe Shackleton firsthand to further assess his suitability for marriage into his family and take the hand of his daughter.

Shackleton spotted an opportunity to impress both Emily and her father, although he did not fully understand their reservations regarding his maritime ambitions. On July 31, 1901, Shackleton set sail for Antarctica on Captain Robert Falcon Scott's *Discovery*. He wanted to lay the world at Emily's feet.

On the eve of his departure, Shackleton asked Emily to marry him upon his return, and Emily accepted. He knew he would have to seek permission from her father when he got back from his travels.

Following the Discovery Expedition, and after a short rest period in New Zealand, he returned to England via San Francisco and New York. He accepted the role of secretary of the Royal Scottish Geographical Society upon his return.

He recalled the sights of San Francisco with its hills and Wild West reputation. He visited the Pacific Union Club, atop Nob Hill, overlooking the San Francisco Bay with the Barbary Coast below and Alcatraz like a jewel in the middle of the bay. Surrounding the area were the neighborhoods of Italians in North Beach, the Sicilians of Fisherman's Wharf, Japan Town, Chinatown, and the towns of Sausalito and Tiburon across the bay in Marin County.

At the Pacific Union Club, Shackleton met with a group of pioneers of the West, people engaged in gold mining, silver mining, and railways, along with inventors and investors. He enjoyed the pioneering spirit of the city and the region, and he appreciated the connections for future endeavors.

When in New York, Shackleton met with Henry Collins Walsh, a historian and explorer of Central America, founder of the Arctic Club. As they talked about the Discovery Expedition, they also discussed and laid down the framework for what in three years would be an establishment known as the Explorers Club in New York.

New York with all its hustle and vibe reminded Shackleton in many ways of London, but at that time of year it was terribly cold and miserable. Shackleton wanted to get home and see Emily.

Shackleton was a good-looking man with a face of determination—a reserved, studious, furrowed brow. He rarely smiled with his lips, always with the eyes. He was a serious man, a man with presence, a man with purpose, but one with a dry sense of humor. It was sometimes difficult to spot the difference between humor and abruptness—a trait of many who shared Shackleton's profession.

Emily Dorman was an attractive, educated woman. Now in her thirties, she had already rejected numerous proposals of marriage.

Upon Shackleton's return, the crew of the *Discovery*, including Shackleton himself, were public heroes. Three months later, he and Emily married, on April 9 of that year.

She did not have her father's hand to walk her down the aisle, as he had passed way while Shackleton was away on his adventures. The explorer hadn't needed to ask him after all, and in a way, he was relieved by that because of the fear of potential rejection.

Emily was as stoic as Shackleton. She took their matrimonial duty to the empire and her own sacrifices as seriously as he did. It was Emily who kept the household affairs in good shape as he, like a gold miner, would leave periodically in the hope of making the next big discovery, that distant land, always going a little farther, one day to return with not just fame but hopefully also fortune.

With Shackleton's public fame and hero status and the sustained periods away from home, Emily led a comfortable but solitary life as she raised the Shackleton children, thankfully with the benefit of her father's legacy and financial stability.

Although Shackleton was famous, a polar explorer's pay was meager, and in Shackleton's case it was close to nonexistent after taking on the credits and then the overwhelming debits of funding new expeditions and failed ventures. That was the explorer's life that they had both signed up for, and they would both stick to it in sickness and health, till death do us part.

Shackleton paused his thoughts and looked out at the ocean thinking about Emily, about the children, about home, and about his life, what it was and what it could have been. It wasn't that he was discontented necessarily; it was his fear of failure that drove him on, always striving for one more step, one more obstacle, one more pinnacle to climb. He often felt like a mouse on a wheel, incessant, never ending, no finish line and no end in sight. He was better when he was distracted, immersed in his responsibilities, having a battle to win, an ordeal to survive, another sea to cross or a mountain to climb.

These moments of solitude were difficult for Shackleton as he preferred to be busy, in the lead—not a passenger but getting stuff done.

9
WAR WATCHING

Day 72
The Endurance
Buenos Aires, Argentina

FRANK WILD WAS BACK AT the helm alongside Worsley as the *Endurance* tracked across the Atlantic and sailed toward South America. Spotting the coastline of Argentina in the distance warranted a celebration. As any sailor knows, after a long crossing over any ocean, the first sight of land is always a welcome occasion, and it somewhat flutters the heartstrings with a sense of adventure, new lands, and achievement. For the crew of the *Endurance*, the sight of Porto Alegre, and the Punta del Este and Montevideo right before them, was a beauty to behold.

"There she is, boys!" Wild shouted into the wind. The crew had their moment of celebration as they cheered and hollered, saluting the sight of land before them.

Most of the crew stayed above deck as they sailed down the Rio de la Plata into Buenos Aires.

Wild remembered a Frenchman whom he had once met in Paris a few years previously. He always recalled the intensity and brilliance of the man, along with the quote he had shared: "One doesn't discover new lands without consenting to lose sight of the shore for a very long time."

Although the Frenchman André Gide was no sailor, his words struck a chord with Wild. He would never forget these words as he whispered them to the wind as a private welcoming of the shoreline of the great continent before him. It made the hairs on the back of Wild's neck stand on end, and that was why he was in this line of work. This is what he did. *This is my purpose,* thought Wild, as he puffed on his pipe, taking in the beauty before him.

The past seventy-two days at sea had been a learning curve for the newly assembled crew, a time of getting to know each other and the many different dynamics—learning each other and, in some cases, learning themselves as men and as sailors.

The son of a schoolteacher, Wild was like a sponge, ever keen to learn, and over the years he had developed an interest in human behavior, specifically the behaviors of his men and his crews, often in times of austerity and sometimes adversity. He was interested by the reaction of men and different leaders and their styles. He would use these learnings and observations in creating and perfecting his own style of management.

Over the years he had observed many different leaders, the standoffish and the aloof, the hands-on and the accessible, the harsh and the fair, and the in-between. He had watched the scolders, the charmers, the ones with character and wit, the ones who relied upon rank in the absence of the foregoing qualities. He had seen how men reacted, and he thought a key measure of success was the loyalty that the men invested in their leaders. And he had witnessed no one better able to inspire such loyalty than the boss, Shackleton himself.

During the passage, Wild observed Worsley's style and realized that he ran a relatively relaxed ship in comparison to some, definitely including Shackleton. Wild took care of the daily routine and the important matter of not just keeping the *Endurance* in shipshape but also keeping the crew disciplined and occupied. This reminded Wild of another of his great sayings: "The devil finds work for idle hands to do." It made the days go quicker, used up energy, occupied the mind, and made for better rest too.

Wild had always been fascinated with how so many phrases used in the English vernacular were derived from sayings of sailors. He held that thought for a moment as he held the smoke from his pipe and then let them go, both at once, into the light breeze as they sailed.

Worsley's style was both relaxed and standoffish. They had discussed how he wanted to allow the crew to express their personalities, come out of their shells, bond, or express their differences. "By the time we get to Buenos Aires, we will know who they really are, Frank," Worsley had coached him. "Anyone who doesn't meet the mark will be replaced when we get to Argentina." Wild agreed as, frankly, once they departed from Buenos Aires, it would be too late to recruit replacements for wayward crew.

Wild had agreed to what he thought was a pragmatic approach.

Lewis Rickinson ran a tight routine with the ship's engineers, performing daily maintenance routines and drills, keeping the engine room in pristine condition, so much so that "you could eat your dinner down there," Wild had observed and commented on more than one occasion, his way of complimenting Rickinson and his team.

Wild had learned many phrases, quotes, and toasts over the years, and he found them more effective than just saying "Good job" or "Well done." His repertoire included something for almost every occasion and served as connecting links with the past, connections and aspirations to the future, and a means of imparting sometimes humor and sometimes praise, but always with purpose.

He and Worsley had discussed the latter's thoughts, and Wild was enlightened by the big Kiwi's perspective, akin to his rugby experiences, explaining that when a kicker misses a kick, if he is a team player and committed to the cause, then there is no need to rebuke him. Often silence is enough, along with a pat on the back and wishing him better luck next time. "No one wants to let their teammates down," Worsley had pointed out. "Carefully select the best team, the most committed, with the right level of skills and experience but also aptitude and attitude, and then the team will become self-governing, and failure will become an obsolete option. Like with a bond, the sum of the parts is greater than the whole." Wild mulled over this perspective, and as time went by, he grew to like and respect Worsley more and more.

Hudson had gained the nickname Buddha because one night, as a prank, he had dressed up in sheets as part of one of the crew's entertainment nights to keep them occupied, and the rest of the crew noted that he resembled Buddha in his golden robes—an image that the crew wouldn't forget. The nickname stuck.

Big Tom Crean had all but adopted the dogs, and by the time they were arriving in Buenos Aires, there were four more little additions to the pack thanks to his favorite of the pack, Sally.

Wild also pondered this phenomenon, big Tom Crean, as tough as tough could be yet displaying real compassion.

He recalled a tale about survival training for the Royal Marines who were given a live rabbit and some potatoes and carrots to survive three days in the wilderness. He was told that most of the marines came back with the live rabbit, having shared the vegetables between them.

At the time Wild was confused, but he came to understand when he'd heard, "We want thinking men, soldiers with compassion. Those few who ate the rabbit weren't right for the Royal Marines. We would send them to the infantry."

Wild smiled to himself and looked over to Vincent, picking yet another argument with yet another member of the crew. He wondered how Vincent had gotten through that test of compassion.

McNish had been busy too, helping Crean build additional kennels for the pups, building a specimen chest for Wordie, and building storage shelving for Orde-Lees in the stores, along with some extra features for Hurley's darkroom. He had presented the wooden carved mascot for the bridge, and Worsley and the other officers seemed pleased with his work.

The geologist, Wordie, had fascinated them all as he told of meteorites from space and their apparent abundance on Antarctica, a phenomenon that had many of the men's heads spinning.

"Yer mean like pieces of stars that come down to earth and fall on the snow?" asked McCarthy.

"So, why do they fall on the pole but we don't see them anywhere else?" asked Alfie Cheetham.

"Are they worth any money, like gold?" inquired Vincent.

"Don't they melt the ice?" asked Crean.

Mrs. Chippy had settled in and was enjoying the attention of the crew as they shared their scraps of food with her at mealtimes.

Orde-Lees kept very much to himself and was somewhat aloof. Hudson, the navigator, was a very quiet man, and apart from the rum-infused Buddha incident, he spent a lot of time writing and sleeping in his bunk.

Macklin and McIlroy had kept themselves busy reading up on all imaginable injuries and diseases possible as if getting ready for the Great War itself, but it was comforting for the crew to known that they had men with that level of professionalism aboard.

Hurley and Marston hung out together, taking photos of the crew, Marston making sketches and paintings. He even did a caricature of each of the crew for fun.

Reginald James, the physicist, was very quiet, and when he wasn't reading, he was writing in his journal or penning letters to send home.

All in all, it was an uneventful trip. The only real worry continued to be John Vincent, boatswain, whom Wild ended up charging for bullying. At one point Vincent had gotten into a fistfight with Orde-Lees. Worsley would deal with that in his report to Shackleton when they repatriated at port side.

The crew were all out on deck as they sailed up the Rio de la Plata and toward the entrance of Buenos Aires, Fair Winds in Spanish, a great naval suggestion of a name for a port, sheltered from the Atlantic, tucked inland, a perfect place to take a rest ashore.

"Look at her, Greenstreet. What a beauty." Wild admired the sight.

"Aye. She sure is splendid. A thing of beauty for sure," he agreed.

Some of the crew had been to Buenos Aires before, but for most it was their first time.

"It'll be good for the men to have a run ashore. We'll be here for a week before we head to South Georgia. The boss is on his way to meet us."

Worsley turned to Wild. "Frank, you need to brief the men downstairs to behave. While it is true that there is plenty of fine food, booze, and women in this city, I will not tolerate women on the ship, overdrunkenness, or fighting. Make sure they know that. There are plenty of sailors in this port looking for a sail, and our men'll soon get replaced if they step out of line," he added.

"Aye, aye, Captain," Wild said in his deadpan Yorkshire accent with a hint of sarcasm.

Worsley looked at him, confused. "I'm serious, Frank. Damned serious. Besides, we need to pick up some additional crew while we are here."

Wild already knew that, and it was his priority once he got ashore.

As they pulled up and moored, the crew stepped ashore, leaving the engineering team on the ship as volunteers to take the first watch.

"It's good to be on dry land, boys!" shouted Wild as the remainder of the crew made their way from the ship to the port side across the bridge.

"Sure is, Frank," responded Crean. "Always a good crack." He gathered the seamen and started heading for the nearest bar.

"I can smell that beer and whisky from here, Franky!" he said as he and the others trotted away to Bar El Federal across the way.

"Well, Tom, just remember what the captain said: no booze, women, or fighting," Wild thought it hilarious just thinking about it, never mind saying it.

Worsley looked at him, almost offended, realizing that he was the brunt of the joke.

"Aye, aye, Captain!" was the last thing they heard Crean respond as he swiftly got out of earshot, homing in on the bar and its delights before them, like a pied piper leading the way, the crew falling in behind the big Irishman as he led the way.

That first night in port passed uneventfully, and for Wild it was a pleasant enough excursion. As the days slipped quickly by while they waited for Shackleton's arrival, it became clear from news reports that the war in Europe was heating up and that the tidings were bad for Belgium, France, Britain, Russia, and everywhere else where the war raged. Wild took stock of the latest news:

> German submarines sank three British ironclads, killing over fourteen hundred sailors, and the RMS *Oceanic*, the sister ship of RMS *Titanic*, sank off the coast of Scotland. The Germans had defeated the Russians at the Battle of Tannenberg, with over thirty thousand dead on each side and one hundred twenty-five thousand Russians taken prisoner. Japan had declared war on Germany in line with their 1902 alliance with Great Britain.
>
> The Battle of the Masurian Lakes and the loss of the Russian First Army ended in another defeat for Russia and a further one hundred thousand prisoners of war.
>
> Turkey joined forces with Germany. Russia declared war on Turkey, then the British and French followed suit.
>
> The German forces continued their advances, and all hope of a quick war seemed impossible as all sides dug in, literally, creating a series of trenches with hundreds of thousands of men all along the western front.

Wild almost felt guilty about not being in the fight, but he understood that the expedition had to come first. They were all doing it for the adventure and for the prestige of the empire.

The *Aurora*
Woolloomooloo Dock, Sydney, Australia
October 9, 1914

Captain Mackintosh stood on Woolloomooloo Dock in busy Sydney Harbor and coolly surveyed the *Aurora*, the 600-ton, 165-foot steam yacht Shackleton had secured for the Ross Sea side of the expedition. He did not like the looks of her. She clearly was in no shape to brave the Southern Ocean and the ice of Antarctica, not without a significant refit, a refit that the expedition could ill afford.

The weight of it all fatigued Mackintosh, and he hadn't even left port yet. Shackleton had appointed him as captain, and he'd also recruited several men who accompanied Mackintosh on the journey, including the two Ernestes, Ernest Joyce and Ernest Wild the younger, the latter being the brother of Frank aboard the *Endurance*; the chaplain and photographer Reverend Arnold Spencer Smith; the biologist John Cope; Alexander Stevens, the chief scientist; and Richard Richards and Andrew Jack, both physicists.

Some of these appointments had been rapidly made. Mackintosh was very conscious of the enormity of the task that lay ahead of him and his crew.

Given that the Norwegian Roald Amundsen had already won the prize of reaching the South Pole, the Imperial

Trans-Antarctic Expedition was seeking to trump that achievement with the first crossing of the Antarctic continent from one side to the other.

Shackleton was to make land on the north side across the Weddell Sea, and Mackintosh and the *Aurora* were to make land on the south side, coming from New Zealand and the McMurdo Sound. There, they would lay a series of supply depots across the Great Ice Barrier from the Ross Sea to the Beardmore Glacier, along the route established earlier by Antarctic expeditions, in effect the last four-hundred-mile leg of the traverse of the continent. They would meet Shackleton and his five appointed men, then trek back with them to accompany them on the last leg of the journey— eighteen hundred miles in total and a world first—returning the Antarctic explorer's crown back to the British, to the king, and to the empire.

Mackintosh knew it was a big ask, an ambitious plan, and when he arrived in Sydney to inspect the *Aurora*, he knew it was even more challenging. After his initial inspection, he made his way back to the Woolloomooloo Hotel, where he met the others. He ordered a drink and gazed out at the hive of activity on the port side. The *Aurora* sat in the water, waiting. Across from him was Joe Stenhouse, first officer, and Alfie Larkman, chief engineer.

"Looks like Mawson stitched us up," Larkman said.

"Well as may be, but we have a problem to fix, and quick," said Stenhouse. "Our funds have dropped from two thousand pounds down to one thousand pounds. We don't even have enough to pay the crew," he added with a grimace.

"We can sort that out upon our return," responded Mackintosh, trying to keep the tone of the meeting positive. "We need to get the ship properly registered and stock it with stores and provisions. In addition to the one thousand pounds, we will have to beg, steal, and borrow however we can to get her stocked up for the journey." He looked across at the two for their agreement and signs of willingness to rally. They both were nodding, which Mackintosh saw as an agreement.

"So, I will take care of getting her registered with the port authority. I would like you two to get the inventory list and get it costed out by at least three chandlers. We will then work out what we can afford and what we need in terms of donations. Agreed?"

The two men, willing, continued to nod in agreement.

"In the meantime, I will get a hold of Edgeworth David in London to see how his fundraising efforts are going and find out if he has any good news for us. I will also check in with the British Consulate to see what support we can get from them. We need to get south and start laying those depots. But we have to make certain that the ship is seaworthy. Right now, she's in need of enough work to delay us for weeks—weeks we don't have."

Funding wasn't Mackintosh's only concern. Inexperience was a key theme as many had dropped out at the last minute. He would need to recruit some general assistants and able seamen from port side and heavily support some of the crew, including Donnelly, second engineer, with no seafaring experience, and the wireless operator, an eighteen-year-old electrical apprentice.

Although clearly Shackleton's crossing would be the main feat of the expedition, Mackintosh's task was critical to their overall success. He knew that the lives of many men depended on him, and the burden and anxiety he felt increased.

Is the expedition doomed from the start? he wondered.

10
STOWAWAY

Day 77
The *Endurance*
Bar El Federal
Buenos Aires, Argentina

PERCE BLACKBOROW SAT AT THE bar sulking over his beer, not knowing what he would do next. He had escaped the coal mines of Newport in his homeland of Wales and had traveled to seek an adventure, an alternative.

He had met up with William Bakewell, originally from Illinois in the United States, who was making his own escape, in his case from the railroads, and the two had hatched a plan together to head down to Buenos Aires to jump a ship and venture to new lands and distant shores. In the past couple of decades, fueled by the exports from the Pampas, the city had become major on a global scale, exporting produce to the rest of South America, the United States, and the rest of the world. With over half the population of Buenos Aires being of foreign origin, the city was cosmopolitan.

Earlier that day, Blackborow had met at the dockside of the *Endurance* and interviewed for one of the roles on board, only to be told, at just eighteen, that he was too young and inexperienced. And now his traveling mate, Bakewell, had landed a place on the crew and would be leaving him behind, on his own.

Bakewell and his newfound friend Walter How were celebrating their new ship. They were at the local hostelry, Bar El Federal, Carlos Calvo, just across from Puerto Madero, within easy reach of their new ship. The night was young, but the pair had been celebrating for a while and were somewhat the worse for wear.

Blackborow continued searching the bottom of his glass, trying to work out what he would do next. He ignored Bakewell's and How's antics and their drunken tomfoolery. He was in no mood; he was not celebrating. *What am I to do on the other side of the world alone, running out of money and with no way out of here?* He played the thought time and time again in his head.

How was apparently from Bermondsey, London. He and Bakewell had hit it off as newfound shipmates. How had been on the long sail down from Plymouth on the *Endurance*. Bakewell and How were also toasting their newfound friendship.

"Oh, come on, young Perce, you'll be right," said How. "You'll catch another ship."

"Yeah, right," was the response. "Maybe I should just head back to the bloody coal mines of Wales," he said as he slumped at the bar.

"Well, that's a heap better than working on the railroads," stated Bakewell with more than a low level of conviction in his tone.

"What the hell would you know?" Blackborow didn't expect an answer.

The *Endurance* was leaving at 8:00 the next morning. They had to be on board by 5:30 a.m. in readiness for their departure. Bakewell and How were determined to have fun before they left.

One of the several women of the establishment was stroking Bakewell's thigh for drinks, and Bakewell was obliging. She was also suggesting a *private dance* in one of the private rooms. The more drinks he consumed, the better and better that idea sounded, and the better-looking the temptress became.

How was trying to talk to Blackborow and fill him full of the hope of opportunity, but it wasn't working. Blackborow, usually an optimist, a joker, couldn't see anything humorous in his current situation that night.

"What the hell am I going to do?"

Bakewell eventually took the bait. As he was being escorted upstairs by the hand to whatever delights awaited, Walter How showed his appreciation too, but he turned to Blackborow. "Come on, son, let's work out a plan, my old mate."

"Oh yeah, what's yer plan, boyo?"

How knew the *Endurance*. He had already sailed on her over the past three months, and although Shackleton hadn't been on board, he knew the crew well. He knew Worsley, the captain, and knew from the sail down that Worsley ran a relaxed ship. How believed that joining uninvited could well be an option for Blackborow.

Blackborow's eyes widened with a sense of hope. "Really? You think so? How would I get aboard?"

"Details, details, details, my son." As another of the Bar El Federal women came to pay attention to How, his attention to the conversation with the young Welsh boy about his demise faded, his having been distracted by the young woman and her talk.

Moments later, like part of a tag team, Bakewell returned with a big grin on his face, and How repeated the process of being escorted hand in hand to the private rooms somewhere in the depths of the building.

Blackborow had no interest. His only concern was about what he was going to do. Bakewell ordered another American bourbon and smiled at Blackborow, who was sipping his beer.

"So, my little friend, have you worked out what you are going to do yet?"

Young Blackborow was usually a happy enough chap, always up for a laugh and seeing the bright side, but he was clearly not in that frame of mind tonight, although he was seeing a glimmer of hope.

"Walter reckons there might be an angle to get me aboard."

"How?"

"Yes, How!" Blackborow rolled his eyes at the pun.

"No. How does How propose that we do that?" he asked.

"Not sure exactly what he has in mind, but he knows the ship and knows the captain and reckons it could be an option," Blackborow said.

"Sounds like a great plan, my little Welsh friend."

"Well, it's you that's bloody deserting me since we came down here together."

"Okay, okay. Settle down. Let's work something out when he comes back from upstairs. Besides, what the hell are they going to do if we get you on board and we are halfway to the bloody South Pole?"

Bakewell had made a good point, and that stayed with Blackborow as they both thought through the situation, weighing the opportunity and the risks. The alcohol-fueled optimism won the moment.

Blackborow looked around the Bar El Federal, apparently established in 1864, with its tile floor, wood bar, stools, and tables. Its patrons were miners, cattle herders, and seamen, all pioneers with money in their pockets and in most cases willing to burn a few notes in exchange for memorable moments whether on the sea, underground, or on the Pampas—all three very different lines of work, yet very similar too.

How came back down eventually, with an even bigger smile on his face. "We have a plan, me shipmates," he announced.

Blackborow and Bakewell paid attention.

"Let's get our little Welshman here on board tonight, and we'll work it out once we get to sea. What are they going to do, throw him overboard? turn back? No. Are they bollocks?"

"Sounds like a plan to me," How said.

"I guess it could work," Blackborow replied.

"Sod it! Let's have another drink," How suggested.

"Whiskey, bourbon all around!" Bakewell said, waving the bartender over.

"Bloody good plan." How laughed, shaking his head. "A bloody good plan indeed. That way, we don't leave a friend behind on the beach."

And that was it: the plan was decided, and the whiskey sealed the deal. The next thing would be how they would execute it—an often-forgotten detail of well-hatched plans at bars involving excessive libation. They would work out the details later. Of that, Blackborow was sure.

Day 88
The *Endurance*
Grytviken Whaling Station
South Georgia, Southern Ocean

Wild stood on the quarterdeck of *Endurance* as the helmsman. He maneuvered the ship into the snug, horseshoe-shaped harbor of Grytviken whaling station. The desolation of the place struck Wild. A few dozen buildings hugged the shoreline, and there was a little church perched on the summit of a hill that rose above the harbor, almost like a priest looking down upon his flock.

This would be their last stop on land before they made their way down to the Antarctic. It was a welcome sight, although Wild often wondered what had possessed these people to sign up for a permanent life in such places around the world, facing the elements and the extremes amid a sparse level of civilization. It must take a certain type to sign up to this life. As an explorer, he always had a home to look forward to. For these people, this was it, he mused.

Compared to Buenos Aires, this place would be a letdown for the crew. There was little to no fun to be had here, just warmth and comfort from the elements as they refueled, refired, refreshed themselves, and traveled onward.

Miraculously, this place was home to almost two thousand souls, Norwegian whalers and their families, a hearty bunch whom Wild was certain the crew of the *Endurance* would connect with. He had encountered similar communities on his travels at both extremes of the globe and in other places too.

They would be here for a week. They'd wait for the incoming mail boat for much-anticipated news from their loved ones, their families, England, Europe, and the world, and then be on their way south.

It had been largely an uneventful trip down from Argentina. There had been some incidents of fighting and drunkenness that Shackleton dealt with, including the inevitable demotion of Vincent to able seaman. He had stepped over the line one too many times, and the punishment was necessary not only to bring Vincent down a peg or two but also to appease the rest of the crew, who were sick of his bullying.

Wild knew from the first leg of the trip that Worsley was a different type of leader from Shackleton; they showed a difference in styles that Wild was very attuned to. He had concluded over the years that one's style wasn't really the thing; the important thing was the ability to get things done, meaning that ultimately the results were as important as, if not more important than, how one reached the destination.

That said, Wild also knew that there were certain acceptable rules as to how one got there, and there were certain taboos as well. He had worked out that it was probably a balance, and the test of success was actually really quite simple: Did the captain achieve the desired result? And would the crew gladly join him on his next expedition?

It was quite straightforward in Wild's mind. That was how he approached his business of managing the crew, albeit from a lower level than Worsley and Shackleton, both of whom he now held in high regard. He just recognized that they were different leaders.

That said, Shackleton did run a very tight ship.

Three days out from Buenos Aires, successfully smuggled aboard, Blackborow was found hiding in a locker beneath a bunch of clothing. Wild was first on the scene, and he summoned Shackleton from his quarters. The stowaway was sitting on a stool in the Ritz.

Shackleton and Wild both recognized the boy from a few days ago as they had interviewed him in Buenos Aires. They both had agreed at the time that he was too young and inexperienced, but it was clear to them that he was deeply disappointed by their decision. They had looked at each other at that time, and although they felt for the boy, their responsibility was the safe passage of their crew, no exceptions. They were supposed to ensure there were no weak links, although they both admitted there existed a few.

But somehow Blackborow had gotten on board the ship. Shackleton was as interested in who the smugglers were as he was in who the smuggled was.

Shackleton called the entire crew and headed into one of his rare but impactful rants. Most everyone knew not to mess with the boss. Those who didn't know would very quickly learn.

"How dare you board my ship without permission?" he yelled at Blackborow.

Wild could see that Blackborow was shaking, but some of the less experienced members of the crew were shaking even more, as were some of the more senior ones. The likes of Crean and McCarthy just took it in their stride. Vincent wore a look of almost contempt, and McNish was calmly stroking his cat as Shackleton went through his routine.

Wild was bemused as to how this would work out. He knew there weren't too many options here. It wasn't that the boss was going to turn back anytime soon. It was unlikely, Wild thought, that they would leave the boy in South Georgia. And Wild knew the boss like no other, including his compassionate side. He had his prediction of how this would work out. Wild watched on, learning.

"We are sailing with the king's blessing, and any man on board this ship, my ship, without my blessing is committing a crime." He looked around at his audience, his fists clenched in a show of fury.

"And those who helped this boy onto this ship have also committed a crime, maybe a bigger crime than the stowaway himself." He glared at the audience, daring any one of them to make eye contact, working out the perpetrators before him. Mrs. Chippy now sat between McNish's feet, looking on.

"I take it from your reactions that you two were involved?" He pointed to Bakewell and How, who were looking down at their boots in fear of the now imminent and looming consequences of their alcohol-fueled "seemed like a good idea at the time" actions.

Wild was developing his own style, and it was easier for him to be closer to the boys. He was more one of them than he was one of the boss's, and his reputation and no-nonsense approach demanded respect from the crew, an essential element to gaining a position of accepted authority, a position of respect. Wild also knew that respect was a two-way thing, and the fullest-impact mutual respect was the most potent type. "Treat folks as you like to be treated yersen" was one of his own father's many sayings. The thought flashed by Wild, not for the first time, that maybe that's where he'd picked up his liking for his repertoire of sayings.

Wild was like the big brother. He knew the crew, they trusted him to get stuff done, and he often knew their secrets before even they did, never mind the expedition leadership. Wild had known about Blackborow within a couple of hours of leaving Argentina, but he would never admit it. He'd realized even then that there wasn't much he could actually do about it, so he thought he would wait and see how it played out—and here they were.

Wild watched on as Shackleton turned his show of anger to the boy who was seated on the chair. "And as for you, young man."

Shackleton was putting on a show. It was hard to say how much of it was show and how much was sheer anger. With his chest out, his fists clenched, and his arms to his front, his eyes bulged and his voice bellowed like that of a regimental sergeant major dressing down the privates on parade.

"Did you know that on expeditions like this, with extra uninvited passengers—*stowaways*," he said, emphasizing the last word, "that the men often get hungry as their own rations deplete?" Shackleton paused for effect. "And did you know that in these circumstances, when the men get hungry, the first thing they eat are the stowaways?"

Blackborow mumbled something under his breath. A couple of the crew closest heard it and smirked. Shackleton flashed them a glance and then turned his anger back to Blackborow.

"What was that, boy? Speak up if you have something to say."

Blackborow, head down, looking out from beneath his eyebrows, feeling the level of tension, said with a sense of humor, in a likable, court jester type of way, "I said that they would get more to eat off you, sir!"

Several of the crew members smirked, trying their best not to laugh, looking at their feet as they fought off the unstoppable. Even Shackleton himself had found it amusing and let out a smile. What was he going to do, turn back? throw the boy overboard? No, of course not. Given that it was three days into the sail, he would have to let him stay. He looked around the Ritz, padding the moment out. "Charlie Green, it looks like you have yourself a steward," Shackleton announced.

"Yes, sir, I'll keep a good eye on him," Green acknowledged. The tension of the Ritz released—almost.

"Mr. Wild?"

"Yes, sir?"

"Make sure these two get extra duties for a month for their treacherous deeds," he ordered, pointing at Bakewell and How, who were still looking at their boots in guilt.

"Any repeat of ill-discipline will result in captain's orders. Understood?" He eyed the two culprits and the rest of the crew. "Disobedience of any order will not be tolerated on my ship. Understood?" He glared at the crew one by one.

"Yes, boss," came the chorus from the crew.

"Get on with your duties. Dismissed." Those were his final words on the matter. "Show over."

As they moored up in the whaler's harbor, they were one of two visiting ships in Grytviken, the other being a German ship that caught Shackleton's, Worsley's, and Wild's attention.

Pro-German sentiments were growing around the world. On the way down from Plymouth, in Madeira, the German ship SS *Hochberg* had rammed the *Endurance*, causing minor damage. The German captain had claimed that it was accidental, but Worsley wasn't convinced. Despite the Germans' arrogance being clearly on display, Worsley demanded the German crew fix the damage, which they did, begrudgingly under the very close supervision of Worsley and his crew.

The crew were all keen to learn what was happening in the news. Shackleton headed to the stationmaster's office to register their arrival and gather news from Europe. He returned an hour later and gathered the crew for a briefing.

"Gentlemen," Shackleton said, "I'm afraid the news of the war isn't good."

And then he relayed what he'd learned.

British and German troops had engaged in fighting in Belgium. Germany had completed bombing raids on Paris. The First Battle of the Marne had started with British and French forces preventing the German advance. German submarines had been sinking British ironclads with thousands of men and women dead. The Canadians had sent more than thirty thousand troops to Europe.

The pro-German Boers in South Africa were rebelling against British rule, as were the Irish nationalists. Countries were joining the axes of the two major alliances then declaring war on each other. What started with an assassination had spread across Europe and the world.

These unprecedented events in Europe were difficult for the crew to comprehend at such a distance; nevertheless, the gravity and seriousness was not lost on them. They would have a week here in Grytviken to make the final preparations, wait for the mail boat, and then push south.

There was a rising arrogance and a divide between the two great axes of power at that time. The British, the Dominions, and the alliances of the empire were clearly on one side, and the Germans and their alliances were firmly on the other. Because of this, Shackleton had deliberately stayed away from the Falkland Islands and navigated the oceans, making a point to stay away from the obvious routes and the places where warships on either side might be lurking. The German ship at Grytviken had been a surprise.

When the *Endurance* had arrived, it was obvious that the crew of the German ship shared the same level of arrogance as previously witnessed, and Shackleton made a mental note to keep a very close eye on them and limit the chances of exposure between the two ships' crews, Shackleton sensing and anticipating the potential outcome.

There wasn't too much for the men to do in Grytviken, but of course there was a beer hall, *ølhall*, in this predominantly Norwegian great Viking town. It was a simple affair, a long shed with two rows of wooden tables in the middle, probably enough wooden bench seats for two hundred fifty men. There was a bar that ran the length of the shed on the left-hand side with a dozen taps running, and behind it was whisky, vodka, and rum. Steins and shot glasses were the only two choices.

The ships' hands had gone for a run ashore, knowing that they were nearly ready to set sail and that this might be their final blowout. So with big Tom Crean in the lead, the boys went about their merriment.

Shackleton was aware of their excursion, having warned them not to drink too much, but Wild and the other senior officers knew that was as futile as asking a young child not to jump in puddles. Wild watched them from the bridge as they headed over to the ølhall. He also watched the crew of the German ship heading over twenty minutes later.

He knew the combination of two countries at war, along with rivalry and national pride mixed with arrogance, beer, and spirits, wouldn't be a good thing. But Wild understood that Shackleton was also a patriot. He knew his men. He had been around long enough to know the score, so rather than act, he deliberately allowed the scenario to play out.

This was a lesson Wild had often applied: rather than force a situation, change the course of events. Sometimes it was interesting to let events take their natural course, sometimes for different reasons, but his reason today was a little mischievous. Wild knew exactly what the outcome would inevitably be. He took a puff on his pipe and giggled to himself.

Shackleton went about his final briefings with his senior officers. They had opened a bottle of Mackinlay's from Wild's "treasure chest," all with their pipes in hand. It was a good time for the officers to bond and for the boys to have their fun, Shackleton explained.

"Well, gentlemen," he addressed his audience. "This, my friends, is where it starts getting really serious." He took a puff on his pipe and exhaled, blowing smoke rings into the overheads.

"We are in shipshape. The men are ready; the dogs are on board, fed, and happy; the stores are full; the galley is stocked; and we are ready for our great adventure."

Worsley cleared his throat to interject. Shackleton looked at him. "Yes, Captain?"

"I was just going to add as a reminder to all that the ice is closing in."

Hudson, the navigator, piped up. "The whalers are telling us that they have not seen conditions this bad, this early in years."

Shackleton cut him short: "Yes, yes, we have been through that already."

The men looked at him, clearly wanting more of an explanation. "We don't have the time or the funding to wait, gentlemen. We have no choice but to press on, or else abort, and I am not about to do the latter."

The men agreed, for the most part. Worsley called a Mackinlay's toast. At the clinking of the glasses, the men were reunited again; the moment of doubt had passed. They were explorers, they were pioneers; they feared nothing.

After they moved on to the serious business of the expedition itself, once they had arrived at the pole, they talked about the war, the implications, the sheer ripple across almost all of Europe as it spread to Russia, Japan, Canada, Australia, and New Zealand. There was speculation as to if the United States would get involved and speculation on how long it would take the British allies to defeat the Germans, the latter not realizing their own arrogance and seeing themselves as invincible. Heaven forbid.

Alexander Kerr, the second engineer, and the stokers who had joined Crean's party later at the ølhall came bursting into the bridge. "Boss, boss." Kerr was looking at Rickinson, chief engineer, and Shackleton. "You'd better come quickly. It's getting a bit nasty down there."

Shackleton and many of the officers rolled their eyes at the inevitability of this interruption. Shackleton, Wild, Worsley, and Rickinson went ashore to see what was going on.

On the way, Kerr gave them a running commentary in his London, East Ham, Cockney accent, describing how the last couple of hours had taken shape.

He went on to explain how the Germans had come into the bar twenty minutes after they had arrived and how, at first, they stayed together at opposite ends of the bar. But as the beer and liquor flowed, the atmosphere grew tighter, and there had been some exchange in the toilets, the heads.

"What sort of exchange?"

"Well, boss," started Kerr, "they don't speak too much English, and we don't speak too much German either, but it comes to a point when they call your mother a whore."

"I see," said Shackleton.

"And who called whose mother a whore?" Worsley asked.

"Well, it was young Blackborow who went into the heads and came out with a black eye."

"So, was he being fleet of tongue?"

"No, no, it wasn't like that," said Kerr.

"What was it like?" Shackleton asked.

"Well, apparently this big blond German called his mother a—you know."

"And?" asked Worsley. "C'mon, spit it out, Kerr."

"Well." He hesitated.

"Spit it out, Kerr," came the chorus.

"Blackborow pissed on the German's boots."

Wild laughed, along with the other officers, who were highly amused by the thought and the picture of the young, cheeky stowaway urinating on the big German's boots.

As the officers walked into the hall, the place was raucous. Big Tom Crean was boxing three Germans, and Vincent was taking on another three. McCarthy, McLeod, Holness, How, and Stephenson were all in the fray of things, even Bakewell and Charlie Green. McNish was protesting for everyone to stop, Mrs. Chippy stuffed inside his peacoat. Shackleton turned to Wild, held out his hands, and shrugged his shoulders as if asking a question. Wild returned the signal and asked the same question with a big smile on his face.

After few more moments of watching the fighting, as Crean was about to crash one of the benches over the back of a blond German giant, Shackleton just stood there and bellowed at the top of his lungs, "*Stop!*"

Like a grenade had gone off, the men on both sides stopped still, punches in midair, furniture ready to crash on their opponents, bottles ready to swing, and in the moment, their hands lowered to their sides slowly.

Shackleton stood there and pointed to each member of his crew.

"Crean, out. Vincent, out. McLeod, out. McCarthy, Holness, How, out. *Now!* All of you get out and get lined up outside. *On the double!*" Once again he sounded like a regimental sergeant major.

Without saying a word, Shackleton marched them back to the *Endurance* and got them on board, the men fearing the worst of Shackleton's wrath.

"Bloody idiots," he said with a smile. "Good to see that you gave them something to think about. Now, Charlie Green, get a steak for Blackborow's eye, will you?"

"Mr. Worsley, set sail. To the Weddell Sea."

"Yes, sir."

The *Aurora*
Sydney Harbor, Australia
December 15, 1914

Despite the difficulties, the *Aurora*'s captain Mackintosh gave the orders to set sail to Hobart on their way south. The *Aurora* had a full complement of crew, and by hook or by crook she was fully laden with coal, supplies, equipment, and food. The work to make her as seaworthy as possible had also been completed.

They were finally on their way, three weeks later than planned, but they could make that up by burning a bit more coal on the way down.

They would pick up some additional stores in Hobart and then head straight back out on Christmas Eve. They'd travel onward and reach Ross Island by mid-January, where they would find a safe mooring for *Aurora* and begin their work.

First, they would lay one depot near Minna Bluff and then another in quick succession. Mackintosh wanted to get depots established as Shackleton might want to attempt the crossing this season.

II
SILENT NIGHT

Day 138
The *Endurance*
Vahsel Bay

WILD STOOD BESIDE SHACKLETON ON the quarterdeck near the wheel, their morning pipes and mugs of hot tea in hand. He glanced over at Shackleton and saw the worry furrows on his brow. He knew the whalers had been right about this being a particularly bad ice year. But Shackleton pressed on, despite the increasing danger. Today Wild sensed an unusual level of apprehension in the air. He looked toward the bow, which was partially obscured in the early-morning mist. Large chunks of blue-and-white ice thumped against the bow and scraped aft as the ship made its way through a dark, heaving sea covered in thickening layers of pack ice that would soon, no doubt, stretch white out to the horizon.

He knew the level of weight that Shackleton felt on his shoulders, not only the responsibility of getting the empire back in its rightful place as leader of pioneering, not just the pressures of funding and tighter than comfortable budgets, but also the inordinate pressure of planting the king's flag, stowed carefully below in the depths of Shackleton's cabin.

They had been through a lot together, and Wild didn't doubt that there was a lot more to come on their journey. He puffed on his pipe in synchronicity with his friend in the hope that it would signal his camaraderie and moral support.

It was Christmas Day. The crew were determined to make the most of it.

Wild attempted to deflect the focus. "The Christmas menu looks pretty damned good," he offered. "I heard Charlie has even knocked up some Yorkie puds." Shackleton winked. Wild was pleased with himself that his diversion had seemed to work.

"Aye. Me old mum's recipe, no less. By 'eck, she knew how to cook up a storm," Wild said.

Shackleton nodded. "The prowess of Mrs. Wild's culinary capabilities is legendary," he said, smiling back at Wild.

"Who would ever have imagined that her recipes would have made it all the way from Whitby Bay down here to Vahsel Bay at the opposite end of the world?" He looked over again, puffing his pipe, and smiled with the corner of his mouth. "Aye, old Mum would be proud for sure, boss," Wild said.

Charlie Green and young Blackborow had cooked up a feast in the galley from the provisions they had picked up in Buenos Aires. They had turtle for soup, whitebait, and jugged hare, and the potatoes, carrots, and turnips they had saved were still good for mash—tatties and neeps—which would keep their Scottish contingent happy. And of course there were the Wild Yorkshire puddings. And then for after, there was lusciously rich Christmas pudding with dried fruit in a dark sponge and mince pies with dried fruits in syrup and wrapped in pastry with a dollop of Wild's treasure chest rum butter. Perfect!

Wild had earlier visited the galley, where he'd inspected, tasted, and sampled the feast, approving it. He had been generous with the whisky in the neeps and the rum in the pudding.

As he'd dipped his finger into each of Charlie Green's delights, he nodded and smiled with approval. "Bloody fantastic, boys. Bloody fantastic!" Giving the Yorkshireman's highest level of approval for such things, and slapping Blackborow on the back, he added, "Not bad for a stowaway, young man."

Blackborow blushed with pride. "Needs a Welshman's touch, boss," he replied, his quick wit countering Wild's.

Wild recalled his own mother, back in Yorkshire, a lifetime ago, in front of the open stove every Sunday, tending the delicacies inside. Most memorable were the aromas seeping from the kitchen and traveling throughout the house. It was a living memory that would never fade from Wild's mind, one he had often used in times of adversity and malnourishment to keep his spirits high.

No matter what Wild faced, he always kept his spirits high, which was the Wild way. Always. He knew from experience that positivity was essential to success, the opposite being potentially disastrous, especially in hazardous and dangerous conditions, to which the crew were regularly subjected. Therefore, maintaining that level of positivity was an important element of Wild's approach to the management of his crew.

He had organized the opening of his treasure chest and had plenty of Argentinian red wine from Mendoza, Norwegian beer for the boys, some port that the boss had brought with him, rum, and scotch whisky. He also had some gin; lemons, not limes; and tonic water for the more discerning, the officers of the crew most likely.

"No matter your tipple, we have something for everyone here, boys!" Wild declared to the crew, proudly showing his wares.

Harry McNish had taken the lead in decking out the Ritz in boughs of holly or whatever they could lay their hands that would resemble Christmas. McNish fashioned some spare timbers into a do-it-yourself tree, and Orde-Lees had made some table decorations, including candles for the occasion.

"Anyone can slum it. It takes a certain class to do these things in style," commented Orde-Lees as they went about their tasks.

"Aye, if you have a silver spoon when yer a bairn," McNish observed aloud. The pair laughed together in good-hearted camaraderie.

Despite the boss's doubts about both these men, Wild was warming to them both, the dour Scot with a sense of humor drier than the Sahara, and the all-around action man Orde-Lees, parachutist extraordinaire. In Wild's book, diversity of character added dynamics to the crew. As they got closer with time, their diversity of character made them stronger.

Now it was true that you couldn't have a whole crew of Shackletons, nor a whole crew of Worsleys, McNishes, or Vincents, but just like Wild had said in conversation with Worsley, it was the sum of the parts that made the whole. *Just like a rugby team,* Wild thought, *we need the props, the flankers, and the hookers as much as we need the scrum half, the wingers, and the fullback. This is a true team game.*

Worsley had opted to take the wheel and let the boys enjoy their festivities below. The sea was calm as they continued their trudge through the ever-thickening soup of slush and ice. He could hear the start of the festivities below, but he was happy at the helm of *his* ship, in the solitude of his own company, a state that many folks of his ilk enjoyed the most.

As the *Endurance* rocked slowly back and forth, he thought about his own journey and of his homelands in New Zealand. From a rugby family, and a former number eight in the pack, he was used to, and liked, keeping the rear guard in control, in safe hands. He was reliable and at the same time was a team player, but with his own stamp and mark on that title and role.

Standing at the helm, one hand on the wheel, his pipe in the other, he had his own thoughts in his mind. He turned his thoughts to the haka, the Kiwis, the Maori, the camaraderie, the friendship, the laughter, the loyalty, and the crack.

Listening to the silent symphony of the slush and ice playing with the double-crafted hull, he gripped his pipe between his teeth, slipped his hand inside his peacoat, pulled out his flask, and took a swig of the Mackinlay's it held, a dram that he had come to know recently through his new acquaintances aboard the *Endurance*, Shackleton and Wild.

Worsley recalled the story of legend, how Shackleton himself had placed a special order for twenty-five cases of Mackinlay's Rare Old Highland Malt to lift the spirits of his crew on the 1907 Nimrod Expedition. He recalled how he had discovered the fine golden single malt from Glen Mhor at Charles Mackinlay & Co. in Leith, Edinburgh.

"A fine wee dram," he said to himself, mocking his Celtic colleagues belowdecks.

He thought about Shackleton, the legend, and all those on the *Endurance*. He wondered what would become of them, how this adventure would turn out, and even if the crew would join the boss in his legendary status. It was true that Shackleton wasn't the only one brushed with the tinge of fame, but he was head and shoulders above them all in notoriety, even above Wild, Crean, and the most decorated expeditioner of them all, Ernest Joyce, with the Ross Sea party on the *Aurora*.

Young Blackborow appeared from the depths of the ship. Worsley appreciated and thanked him. He had willingly fetched his meal, including a half bottle of the Argentinian red, with cork in the top, and a glass.

"Thank you, my boy." He winked. "I told the boss that we shouldn't throw you overboard." He patted Blackborow on the back. "Good man."

"Thanks, Captain. I told you I was a good catch."

"That you are, my boy. That you are. You may be the stuff of legend yourself in years to come." Worsley grinned at the young Welshman.

Blackborow looked at Worsley, paused for a moment, and smiled. "Yes, sir. I do hope that we are."

"Just for a day." Worsley patted him on the shoulder.

"I'll be back up with Christmas pudding at halftime. Don't forget the soup. It's in the mug, and it's *delicious!*"

Blackborow scampered off and looked back at Worsley at the helm once more before returning to the Ritz to join the rest of the crew. "Give me a shout if you need anything, Captain," he'd called back as he left the bridge.

In line with tradition, Wild and a few others readied themselves to serve the crew their Christmas feast. The serving squad included Shackleton and First Officer Greenstreet, with Charlie Green, the cook, and Blackborow as steward. Between the five of them, they would wait on the rest of the men in the Ritz.

James Wordie opened the festive feast with grace. "For what we are about to receive, may the Lord make us truly thankful. Amen."

McNish accentuated the *amen* for the benefit of the less religiously educated men around the table, sending a glare to Vincent in particular. Shackleton followed with a toast. "Gentlemen, I propose a toast. To the king." He raised his glass.

A moment lapsed, and then came the chorus of the entire crew: "The king!"

Wild added his own sentiments to the occasion: "To absent friends, over land, overseas, or upon distant shores. Safe travels, good winds, and luck along the way." Wild raised his glass.

"Absent friends," the crew chorused to a clinking of glasses and mugs. They liked toasts.

"Happy Christmas, boys!" Shackleton announced as he served the last bowl of soup and sat down to sample his own food at the head of the main table. Charlie Green had made some bread to dip into the rich and tasty broth. "Tuck in."

Green and Blackborow remained in the galley, busy preparing the next course. Blackborow was in charge of the veggies and gravy, and Green was keeping an eye on the progress of the Yorkshire puddings, under the watchful gaze of Frank Wild.

"It's a tricky thing, yer know, getting these just right." Charlie Green nodded and rolled his eyes. It wasn't the first time that he had heard this lecture. "Batter at the right consistency, not too runny, not too thick, just right. Heat the tins as hot as yer can, then go ahead and pour her in." Wild mimicked pouring the batter into the pan. "Then lock 'em up, don't let 'em out, and watch 'em rise before your very eyes." Wild raised his eyebrows and smiled his big Yorkshire smile. "That's how yer make me mother's Yorkie puds, Charlie."

Charlie Green nodded. "Yes, Frank, thanks for that—again."

They laid the feast out family style, handing out the plates full of food and passing the jugs of gravy.

Wild pulled out a jar of horseradish sauce—a rare commodity, especially out at sea. Wild made sure that everyone's glasses were topped up, no matter their tipple. "To me mother's Yorkie puds!"

The crew raised their glasses. It had become a joke over the past week. "To Mrs. Wild," they all responded, Shackleton leading the chorus.

"And all that sail on her," added big Tom Crean, probably the only one in the Ritz who could get away with such a pun. They all belly-laughed and cheered each other.

The Ritz quickly fell into a concentrated silence as the men got down to the serious business of eating, the only noise being the noise from the galley and the rattle of knives and forks on the tin plates. Every now and then Shackleton would provide callouts of individual praise or endearment to key members of the crew, and although it was a celebration, he pulled in key aspects of their preparations for the weeks to come.

As they ate, Wild observed the individuals around the table and assessed his team-building efforts over the past weeks and months, understanding the need for balance and harmony but also recognizing some of the weaknesses in the personalities and dynamics. Orde-Lees was isolated, aloof, and somewhat arrogant. Vincent was a bully, but following his dressing-down and demotion, he seemed to be towing the line. Hudson was unusually quiet and withdrawn, and McNish just seemed constantly irritated with the others, considering his zeal for his Scottish Christian beliefs.

Apart from these things, Wild assessed that the crew formed a cohesive team. *They will all find their places,* he thought. His assessment was continual. Even young Blackborow was proving an asset with his chirpy wit and happy-go-lucky attitude. His contribution was becoming really valued by the crew. Then there was Shackleton, and Crean, and Worsley, like solid rocks.

Even Mrs. Chippy seemed happy, sitting underneath McNish's feet and lapping up the feline version of the feast smothered in gravy. *A ship cat's life isn't so bad after all,* he thought.

Shackleton was relating his version of events with the Germans in the beer hall in Grytviken, saying how as he had walked in his men were in various states of combat with the crew of the German ship, and how he had reacted when he heard about Blackborow urinating on the big blond man's boots. Blackborow was embarrassed, red-cheeked. "Well, he did call me ma, well, a you-know-what," was his defense. The Ritz broke into laughter again.

"So, boss, if yer knew we would get up ter nay good, why did yer let us gan in the first place?" asked big Tom Crean.

Shackleton didn't answer, just raised his glass again. "For king and country," he shouted.

His audience responded, "To the empire." They all got the humor, apart from Blackborow, who was muttering on about the German's disrespect toward his mother.

The Christmas pudding came in, flaming with rum. McNish played on the bagpipes like it was some Robbie Burns event. McNish continued to do the blessing of the wee beastie, a bit of a long-winded affair that got the eyes rolling, especially Vincent and Orde-Lees. Wild spotted the frustration and started his applause, cutting off McNish and saving the audience another seven verses of the obscure but fun Burns poem.

There was a round of applause, cheers, and toasts. By now Wild had switched everyone over to either whisky, rum, or port.

After the meal was over, the boys were finishing up, telling their stories, chatting, and joking. Wild and Shackleton sat at the head of the table with a bottle of port between them. They presided over the party like parents over their family, as fathers over their boys. With pipe in hand, Wild reminded himself that it was moments like this that made their lonely lives as explorers worth it—the feeling of camaraderie, the sense of togetherness, of family.

"Charlie Green, that was fantastic. Christmas Day, thousands of miles away from home, and just like I was back in England," bellowed Shackleton. "I propose a toast to Mr. Charlie Green! *Mr. Charlie Green.*"

It occurred to Wild that there were few or no signs of toast fatigue. It was after all Christmas Day, and toasting was their way of introducing fun into what often was a dull and routine life on board.

"And not forgetting our young stowaway boy here!" Wild added. They all cheered again. Blackborow took a theatrical bow, ever the jester.

"I told you I was worth it, boss!" Blackborow added with his usual cheeky but likable wit. "Better than eating a young boy from Wales." He cast a big grin from the galley.

Charlie Green and Blackborow joined the table. Shackleton moved his chair to make some space, and Wild grabbed a pudding and a bottle of whisky to take to the bridge for Worsley.

He found Worsley at the helm and offered him his pudding.

"Get your chops 'round this, Captain. Bloody fantastic!" offered Wild.

"Yep. That dinner was pretty darn good too. He was a pretty good catch."

"You mean Green?"

"Yes, but the young kid too."

"You mean the stowaway?"

"Yes, I think he's a good balance for the crew. He adds a different dimension, you know, a bit of humor." They agreed.

"Mrs. Wild's Yorkshire puddings weren't too bad either!"

They stood together and looked out from the bridge, the pack ice closing in around them. Conditions were still good enough to push forward. Wild knew that the pack ice would slow down their progress and put into jeopardy their carefully laid-out plans and the delicate timing of their arrival to the Antarctic continent. Wild was worried. He could see that the captain was too.

As they smoked their pipes and Wild poured them each a mug of whisky, Worsley and Wild looked out at the ocean as the day was coming to a close. They could hear the crew belowdecks singing. The two went silent in the comfort of their own company, smoking their pipes, drinking their whisky, and just thinking about the path ahead. It was a respectful and comfortable silence—two pioneers together, side by side, shoulder to shoulder. They could hear the voices below singing "Silent Night."

PART III

CRUSH

12
WITHIN REACH

Day 159
The *Endurance*
Close to Vahsel Bay, the Weddell Sea

THE *ENDURANCE* CONTINUED TO ENCOUNTER polar pack ice. Progress was very slow and as the ship worked its way through the pack. They were averaging less than thirty miles a day, frustratingly slow progress.

Wild joined Shackleton and the other officers each day at dinner to discuss the day's progress. The ice was an occupational hazard in this part of the world, and although it was thick and awkward, and unusually heavy for this time of year, they maintained their optimism and spirits, despite the fact that the ship had slowed to almost a crawl as the engine worked overtime to push the vessel through the ice.

Wild kept the crew busy with their daily tasks and routine, keeping the *Endurance* shipshape.

In line with their Christmas festivities, they had also celebrated New Year's Eve in similar, but perhaps not so resplendent, fashion with more booze and less food and the men taking it in turns to put on a show for the others.

Hudson did another skit dressed in his sheets that had originally earned him his nickname, Buddha. The Irish contingent, Crean, McIlroy, and McCarthy, and the honorary Irishman Bakewell did a rendition of "The Irish Rover." The Scots, Robert Clark, McLeod, and McNish, led by James Wordie, the geologist, sang "Flower of Scotland." Harry McNish with Mrs. Chippy did a cameo skit of Robert Burns's "A Red, Red Rose," and the boys from London sang the old Cockney favorite "Roll Out the Barrel."

A good night was had by all, although the tensions between Orde-Lees and Vincent were visible again. It was clear that they didn't care for each other—Orde-Lees being standoffish and aloof; Vincent, loudmouthed and uncouth.

Wild's treasure chest proved popular again that night as they sang into the night and toasted the accursed ice surrounding them.

By January 15, they had made it within two hundred miles of Vahsel Bay, their intended destination, but with a greater quantity of—and heavier—pack ice and an incoming wind, progress was proving impossible. Shackleton ordered that the ship take shelter beneath the refuge afforded by a large grounded iceberg close by.

After two days of shelter, the storm and its wind subsided, and the crew set full sail, making a dash in the break in the weather. The dash worked well for a few hours, but by teatime, they encountered ice again, although different this time. This ice was much thicker, soft brush ice.

The wind returned and blew for six days, northerly in the direction of land. By January 24, the ice had completely compressed, and the entire Weddell Sea was a mass of floating ice. The *Endurance* was icebound.

The crew waited for southerly winds to push them toward their destination, but in the grip of the ice, the *Endurance* just drifted in the direction in which it was taken with no choice in the matter.

These most powerful forces of nature were uncompromising.

Day 174
The *Endurance*
The Weddell Sea

The *Endurance* had been icebound now for days. Wild looked around, shading his eyes against the bright glare of the sun reflecting off the snow that extended as far as the eye could see. He wondered when the ordeal with the ice would end.

Life on board the ship was monotonous, whether in open seas for weeks and sometimes months on end or, in their case, trapped in the ice. This wasn't an unusual occurrence for polar explorers, but nevertheless it was frustrating.

The crew were all keen to learn of news from the homeland. They had a radio receiver, and each month they had tried to connect to the radio signal from the Falklands monthly broadcast, but at 1,630 miles away, it was just too far for them to pick up. They kept on trying but to no avail.

While stranded in this position, they occasionally made some progress as channels in the ice appeared, but these quickly closed again. The main priority was to accumulate a stock of seal meat to feed the dogs and slow the depletion of their own rations aboard the ship. The bonus of emperor penguins, and the double bonus when they had freshly consumed fish in their stomachs, was a welcome surprise and an early sign of the harshness of polar exploration for some of the crew.

The occasional killer whale would pass by, aggressive as its name would suggest.

Wild was a calm, patient man, but even for him the frustration was almost unbearable. He observed the human effects on the men. Shackleton was quiet and somewhat withdrawn and spent more and more time in his cabin reading and, Wild suspected, drinking too much.

Hudson was more and more withdrawn, Orde-Lees said little about anything, Vincent was sulky most of the time, and McNish just kept himself to himself, mainly with his little leather-bound book. Crean had immersed himself with the dogs and was quite the kennel master.

The crew's morale fell on the shoulders of Wild, Worsley, and the ever optimistic Hurley, always cheery and making jokes, and of course Charlie Green, who kept the morale up through his culinary creations. Blackborow, the always cheeky jester, tried his best to help given the obvious situation in front of them.

Wild knew from previous expeditions and experience that keeping the crew's spirits up was of paramount importance. Without that, he knew it was very difficult, and when men lost the will to live, it was irreversible and almost usually ended in tragedy and always disaster.

It was a tale of daily frustration as they flirted with the uncompromising power of the ice and attempted to make progress, seeking channels and making way some days, then being locked in ice on other days. They'd be chiseling ice from the *Endurance* one day and sitting in a pool the next. Making progress, or trying to, was a daily struggle for the entire crew.

The pack ice closed in like an iron fist, except there was no iron. There was just the horrifying cold, the deep blue of exposed ice under snow cover, and the persistent frost that accumulated on everything above deck. Wild stood on the quarterdeck, facing aft, and simply stared in dull nonthought at the nothingness of white that surrounded the stranded ship. He fought off the deeply frightening thought that this expedition could be defeated by the power of Mother Nature and the ice below him.

Despite Wild's attempts to maintain the at-sea routine, it was becoming increasingly difficult to justify the often-needless chores. By the end of February, the crew had ceased to observe these routines, but Wild would create new ones that had more relevance to their current needs. They needed to convert the *Endurance* into a winter station. With McNish in the lead, Wild and the men were busy with the conversion, making the *Endurance* a more comfortable homestead in the sea of ice around.

The quarters of the ship were made snugger for the winter with Macklin, McIlroy, Hurley, and Hussey in the Billabong bunk. Clark and Wordie, the Scotsmen, were in Auld Reekie;

Cheetham and McNish, in the Sailors' Rest. It was the Nuts for the engineers; the Anchorage, Fumarole with Wild, Marston, and Crean; and Worsley in the Wardroom.

The men built igloos on the ice for the dogs and their pups, renaming these as dogloos.

Humor was an important factor for building and maintaining morale. Wild knew this not just from his previous polar expeditions but also from the lessons learned generally in the management of men. Even in the most austere times, the use of humor to deflect desperation, horror, or sheer squalor was a way to deal with the situation at hand. What he did know was that dwelling in reality was not good for morale, even his own sometimes.

Wild maintained the routine was still a critical part of maintaining discipline. The winter station routine was different, and through the skills of Charlie Green and the galley, and Wild's treasure chest, with regular entertainment, Wild managed to maintain a positive tone despite the crew's circumstances.

Wild was concerned about several of the crew but no less so than Shackleton himself. The reasons for Wild's concerns about Shackleton were not as clearly evident to the rest of the crew as they struggled with their own daily mental torment, but Wild knew Shackleton better than anyone, and he recognized the signs of pressure and pain as Shackleton spent more and more time in his private cabin, more and more often taking his meals in there and not with the rest of the crew.

Shackleton had stocked his cabin with an extensive library of books, everything from encyclopedias and other reference books to classics and novels, and would retreat to his private quarters to read alone, often accompanied by a glass of whisky, or two, or more as Wild suspected.

Like many of the others, Shackleton also kept an extensive diary of the daily events as the expedition unfolded, no matter how mundane at this point.

Like many great leaders of the time, and before and since, Shackleton bore the full burden and weight of responsibility on his shoulders and flirted daily with his own black dog, but this was never visible to his men, apart from Wild. For many great men and women, depression was an issue as they bore the responsibility on their own two shoulders. Some took solace in a book, painting, writing, or poetry or the contents of a bottle of whisky.

It wasn't just the responsibility; it was also the loneliness— the loneliness of making necessary decisions on the behalf of others, potentially affecting their lives, sometimes on matters of life and death.

Then there was the personal loneliness—of wives and children far away and badly missed. The longer families were apart, the more difficult it was to stay in touch and share common interests, values, and thoughts. Wild knew that Shackleton, like him and many of the men, had drifted apart from his loved ones at home. He knew also that the same happened in reverse as wives bemoaned husbands who spent months, sometimes years, away in what they saw as the frivolous pursuits of an explorer.

Wild knew the critical importance of the success of this expedition for them all but especially for Shackleton. He had a lot riding on this: his livelihood, the investors' interests, his reputation, and his promise to the king.

The financial success of this expedition was critical too. Shackleton planned to sell both ships, the *Endurance* and *Aurora*, at the end of the expedition to recoup his money to pay his debts and to monetize the assets produced by Hurley, Marston, Wordie, and the other scientists. He'd been contracted to publish an account of the expedition and had every intention to bask in great success once they had conquered the continent, crossing from one side to the other, via the pole, for the first time. Both the explorers and the empire would be victorious.

Shackleton bore the burden with grave personal responsibility, and as would be attributed to another great leader of the time, he would *never, never,* ever *give up.* That was his mantra. This was his passage. This was his purpose, and no one knew that better than Wild, his right-hand man.

The Great War
Gallipoli Peninsula, Turkey

The landing craft pitched in the steep chop off the beach. Jimmy Smith figured they had two hundred yards to go before they hit the surf. The noise was horrific, deafening. Smith glanced over at Richie Blundell. He could see that he was scared witless and wanted nothing more than to go back to their hometown of Bolton. He thought they all were frightened.

Artillery shells screamed overhead and exploded nearby. The rattle of enemy machine guns reached Jimmy, causing him to tremble in fear, especially when the clang and thwack of bullets rang out when the landing craft came under fire. Dense black smoke rose from the beach as Allied incoming artillery bombarded Turkish positions.

The incoming rounds made all the men in the landing craft duck, hands holding their helmets. Smith looked around, peering out from beneath the rim of his own helmet. He wondered what in the hell he'd gotten himself in to. Suddenly the landing craft heaved to the left as an .88 round threw another geyser of spray thirty feet in the air to his left.

Jimmy looked over at Richie, his old friend. They maintained eye contact in fear and to reassure each other that it was going to be all right, but neither of them were convinced. They would have held hands if they could.

"Bloody hell! That was close," shouted Jimmy Smith, stating the obvious.

"Too bloody close" was the response. "Let's get off this rusty blood bucket before we're shot out into the water." Although the prospect of the landing wasn't much better, at least they could run and hide instead of being the sitting ducks they were at this moment.

"Can we not just go home, back to Bolton?" Jimmy asked pointlessly.

The bullets kept hailing in, red crimson streaks spattering across the boat, helmets blown off with the force of God, men falling all around, bleeding, crying, wailing, and dying.

In the last few minutes, the horrors of war had erupted all around them. The high hopes and confidence that they would be home soon after giving the Turks a bloody nose had long evaporated. The look and smell of fear was all around them, as was the terrifying noise of the onslaught against them.

With the gates of the landing boat released, the tin soldiers Jimmy and Richie made the breach and clambered onto the beach with big brave hearts, amid slaughtered men and surrounded by the body parts of brothers and comrades in arms, all the way from their valleys and their farms. The water lapped red around them as they made it to the shore.

The rude awakening continued up the beach with just a few making it within reach of relative safety and the cover of ground to dig their trenches. The bullets, the shells, and the explosions resounding around them, the grown men and boys, wounded, injured, and mutilated, were crying for their mothers like babies.

As the Australians had their own battle band, so did the British in the form of the trusty Scottish regiment's marching band, which had motivated armies for centuries and instilled fear in their enemies. The wailing banshees' fighting tunes and merry dances spanned the distance, traveling on the wind to announce their presence.

Pipers on the Wind

The pipes in the distance utter my name.
The dying, the wounded, the dead, and the lame.
The machine guns incessant with their rat-a-tat-tat.
I am lying here with me, me gun, and me tin hat.

I pray for the day to be back at hame
With my wee Lizzie Littlejohn and ma wee bairn.

I listen to the wailing of the pipes and the men.
It takes me back to Glasgee and the rolling glen.

Dancing around like the notes on the air.
The splutter and splatter of red without a care.
Brave men and soldiers they be,
Giving their lives, their souls, for George V.

13
THE RACES

Day 278
The *Endurance*
Weddell Sea Ice

VINCENT, AT THE CHALKBOARD, SET up the bookie's stand for the big race, the Weddell Sea Derby. The men were betting money, chocolate, cigarettes, or in Alfie Cheetham's case, bottles of champagne in the pub that he would open upon their return to England.

The course had been laid off from Khyber Pass at the eastern end of the old lead to a point clear of the jibboom, around seven hundred yards.

The betting was fierce and the spirit of competition sharp with a sense of fun and camaraderie as a highlight amid what was otherwise a very bleak situation.

With Shackleton as starter, Worsley as judge, and James as timekeeper, the race was all set.

The odds were set with Frank Wild as favorite at 2/3 on; evens for Crean and Hurley, the crafty Antipodean; at 2/1 Macklin at 6/1; and the "outsider" McIlroy at 8/1.

The rest of the crew were ready for the race, and the dogs that weren't competing were howling in excitement. It was just like a day at Epsom Park. Well, sort of. That's how many imagined it.

Crean and Hurley took an early head-to-head lead, battling their way across the first two hundred yards with Macklin and McIlroy trailing and Wild close behind in third.

As they skirted around the snowdrifts in the center of the course, staying on clear ice for greater speed and traction, Wild moved into second, close behind Hurley, with Crean dropping to a close third.

Neck and neck, Hurley and Crean passed the five-hundred-yard marker, but with Wild's momentum and better line, he took the race on the line by a nose in a time of two minutes sixteen seconds, or an average of ten and a half miles an hour.

The crowd of men and dogs roared as they crossed the finish line, Wild with a victorious fist pump as his lead dog crossed the finish line and looking over at Hurley with his big Yorkshire smile.

"Get yer next time, Yorkie!" Hurley shouted.

"With a bit more practice, my Aussie friend."

After the race, Charlie Green made hot milk and cocoa and bannock cakes to celebrate. Wild went off to his treasure chest and topped up the steaming mugs with rum.

Although the races were fun for sure, there was method to Shackleton's and Wild's madness. Not only would these races keep the boys busy and break up the monotony, but also they would serve as useful fitness training for the dogs and their drivers. Who knew how much the dogs might be needed later?

Wild came to realize that his concerns about Shackleton's periods of solitude in his cabin were unfounded. Shackleton had used that precious time to plan for every eventuality in an increasingly uncertain future. The Weddell Sea Derby was just one of his many clever ways of keeping his men preoccupied and less prone to doubt and worry about the menacing ice surrounding them and their ship.

Wild noticed this, and his admiration for the boss's tactics grew daily.

The *Aurora*
McMurdo Sound, Antarctica
May 1915

The captain of the *Aurora*, Aeneas Mackintosh, and the ten men of the shore party hunkered down in the supply depot just up from the shore, keeping out of the brutal subzero winds. The captain knew that the danger of getting disoriented and lost in whiteout conditions like these was quite real. They'd have to stay put until the worst of the blow had passed. As the wind howled, Mackintosh worried about what was happening aboard *Aurora*, moored just offshore in McMurdo Sound.

First Officer Joseph Stenhouse tried not to panic as the wind increased, slamming *Aurora* against her moorings. He could literally feel the ship straining and fighting to get free in the incredible storm. The captain insisted on leaving the bulk of the crew aboard the vessel, saying that it was the safest place to be. Stenhouse wondered if it would have been safer if they'd all gone ashore with sufficient supplies to last throughout the duration of the coming winter months.

As the hours passed, the storm worsened. The wind shrieked in the ice-coated rigging. Mackintosh would have thought the waves would have washed over the ship, but there were no waves. The ice cover made it as if they were aground or hauled up on dry land. Suddenly he felt the motion. It was subtle at first, almost indistinguishable from the motion imparted by the force of the wind on the superstructure spars and rigging, yet something had changed.

Dressing against the elements, Stenhouse made his way up the companionway stairs to the hatch leading to the quarterdeck. He carefully opened the hatch and was immediately met with a blast of freezing air that burned his lungs. No man or dog could live in such atrocious weather. Death would come in minutes. He strained to see around him in the light of the dawn, but in the whiteout conditions, visibility had dropped to zero. Or almost.

To his horror, he could see that *Aurora* had come unmoored. The ice floe they'd anchored her to was adrift, having broken free of the pack, and was on the move. He could scarcely believe his eyes as he stared at the patch of dark water that stretched beyond the scope of his vision. Still, the sea was relatively calm because there was no fetch for waves to build on. It was the strangest sensation, being in a full gale at sea with no discernible waves to buffet and threaten the ship.

"Oh my God," Stenhouse whispered, wondering what would happen to the men stranded ashore as *Aurora* set a course north with no engines or sail to power her. In the coming hours, with Stenhouse and the rest of the crew helpless to act, the force of the wind carried the ship out of McMurdo Sound and into the midst of the Ross Sea. Then she lost her rudder. Stenhouse and the men worked hard to make repairs, but none could be made, so he and the crew were helplessly carried ever northward.

When the storm abated, Captain Mackintosh and his men exited the small shelter of the supply depot they'd established. His heart sank. The ship, his ship, was gone, blown away in the storm. Fighting back his panic, he calmly said, "Well, men, it looks like we're going to have to trek to Cape Evans. It's the only hut suitable for us to survive the winter."

"But surely the ship will return. First Officer Stenhouse wouldn't just leave us here," one of the men said.

Sighing and shaking his head, Mackintosh said, "He might not have a choice. After all, he can't very well sail through the ice. Even with a working engine, it would be almost impossible to get back to us."

The captain could see the despair in the facial expressions of the men. He could hear it in their voices.

"We'll survive this!" he said, trying to be enthusiastic for the sake of his men.

The captain told the men to get ready to go when he returned to the supply depot. He was thankful that the efforts of previous expeditions just might save them, for there were other supply depots, other huts.

Such huts included Hut Point, constructed by Scott's men during his Discovery Expedition of 1901 to 1904, otherwise known as Discovery Hut. It was used as a large storehouse and had not been designed to be a shelter for men.

Cape Royds, constructed by Shackleton's men during his Nimrod Expedition of 1907 to 1909, was designed to be lived in and had a large stove and enough provisions to last a team of fifteen men an entire year.

Cape Evans, constructed by Scott's men for the Terra Nova Expedition of 1910 to 1912, was a much larger hut than Shackleton's, complete with ancillary stores and stables.

Mackintosh figured that with any luck they'd have enough provisions to last about one year. If *Aurora* made it back to civilization, they just might stand a chance.

Day 290
The *Endurance*
Weddell Sea Ice

Halfway through the long darkness of the Antarctic winter, it was time for another celebration dinner at the Ritz with speeches, songs, and toasts and "God Save the King." These moments were what kept the *Endurance* crew alive in both spirit and soul.

There were skits from the crew, this time led by Hurley, doing a rendition of "Waltzing Matilda," accompanied by Crean, McNish, McIlroy, and James on percussion.

Charlie Green and Blackborow did a *Punch and Judy* show featuring Shackleton, Worsley, and Wild as the main characters. Then the Irishmen clubbed together for "Danny

Boy" with the rest of the crew joining in midway, the finale being a lung-fueled "God Save the King" that sounded like it was intended to travel the thousands of miles back to London and King George V himself. "God save our gracious king! Long live our noble king! God save the king! Send him victorious, happy, and glorious, long to rule over us. God save the king!"

A Day at the Races

It's a day at the races on the Weddell Sea.
Vincent, the bookie, with the odds on display.
Shackleton the starter, Worsley the judge,
James keeping the time and giving them a nudge.

Wild, Crean, and Hurley taking the betting lead,
The rest of the field falling behind the steam.
Excitement builds as they set on their way
To Khyber Pass and a spectacular relay.

All the way out and then to the turn
Hurley and Crean in the lead, but Wild will return,
Building momentum as his team gets the taste,
Winning by a nose in this Antarctic race.

Keeping the men preoccupied was a major effort for Wild and the other leaders. Pleasant distraction was a hard concept to grasp in such desperate times, but it was a focus that Wild knew would be their savior. They engaged in skits, sing-songs, poetry nights, and the races, and just like the men on the western front, they played the empire's favorite game, football, a most diverting pastime.

Vahsel Bay Warriors and Weddell Sea United were born a long way from their favorite teams, Manchester United, Liverpool, and Arsenal, and a very long way from Jimmy Smith's favorite, the Bolton Wanderers.

Frank Worsley, manager of the Warriors, and Wild, manager of United, were set for their own World Cup at what seemed a million miles from anywhere.

The talented Orde-Lees was in the goal for the Warriors. In front were Worsley, Clark, Wordie, and Rickinson, with Greenstreet, Holness, Hurley, and Macklin in midfield and the big McCarthy and the agile and fit Bakewell up front, ready to poach the goalmouth.

Worsley had a dynamic team capable of good defense with their upfront duo, capable of scoring a goal or two.

Wild's team was equally impressive. Big Tom Crean in goal was almost unpassable. James, the fit and feisty marine, and Vincent were sweepers. McLeod, Wild himself, Chatham, the young Welsh boy Blackborow, and Hussey were in the midfield. Hudson, McIlroy, and How formed the three-man strike partnership.

Shackleton blew the first-half whistle, and within a minute, Wild, taking the kick and passing to How, played a one-two, one-two. They were suddenly in the box, and How blasted the leather-bound ball straight past Orde-Lees, to his left, too far away to reach, the ball glimpsing his gloved fingertips for a goal. The score was 1–0 United. They celebrated their early goal with Orde-Lees, Worsley, and the rest of the team making their appeals to the referee, Shackleton.

The men had cleared the surface snow to make the pitch as even as they could. Their boots were slipping on the ice. The determination on both sides to win this Antarctic Cup was clear.

United held their lead for twenty minutes until Orde-Lees launched a big kick down the middle of the field. Worsley headed and found McCarthy, who dribbled it toward United's goal, tackled, and slipped it past Vincent and into the running path of Bakewell, who slipped it side footed past big Tom Crean for a score of 1–1 at halftime.

The players sipped on hot tea and milk while the two managers briefed and rallied their teams with their various halftime tactics. After five minutes, Shackleton called them back to play for the second half.

It was a competitive game with both sides determined to win, helped with the side bets of chocolate rations and tobacco and the promise of goods and services upon their return to civilization, including bottles of champagne and construction projects. Wild even offered to be a personal butler to Worsley for a month.

With five minutes to go to full time, Bakewell scored a second goal, and Hudson an equalizer, for a score of 2–2.

Wild picked up the ball in midfield from a wayward pass and charged toward the Warriors' goal, and Orde-Lees, shimmering as he reached striking distance, pulled the ball back with his favored right foot and launched the leather ball to the top right of the goal, past the keeper's hands, to score: 3–2, United. Shackleton blew the whistle, signaling full time—game over. United and Wild were victorious.

A few days later there was another race between the two crack teams, Hurley's and Wild's, and a rerun of the rivalry, along with the #1 and #2 from the previous Antarctic derby. Ever since the last race, Hurley and Wild had been winding each other up. It inevitably came down to a rematch between the two.

The buildup was even more intense than before. The rules were the same as before, but this time there was a weigh-in to make sure that they were both on equal footing, the weight being a total of 910 pounds or 130 pound per dog.

Vincent again ran the book, Alfie Cheetham betting more of his yet to be seen bottles of champagne, and the now usual bets of chocolate and tobacco.

The two sleds, the dogs, Wild, and Hurley were at the start line, the packs barking and howling as a signal of their appetite for the race ahead. The blade runners on each of the sleds were feeling the pressure, the buildup, the growing momentum to move forward. Wild and Hurley were doing their best to hold on until the signal to release their dog power and commence the race.

The crew were howling, as were the dogs. It was an exciting spectacle on the Weddle Sea ice shelf, the deep, dark, icy, and deadly blue of the frozen ocean below them.

Shackleton, Worsley, and the rest of the officers, pipes in hand, overseeing the races of the day, sat in their directors' chairs with hot tea and rum before them as the signal went up. The two teams, one headed by Wild, the other by Hurley, sped off from the Khyber Pass, neck and neck. Everyone there had a bet, real or not, on the race. Cheetham had bet on Hurley with his promise of champagne to come, Crean had bet tobacco, McNish had bet his wooden knickknacks, Vincent had bet rations he had shelved from the galley, and Shackleton and Worsley had bet real, hard cash, not that there was anywhere to spend British sterling within approximately eighteen hundred miles of their desperately ice-locked location.

Of course, Wild had the leverage of his treasure chest for bets and promises, and Hurley had hero-making photographic opportunities and wherewithal.

As the crew watched the whole race, Hurley had a nose on Wild, but then Wild picked up momentum and gathered pace. Neck to neck, they ate the last part of the course, and eventually Wild beat Hurley by a yard and an impressive two minutes and nine seconds, or eleven and one-tenth miles per hour, with Hurley a close seven seconds behind.

Shackleton was pleased with the improvement in speed and was delighted that the men had yet another outing to try to forget their desperate situation.

There was controversy, however. On the weigh-in after the race, Worsley reversed the result and gave the race to Hurley on the grounds of his compliance with the weight requirements, whereas Wild apparently had not complied.

Afterward, with lots of joviality and banter, the men drank up the hot milk and devoured the bannocks, but this time Wild didn't venture to his treasure chest. He was visibly miffed at the technical loss.

"Better luck next time," Hurley teased Wild. Wild ignored him.

It was a long, dark winter. On July 26 was the first sight of sun for seventy-nine days. Living without the blessing of the sun wilts the soul. The sighting was of immense relief and uplifting to all the crew, including Shackleton, Worsley, and Wild.

Wild stood on the deck watching the sun slowly sneak toward, then rise above, the horizon, the first sight of the sun for so long. He enjoyed the warmth of its glow as it rose in the morning sky. Wild stretched his arms skyward in a welcoming and warming salute. Shackleton joined him, coming up by his side. Slowly, one by one, each of the crew joined them on the upper decks in wonder of this sight, the sight of the sun that seems so normal a part of life, yet for these men it had been missing for the past two months or more, which time they'd spent in darkness.

Sunday Sunset

The sun comes up in the morning light
Just as the day is dawning bright.
A welcome sign to awaken me
As I set about my daily routine.

I busy my way throughout the days,
Monday, Tuesday, and Wednesday rays.
I think about the sun on my skin
And how it helps my day begin.

Thursday, Friday, and Saturday pass by.
It's always more pleasant when you are in the sky.

Sunday comes, and it is always a good bet
When the close of the week sees the sunset.

That evening, the men thought the captain had gone mad as Worsley was having an ice bath on the floe. Stark naked except for his woolen hat, he, like a madman, bathed in the ice, freezing cold for a while, with just his pipe and a crazy smile.

His intention was to have a bit of fun, to lighten up the mood. Worsley invited others to join him. However, the crew left the frozen captain to it, laughing out loud as Worsley succumbed after just two minutes and rushed back to the warmth of a bath he had prepared with steaming water.

They all assembled later in the Ritz, and once again Wild ventured into his treasure chest.

Shackleton, Worsley, and Wild understood the importance of not only maintaining the ship's routine but also creating some fun moments to boost the morale of the crew.

Regular games of football, skits in the Ritz, dressing up, and evenings of plays and poetry were the order of most days, most often with McNish taking the lead with Robbie Burns–style poems that he would read from his closely guarded little leather-bound book.

Wild wrote in his journal of how difficult it might be for those never exposed to such adversity to comprehend that the crew had these regular celebrations and events and seemingly did everything they could to stay upbeat and confident no matter how bad their circumstances. It was this type of fortitude that had built the British Empire, the maintaining of a stiff upper lip and expressing no complaints even on the darkest of days, the use of humor to dissipate anxiety, and the mental strength and determination to overcome danger and the greatest of all fears.

These men were pioneers and explorers. Their mission was for king, country, and empire. Fear paralyzed, and anxiety was only counterproductive. Supreme confidence to overcome anything was the only way forward.

These were very extraordinary times indeed.

14
UNDER PRESSURE

Day 360
The *Endurance*
The Weddell Sea

THE ICE WAS RAFTING UP to ten and fifteen feet around the *Endurance*. On August 1, she listed ten degrees under the pressure and sheer force of the millions of tons around her. Ice smoke puffed out because of the sheer pressure and friction underneath. The haunting sounds from the ice below preyed on the mind and whittled the soul.

Even the most optimistic and calmest of characters, Frank Wild, started to think that they were in a precarious position, although that was probably obvious to most. This was getting serious.

The earsplitting explosion of ice, thick ice, breaking and sheering upward against the ship startled Wild. He couldn't believe the forces at work against the reinforced wooden hull of the *Endurance*. He feared that it was only a matter of time before Mother Nature won the war against her. *And what then?* He dared not go there or even consider the implications. *What were humans anyway?* Humans were proving to be nothing more than animals in the trenches throughout Europe. Maybe for Wild, defeat on the ice was his calling, his fate, after all.

Wild dispelled these defeatist thoughts, knowing how destructive they could be, and he went below deck to Shackleton's cabin. He quietly and politely knocked on the door.

"Enter." Upon hearing Shackleton's familiar booming voice, he opened the door and walked in.

Although the cabin was by no means opulent, it was certainly more luxurious than the other quarters, and private. Privacy was not on the list of an explorer's life, and Wild, in the company of his old friend, felt the momentary delight of just the two of them in one room.

The shelves of the cabin were stocked with Shackleton's many books. The aroma of pipe smoke and whisky was in the air. His journal was on the desk with scribbles and notes. Shackleton was a disciplined man with a disciplined mind. A bottle of Mackinlay's and a whisky glass were neatly in place in his cabinet. His outerwear was hanging neatly in the corner, and his bunk was made, so neat and tidy that it would do any military man, even a cavalryman, proud. Wild thought you could bounce a penny off the taut blankets and sheets, like a trampoline.

Wild knew the importance of self-discipline and mental strength. Not all had it 100 percent between their ears or in their hearts, and the many who didn't, and the few who could succeed without their full ration of blessings, could make up for it by training their minds to be strong. One led to the other, and often vice versa, was Wild's theory.

"You've got to make your bed in the morning to succeed" was another of Wild's favorite sayings, and given his recent concerns about Shackleton, he was both pleased and relieved to see these signs of a heightened level of self-discipline that didn't exist in many, especially during these times of extreme anxiety, uncertainty, and potential peril.

It took a special man to be this way, and he knew that his friend, the boss, was a very special man indeed.

Shackleton looked up from the map he was studying on his desk. Wild could see the drawings, the notes, and the apparent escape routes that the boss was clearly working through his mind, not that there were many options available to them.

"Morning, Frank. How are you?" Shackleton asked with a knowing look on his face.

"The boys are getting worried, boss." Shackleton was nodding. "What's our plan if she takes us down?" Wild asked. Shackleton turned his gaze slowly back to the map, running his hands through his hair like a mad professor on the cusp of a great invention.

"Well, Frank, the options are limited. We have to have faith in the *Endurance*, her strength of character and resolve."

"It's more the strength of her hull that I am interested in, boss," Wild said. "We need a backup plan, boss. Just in case, you know."

At that moment the ship lurched and tipped another couple of degrees, temporarily catching Wild off foot.

He lunged and caught himself. The screaming of the ice crushing around them came from the depths below like some mad banshee grasping for their souls.

"Yes, yes, you are right of course, Frank." Shackleton pointed at the map on the desk and traced out the route from their current position to a landmass, Elephant Island. "I think that would be our best plan, but we have no choice other than to wait it out to see if she can get through this. Or we wait until the ice releases us."

"What about taking the fastest sleds and making a run ashore?" Wild offered, a common question from his men.

"To what end? And then what, Frank? Even if we got there, across the ice shelf, then what?"

The boss had a point. They had already sent out some pathfinder sleds to see if there was a line of sight to land, but the ice was very unpredictable, ebbing and flowing as it expanded and contracted, causing pools to suddenly open and then close just as quickly, putting the men in danger of being swallowed up and lost in the icy depths forever.

"Heaven forbid if she is taken, Frank. Our best chances are in open water and not at the mercy of the ice. If we get to that point, then the lifeboats will be our saviors."

Wild stood before him, pondering the point, then nodded slowly in agreement. He knew that Shackleton had given it a lot of thought, and who was he to argue with the great man himself?

"Right enough, boss. You're right. But the boys are nervous. You know that as much as I."

"Aye, Frank, I know that. We're all nervous, right?"

Wild nodded and turned about. He was good with that. All the boys needed to know was that the boss had a plan. That would give them some reassurance and keep them calm enough for now.

The added listing, the rumblings, and the horrific groans and screeches from the ice and the timbers around them just added to their anxiety and did everything to test even Shackleton's and Wild's mental strength.

The ice was very unpredictable, one hour retreating, the next advancing, cracks appearing, water rising in pockets and then coming back.

As a precaution, Shackleton ordered the dogs to come aboard, as losing the dogs at this point would be disastrous. He was leaving all options open, and despite his preference to get to open sea, his plan B of not too many more plans was to make a dash for land on the sleds. At average speeds, and certainly slower than Wild's eleven miles an hour, a quick sprint to land might be possible if they found a clear way on the ice, but that was a gamble. Twenty hours at ten miles an hour might get them within reach of the continent, but they also knew the inherent perils with regard to the integrity of the ice below, never mind the ice fields and obstacles that could slow their progress down to a crawl. Shackleton had estimated that such a journey could take more than a month or six weeks, a very big bet to take against the wild and ruthless streak of the enemy around them.

Under the watchful eye of big Tom Crean, Harry McNish oversaw building the kennels on the deck, and in a couple of days the task was complete. Crean had taken a patriarch role with the dogs and their new pups, which were his main source of distraction from the plight the crew were in.

The early pressures the men had experienced as a crew on the way from London to Buenos Aires had subsided as they had learned to get along with each other and faced the stark realization that they were in this together.

With everyone being desperate to find a potential escape route and get back to land, a few days later, Worsley, Hurley, and Greenstreet headed off to a large iceberg they had nicknamed Rampart Berg to explore potential routes off the ice. Just a little way out they quickly turned around as the integrity of the ice was uncertain and unsteady, and the risk of being consumed was too great.

They were well and truly trapped on the ice shelf with the *Endurance* hemmed in like a delicate oasis amid a vast desert of ice. The escape routes to land by sled were limited, if not nonexistent. They needed to stay with the *Endurance* as their best hope to escape once the ice melted, at which point they would be released and free to travel on their way.

Wild noted that as their situation was worsening, the grip on the ship was tightening and the cacophony of the ship's beams strained under the enormous pressure, rivets popping like bullets and the horrific screeching from deep below haunting the crew every minute of every day and night. This was mental torture at its height, inflicted by the most powerful force known to humankind, Mother Nature.

The ice was moving constantly, opening and closing, freeing, then tightening around the *Endurance*. The creaking and groaning of timbers, loud snapping sounds both fore and aft, told the dismal and horrifying story of the strain.

"Do you think she can resist?" Wild asked Shackleton.

"She is the finest ever made, and if anyone can, then it is she," responded Shackleton in a matter-of-fact tone.

"And what if she cannot?"

"As I told you, staying with her is the better bet than trying to take the dogs to shore. The risks are too great, and there is only a limited chance of success. We must rely on the strength of the oak that she was made from and the craftsmen who built her."

Wild knew the pressure of the ice around them was the most powerful force and that ultimately, if it came down to it, and if the ice chose to do so, it would win.

They both hoped that the sun and currents would return to warm the ice shelf and release them into the ocean so they could move forward.

As the ice shifted and moved, the once plentiful seals and penguins had disappeared, seeking safer environments and consequently abandoning the *Endurance*. They were running low on fresh meat for the dogs.

They were running low on morale and resolve.

Day 421

On September 30, the crew experienced their worst squeeze yet as the decks shuddered and jumped, planks popped, beams arched, and the stanchions buckled and shook.

Shackleton ordered the crew to stand by for whatever unknown emergency they may have to face, including abandoning the ice-struck ship.

Wild walked the upper and lower decks, taking time to go see each of the crew, observe the mood, and find out how they were holding up. The obvious signs told him they were not doing too well.

Wild could smell the anxiety in the air. The men had fearful looks on their faces. They were silent about it, but the reality was becoming very grim. Despite that, the off-the-cuff sense of humor was still evident as they tried to keep their peckers up.

The *Endurance* was now 346 miles from Paulet Island, a place where Shackleton knew there were stores from a previous Swedish expedition of 1902. In fact, Shackleton himself had arranged for the provisions to be deposited there years earlier, as they had never been used by the Swedes. He also knew that the island was too far to reach over the ice, even with the luck of the gods. It would be a two-to-three-month journey, and as the ice would seasonally begin to melt, it would become even more perilous, if not totally impossible.

Running short of reserves, stores, fuel, and food, they were also running short of resolve and hope, as the unpredictable forces around them were forever in their minds, as they could see the landscape with their eyes and hear the terrible sounds with their ears.

Wild looked out at the sea of ice around them, rugged and jutting as the power from below and the pressure from around pushed up the pinnacles of ice like carvings at some grand wedding of the gods. He pulled out his pipe, took a few puffs to get it going, pulled out his flask, took a swig, and just stared out across the desperate landscape before him.

It was an anxious October.

The *Endurance* broke free from the ice momentarily and stood upright, proud and tall, giving the crew time to celebrate with a cheer of good hope that their fortunes were changing for the better and, for a moment, dispelling the thought of the unthinkable, getting crushed out at sea, hundreds of miles from land.

"What man could survive such a fate?" was a question on all their minds, especially Frank Wild's.

Their optimism was dashed just four days later. In the engine room, the weakest part of the ship felt the brunt of the squeeze. The noise was unimaginable as the ship's sheer existence hung in the balance.

The propeller was bent at an angle and the rudder badly damaged. Even if they got out of this squeeze, they would need repairs to move on, and fuel to go on without the sails.

The next day, the next wave of attack, the *Endurance* listed over at an impossible thirty degrees, then released the next day. The ice appeared to be a pool of water, only to return with twice the might.

Then on October 27, 1915, a fateful day, the power of nature eventually defeated the brave *Endurance*, crushing her as if she were made of the most delicate material imaginable by the most potent force known to humankind. She was consumed by the ice but bizarrely was still afloat, stuck in the ice but with her hull a sad relic of splintered beams, well beyond repair.

Wild couldn't believe it, and yet the fate of the ship had been sealed long ago. He'd known it, Shackleton had known it, and so had the men. As the bang and the boom of severing timbers carried in the otherwise quiet air, Wild fought back the despair. He clearly saw that everyone else felt pretty much the same way. They were stuck on the ice with no ships and dwindling supplies and were at least 250 miles from land.

Now what?

It was still a matter of hurry up and wait, and that made the situation even worse. Wild made sure that he maintained discipline by providing at least some form of daily routine, while at the same time humoring the men as much as he could. Shackleton, was the leader of granite; Worsley, the stoic Kiwi/New Zealander; and Wild, a man with a treasure chest of delights to keep the men's spirits up.

Crean was a "trump" as Shackleton had described him. Crean rallied the men at every stage with his no-nonsense, dry humor that even in their desperation managed to get some laughs.

Their demise was unspoken. They continued in silence, each man wrapped up in his own private thoughts of what might become of them.

Crush

The roaring of the ice and the floes
Rings in my ears and curls my toes.
Which one will be the final squeeze
That brings the *Endurance* to her knees?

The decks shuddered, the beams arched,
The stanchions buckled, and the planks popped.

Dogs and sleds at the ready
In anticipation of a near future march.

The fatal day came at the end of November.
She had fought a hard fight but in the end couldn't resist.
The thunders and roars and the noises to remember
As she went down in the icy, lonely mist.

What will become of us now
As we sit on the ice floes surrounded by snow?
No sight of land anywhere near.
We only have months to make it out of here.

15
SHIP'S CAT

Day 449
On the Ice, Dump Camp
The Weddell Sea

THE *ENDURANCE*, LIKE A TOY, lay crippled, lodged in the ice with her body crushed and her carcass still floating in the ice floe in which she was trapped. With very heavy hearts, the crew started to salvage what they could—equipment, stores, and provisions—knowing that the ice could lose its grip at any time and send the ship to the bottom of the dark, cold depths.

Wild oversaw the setup of the tents beside her, the dogs back in their dogloos. The crew named their new home Dump Camp.

That night they endured an impossibly restless night on the ice, listening to the groans and moans beneath them, their ears to the ice, trying to sleep. They heard the incessant cracking noises from the *Endurance* as the ice continued to crush her bones, along with the terrible noises from the deep.

Wild joined Shackleton and Worsley and took grog, the sailor's version of tea infused with rum, around the tents in the morning to lift the men's spirits. The men were lethargic, in need of humor to brighten the very dark day and the prospects before them, in need of hope in this desperate situation.

As they served the tea, Wild joked, "If any of you gentlemen need yer boots polished, then just leave them outside." It was the Yorkshireman's attempt to cheer them up, referring to their lethargy. It made some of the men smile, but not all.

"If you think I'd trust you with my boots, Yorkie, you've got another thing coming," parried Hurley with his ever-reliable Australian humor and high spirits.

The day got even darker as Shackleton gave the order that the youngest pups be shot. "We cannot undertake the maintenance of weakness in our journey ahead," he said, as if he were the high court judge, the executioner, or the grim reaper himself.

Wild watched the men keenly, especially Crean, the now self-appointed kennel master. He found it incredibly difficult to witness the big, hard Irishman sob as he heard the three *pop, pop, pop*'s signaling the end of the dogs' short lives. It would be even harder for all the men, never mind Crean, to actually eat them despite the careful preparations undertaken by Charlie Green to make the best meal he possibly could given the dire circumstances.

Next up, Shackleton ordered the same demise for Mrs. Chippy. At first McNish refused to obey, stuffing the cat deep within his peacoat. "Yer can leave me cat alone," he protested.

"McNish, you are under the ship's orders," boomed Shackleton.

"Aye, boss, a ship that no longer sails is a ship that no longer is." McNish nodded his head back toward the *Endurance* behind him. The insinuation was obvious: no ship, no captain, no expedition rules.

"McNish," bellowed Shackleton, "we have to survive together. I know this is difficult, but you have no choice, man."

Wild stepped forward to enforce the order, and he and Vincent closed in on McNish. McNish knew this was an argument that he just couldn't win. With tears in his eyes, he allowed Vincent to grab Mrs. Chippy. He kissed her for the last time. With the tears running down his face, they took her to one side, away from McNish's sight. He could hear the deadly *pop* that marked the end of his beloved cat.

The tears turned to anger. His eyes were red and he glared at Shackleton and said not a word.

"You did the right thing for our survival, McNish. I will tell you that between now and home, we have many more impossible decisions to make if we are to live to tell this tale."

It was very obvious that McNish was angry. All the men, including Wild, hung their heads, looking at their boots, to let the very sad moment of desperation pass.

McNish just stared at Shackleton, drilling a hole through the back of his head with his bright red, bloodshot eyes.

Wild and Worsley followed Shackleton to their tent. Shackleton pulled out the Bible that Queen Alexandra had given to the ship before she sailed, and he read straight from the page that he had bookmarked earlier: "Out of whose womb came the ice? And the hoary frost of Heaven, who gathered it? The waters are hid as with a stone, and the face of the deep is frozen" (Job 38:39–30).

They sat together in silence for a while as they shared a mug of Mackinlay's between them and each lit up a pipe. Wild eventually broke the silence.

"We all have heavy hearts, boss. It was necessary, and as you said, if we are to survive, we will need to make some tough decisions. The boys understand that, but it was hard for them, especially Crean and McNish."

"Thanks, Frank. I appreciate that. And the Mackinlay's." They toasted silently.

"What's the plan now, boss?" The wind and the snow blasted the tent sides. Just as Wild had asked the question, a big gust hit, the canvas billowing around them, almost knocking the three men over.

Shackleton took a couple of puffs, apparently in deep thought. "We need to get the crew mobilized. We need to get onto the sleds as much of the stores and provisions as we can carry and then move toward land, pulling the lifeboats behind us, heading toward Elephant Island. As we make progress, we'll send back the fastest sleds to pick up more provisions from here as we need them.

"Let's leave the crew here while we send a pathfinder party ahead to track the best route, and then we can head out from here in two days' time."

Wild nodded his approval. "Right you are, boss. I will get the boys ready to go."

"Thanks, Frank. You really are a right hand to my left, especially in times of need and desperation."

"As you have always been with me, boss. The feeling is mutual."

Wild felt a surge of emotion, and he battled it back, noting the look of great sadness in his friend's eyes. He had no doubt that his own eyes revealed the depths of what he was feeling, and he didn't care. Wild left the tent to go and get the pathfinder party ready and to brief the rest of the crew on the plan for the next two days. His intention was to keep them focused on a plan and give them a purpose.

Wild had had his doubts about his friend over the past few weeks, troubled by his solitude, his being introverted more than normal—alone, aloof. And Wild suspected he was probably drinking more than was good for him or the expedition. But he knew that desperate times called for desperate measures, and he also knew that Shackleton had an unparalleled ability to dig deep and lead in the most adverse circumstances.

This will be the boss's ultimate test, Wild concluded.

Mrs. Chippy

You, you, you shot me cat.
You, you, you horrible brat.
I get the point we had to survive,
But surely you could have let me keep him alive.

You, you, you didnay need do that.
You could have thought about that, you gnat.
He was a better friend than you all.
For him I would have taken a fall.

I know, I know, we didnay know.
Mr. or Mrs. down in the snow.
But either way, that was fine
And not a reason to put him down.

Day 471
On the Ice, Ocean Camp
The Weddell Sea

Shackleton, Wordie the geologist, Hussey, and Hudson headed out of Dump Camp to find a way forward. Wild watched them as they left and headed into the cold, harsh landscape, disappearing into the cold, icy, and formidable terrain before them.

Wild knew, they all knew, that they had to find a way forward to safer, more solid ice, a way onward to either make a dash to the land over the ice or alternatively, Shackleton's preference, travel by open sea and therefore sail to land. Although the absolute escape routes weren't clearly defined, they knew that staying put was not an option.

Wild stayed in Dump Camp all day, busying the crew with salvaging what they could from the skeleton formerly known as the *Endurance* and gathering the supplies onto the sleds in readiness for their departure, wherever and in whatever direction that may be.

As night started to fall, Wild and the rest of the party were relieved to see the pathfinder party return. They had positive news to report of a path onward with potentially favorable ice fields that they thought could be navigable and allow them to make their way onward, although they all knew that safety at this point was a luxury that wasn't on the menu.

They settled down for another restless and disturbing night, stranded on the ice with nowhere but the tents to call home.

The next morning, they were ready. Having packed up as much of the stores as they could carry, they set off to safer ice to set up the next phase of Shackleton's evolving plan, Ocean Camp.

Over the next week, Wild oversaw the shuttles back to Dump Camp to salvage whatever additional stores could be transported back to their safer, albeit temporary and precarious, position.

Wild was relieved to see Shackleton pick up his game. He was in his element, being a leader who could be relied upon in the direst of situations. Their predicament weighed heavily on all their minds, especially Frank Wild's.

Wild knew that it would be mental strength and fortitude that would see them through their situation. There was no room for self-pity or worry. They had no choice but to survive, floating on thin ice hundreds of miles from land, and then even the prospect of surviving on terra firma was a daunting thought.

The crew were craving a diet that consisted of something other than seal or penguin meat. Wild sent a final foray back to pick up army biscuits, flour, and some potted meats, along with some tobacco, which was always a pick-me-up for the men. After this heart-lifting treat, their immediate priority was to get off the ice.

Conditions in the Antarctic region are without doubt the harshest known to humankind with winter temperatures ranging from a high of minus ten degrees Celsius on the Antarctic coast to minus sixty at the highest parts of the interior. During the summer, it was ten degrees Celsius near the coasts and minus forty elsewhere.

Because of this exceptionally harsh climate, there are no resident plants and no land-based animals. Around the coasts there are penguins, seals, and whales. Five months of the year there is no sight of the sun, between April and September. There are over two hundred snow days a year, and for much of the balance, the winds gust up to almost two hundred miles per hour. Ice is estimated to reach to the depth of nine thousand feet, the underlying land and mountains rising from sea level to over nine thousand feet in elevation.

The Antarctic is by far the most inhospitable place on the planet for mere mortal human beings to survive.

The crew had been at liberty to select their own best clothes for survival for the expedition, and their choices weren't necessarily ones that anticipated the extent of their current predicament.

They knew from the more experienced members that the number of layers of clothing mattered the most. Wild wore a vest underneath a finely knitted shirt and had a variety of layers to add on as insulation from the savage cold.

Worsley had his famous full-face balaclava that protected his head and also insulated his neck from the cutting cold and wind.

Mainly woolen, and without the benefit of modern technology, these garments when worn over the course of time, and wet with salty ocean water, diminished in their ability to insulate.

The men's biggest weapon against the cold was their own resolve and mental strength. Some more so than others had become immune to the pains. Most of the time, their physical pain and suffering wasn't a topic for discussion because, for the most part, these men were stoics who held the belief that complaining never allowed anyone to make any progress anytime soon. *What's the point?*

Protecting the extremities was critically important, so that meant dry socks, good boots, and warm and waterproof mitts. Head coverage was critical, as was where and when to take a pee as temperatures were so cold that the urine could be frozen to the extent that frostbite could make it all the way to the family jewels.

Most of all, good discipline was needed to stay alive. Keep sheltered, keep dry, and take off as many clothes as you can as you sleep in your scratcher to gain the most benefit from putting on warm, dry clothes in the morning, heated and dried in the men's own sleeping bags.

These were some of the basics of survival in these incredibly harsh and alien conditions. Some of the crew knew from experience, and some of the crew were learning as they went.

Wild spotted Blackborow one morning. The young man was pale, shivering uncontrollably, and delirious, realizing that he had slept through the night in his sleeping bag with all the clothes on that he possessed, leaving him with no extra layers to put on in the morning when he awoke and therefore with no additional comfort or warmth to lift his spirits and his body temperature.

Worsley conducted his daily routine using the sextant to get a fix on the sun so he could calculate their position as the floating ice ebbed and flowed some days nearer to land and some days farther away, but overall their position was more favorable, albeit still at least two hundred miles from their target destination.

"Hope yer know what yer doing with that thing." Wild made his attempt at humor.

"Time will surely tell, my friend" was the response.

"How's it looking today?"

"Still a ways to go, Frank." Worsley looked up at Wild.

"We need to get to get to clear water and get the lifeboats—get off this bloody death trap." Wild looked down at the ice beneath their feet.

"The trick is finding it," Worsley said, stating the obvious.

"We will, my friend. We will." Wild walked off to continue his rounds at Ocean Camp.

Day 491:

On November 21, in the middle of the night, the crew heard Shackleton shout out, "She's going, boys!" They all ran to their vantage points on the ice to get a glimpse at the mile-and-a-half distance and to see the *Endurance* taking her last breath as the ice beneath and around her consumed her. She went down bow first, her stern raised in the air, then took a quick dive below for the ice to close over her forever.

The entire crew were silent with heavy hearts and fear. The separation from their ship was now complete and final. It was a desperate sight for all to see her in her final death agony. The men were now stranded on a sheet of ice in the middle of the Weddell Sea with no ship. Who knew how they would get off the ice and make landfall and then, even if they did, how they would get to civilization and safety.

The crew stood there thinking their own thoughts as the depth of their demise weighed heavily on each of their minds.

Wild, seeing the moment, cracked the treasure chest and doled out rations of brandy for the men. He made a toast: "Some ships are wooden, but those ships may sink. The best ships are friendships, and to those ships we drink."

It was if the crew were declaring their independence from the *Endurance* and stating that the strength between them would be the glue that would ensure their survival, like taking a defiant stance against Mother Nature and the power around and beneath them.

If there was any chance of surviving this ordeal, it would be down to the strength of the sum of their parts. Together they would survive and live to tell this tale one day.

Despite Wild's forced optimism, he wondered to himself when that day would be.

16
BANNOCKS

Day 501
On the Ice, Patience Camp
Drifting atop the Weddell Sea

CHARLIE GREEN HAD PERFECTED THE bannock as a simple yet delightful accompaniment to the core diet of seal, penguin, and now dog meat. A bannock is a cake made of flour, fat, water, salt, and baking powder formed into flat rounds and baked on flat sheets atop the blubber burners for ten minutes.

Shackleton had ordered an increase in the rations and more frequent treats from Wild's now diminishing treasure chest to maintain morale.

Clearly the men were in a very perilous and literally precarious position, floating on a vast expanse of ice, although it felt like dry land, and moving up to seven miles a day.

On December 12, Worsley gave his now daily report on their position. They were within two hundred fifty miles of Paulet Island, close to the same latitude they had been a year previous when they'd crossed the circle on New Year's Eve.

It wasn't the best of news. They had made no progress to speak of, and they all knew that just floating on this ice forever wasn't an option. The shelf could break apart at any moment and dump them in the cold beneath, when their survival expectations would suddenly become minutes, not days, the latter of which was where they were at now.

Wild approached Shackleton to press his point. "We need to get to open water, boss, into the boats, and make our way." Although he also knew this was tricky because if they launched the boats and the ice closed back in, then the brutal force would crush the lifeboats like crackers within moments.

"We have to be sure that it's the right one, Frank." Wild nodded and agreed to the inevitable. "Patience, my friend" were Shackleton's words of wisdom.

Patience was a discipline that all sailors, and especially explorers, had to learn. Given the nature of their profession, it was a counterintuitive personality trait, but with months or years on journeys, it was a trait that the most experienced of the crew possessed.

Wild also knew that there was a fine balance between impatience and rash decisions. Crossing that line could land you in trouble quickly. On the other hand, procrastination could result in no action at all. It was somewhere in the middle that some of Wild's teachings fit, one sure foot in front of the other, bravely and boldly, truly and rightly.

The days dragged on. Seasons slowly changed. Gradually the darkness that pervaded for most of the day and night gave way to more day and less night. Spirits rose to a point. Wild knew they were almost out of time. The men couldn't hold out much longer; they needed more than anything to make progress.

"An army with no fire in their belly is an army with no ammunition," Wild said again to Shackleton. "We need to get off this ice, boss, not just for survival's sake, but also because the men will not last. Their patience is thin, as is the ice below us."

Although they largely kept their thoughts to themselves, their demise was demoralizing and their mood was somber as they realized that they were making little progress and their daily efforts were becoming futile. It was now obvious that their only option was to take the boats and head to land, Elephant Island.

As the ice was starting its seasonal melt, the men could see it showing places where cracks could turn into channels, which could in turn lead to open water to launch the boats. On December 22, they decided to have a premature Christmas lunch on the ice as a treat and to prepare them to make a dash for land. They would be ready. Any day now, as soon as the best opportunity presented itself, they would be off.

The feast included the last of the remaining luxuries: anchovies in oil, baked beans, and jugged hare.

The final dregs of Wild's treasure chest were divided up, and the crew had a good sleep before setting off first thing the next day. Wild did keep one bottle of rum for the morning and one bottle of the Mackinlay's for the road ahead. Just in case.

Day 526

December 26 saw another good feed for breakfast to build up the energy and good heart that was needed for whatever journey lay ahead for them: bannocks with the last of the mutton and hot coffee with the final splashes of rum.

Shortly after midday, they set off on their way across the drifting ice to find open water, dragging the three lifeboats behind them. The first two hundred yards took them five exhausting hours to cover, until they met flat planes of ice and an eight-hundred-pound Weddell seal, which boosted their spirits, although apathy was setting in with the hope of survival in the balance.

Since the demise of the *Endurance*, the crew had first set up Dump Camp to remove all they could from the *Endurance* stores. Then they moved to Ocean Camp as they explored icebound escape routes. Patience Camp was where they would launch their ocean-based escape.

Once they had set up Patience Camp, they accumulated their provisions, and Orde-Lees took inventory: 110 pounds of pemmican, 300 pounds of flour, a little tea, some cocoa, a little sugar, some dried vegetables, and some suet.

Hurley and Macklin took two sleds back to Ocean Camp and relayed 130 pounds of dried milk, 50 pounds of dog pemmican, 50 pounds jam, and some potted meat.

The men built igloos for shelter, and a new set of rations was agreed as a daily menu while they built up their energy and morale. Breakfast: half a pound of seal meat and a mug of tea. Lunch: a four-ounce bannock and a mug of milk. Supper: three-quarters of a pint of seal stew.

Given the shortage of food, and to boost the men's food reserves, all the dogs except the two strongest teams were shot.

The men's patience would once again be tested to the nth degree as they sat there and waited for their opportunity.

Day 594

February 29, 1916, saw the men celebrating Leap Year Day. They had only forty days of food remaining in the stores, and they lacked blubber for food and fuel. They had used the last of the cocoa and were being issued three lumps of sugar daily as a treat.

With seals and penguins studiously avoiding them, their lack of food was becoming a very obvious hardship. Even one of the dogs broke loose and grabbed a bannock, chomping as if it had just grabbed a rabbit or some other delicious morsel.

"I'll tell yer, it makes you appreciate the good things when we get home," commented Alfie Cheetham, ever the optimist.

Wild looked at him with a smile of encouragement, while others looked into their mugs of tea, hoping that his prediction would prove true.

Shackleton and Worsley were stoic and determined. Hurley, Cheetham, and Greenstreet were ever optimistic. Charlie Green was a stalwart at the blubber stove, making the best of very little. Crean was stable, but the plight of the dogs was clearly paining him. And the rest were in various degrees of mental instability.

As they went through March, like a mirage, they could see land within reach. They were floating in the right direction and were ready for a dash.

The Ross Sea Party
Beardmore Glacier
McMurdo Sound, Antarctica
March 9, 1916

Spencer-Smith lay on the sled, delirious and suffering from exhaustion, scurvy, and frostbite. Ernest Wild took care of him the best he could in the conditions.

"Where's my wallet? I lost my wallet, my photographs, my brothers," Spencer-Smith kept repeating to himself, one minute shivering and next minute hot, which was bizarre in this freezing cold.

Ernest Wild, the younger brother of Frank, trudged beside him, talking to him, trying to keep his brain engaged as they headed back down from the Beardmore Glacier, two days out, in their return journey to Hut Point and relative comfort.

"Yer should've eaten yer meat," Wild teased, knowing that one of the reasons for Spencer-Smith's condition was that he couldn't stomach the seal meat, their most ubiquitous source of nutrition.

"Have you seen my wallet, Wild?" Spencer-Smith repeated.

"No, Arnie, I have not. It's probably back at the hut."

"It's got my photographs of me and my brothers camping in the woods at home. There's also one of my sister and one of my father and my mother."

"You like yer photographs," Wild responded, keeping Spencer-Smith talking as much as he could. "What's their names?" he asked.

The man on the stretcher wasn't talking or making much sense. He was in the middle of the Antarctic, paralyzed by exhaustion and scurvy—and delirious. Wild knew that he was in serious shape. The night before he had laid him up in their tent, lit a lamp, and left him writing his diary as Wild went for a smoke and a pint of tea with a splash with his pal and comrade Ernest Joyce.

Now, as they trekked back down the glacier, Spencer-Smith was dropping in and out of consciousness, rambling in between as they tramped on. By 4:00 p.m., he had stopped rambling and stopped shaking. Wild pulled up the sled to take a closer look, knowing that earlier in the expedition, Spencer-Smith had been diagnosed with a weak heart. Wild, Joyce, and the rest of the crew wondered if that was a physical condition or a mental state.

Wild called over to Joyce and Mackintosh. "I think he's gone, Captain."

Joyce bent down to check Spencer-Smith's vital signs, listening for his breath and feeling for his heartbeat.

"He's as cold as a cod, no breath and no heartbeat. He's brown bread, sir." Joyce revealed his grim diagnosis.

Mackintosh, not wanting to believe it, also bent down, checking the man's vital signs, and confirmed the lack thereof.

They decided to set up camp for the night. They grilled the seal meat on a blubber stove, made some tea with an extra splash of whisky, and decided what to do with the body.

The next morning, they awoke early, keen to get back to the comfort of the hut.

Wild and Joyce dug an ice grave for Spencer-Smith. After a few words from the Bible read by Mackintosh, he was laid to rest.

On the Ice, Patience Camp
Drifting atop the Weddell Sea

Harry McNish held a deep sadness for the demise of Mrs. Chippy.

Wild noted the deep resentment that Harry McNish harbored toward Shackleton because of his orders to shoot Mrs. Chippy. The man's dissent spread like a cancer, and its infectious qualities worried Wild. If the cohesion of the group dissolved, then they all would most likely die.

Wild often overheard McNish's grumblings.

"Och, what we hanging aboot fer? Let's make a dash for it." He was referring to the proximity of land, estimated by Worsley to be two hundred miles away. "It's a better way than sitting on this ice float waiting for it to melt. I vote to get going and get to land," he announced for all who were listening to hear.

"He got us into this mess. Why would we continue to listen to him? Och, aren't we men ourselves who can make our own decisions about our own souls? I vote that we confront him," McNish said, raising his voice.

Seeing that things were getting out of hand with McNish, Wild spoke to Shackleton and said they needed to put an end to the dissention. To do that meant taking McNish on directly. Wild accompanied Shackleton to the tent that McNish shared with some of the other crew members. Sure enough, McNish was sowing dissent as usual.

"What will you be voting for, carpenter?"

"Voting to get off this ice barge," McNish replied. "We are two hundred miles from land, a fair distance, but it is better than sitting here like a bunch of haggis waiting for culling time."

"And how were you thinking about doing that, carpenter?" Shackleton asked, his voice booming with authority.

"Well, you got us into this, and I think we can make our own decisions." McNish looked around at his audience, who were looking into their mugs of tea, speaking not one word and showing no sign of support.

Shackleton stepped forward toward McNish and, at the same time, pulled his Boer War–model Webley Mark IV pistol from his tunic and pointed it point-blank at McNish's temple.

"Listen very carefully, carpenter. If you want to stay part of this crew, you keep your opinions to yourself. If you have something to say, you say it to me and me alone. Do you understand?" McNish didn't move or say a word. It was obvious that Shackleton was serious, deadly serious.

Shackleton pulled back the hammer on the pistol to cock it.

"Do you know what the consequences of stirring up mutiny on His Majesty's ship are?" Shackleton pushed. McNish stared back with growing hatred.

"I will tell you exactly the consequences. I will give you three options. One, you take the trip off the ice on your own, and two, I shoot you here and now as a mutineer." He paused a moment for theatrical effect and to accentuate the seriousness of his intent. "Which is it to be, McNish?"

It was obvious that McNish was the sole wannabe mutineer, and what previous support for his proposals he had was clearly no longer in existence. Not liking the two options laid down, he inquired, "And the third option, boss?"

"Yes, carpenter, there is a third option, and that is to stay and keep your mouth and your opinions tightly sealed. And if I, any of the officers, or the men hear one of your mutinous ideas, then we will go directly to option two—and I swear to the God above us and the king of our empire, I will shoot you myself. *Do you understand, McNish?*" Shackleton bellowed.

McNish looked at Shackleton, defeated. "Yes, sir. I understand."

Day 627

By April 2, Shackleton ordered the last two teams of dogs to be shot. Wild took Vincent to go and complete the deed. He could not think about passing the task off to any of the others, and Vincent, as a Royal Marine, was a good soldier for this type of task. They chose to do it as well as they could, out of sight from the rest of the crew, but they all knew what was going on. With each shot, Wild clenched his teeth, occasionally closing his eyes in an attempt to rid his mind of the thing he had to do before him. One by one the shots were fired. It was one of the most awful things that Wild had had to do in the name of the king and for the cause of survival.

These were desperate times, he knew. He also knew that such times often called for desperate actions.

They fleeced the dogs and dressed them for food, handing the carcasses over to Charlie Green. As the men closed their minds to the thought of what it was they were eating, they found it tasted somewhat like beef, but even Charlie Green couldn't cook the toughness out of the meat.

It was particularly difficult for Tom Crean, but the big Irishman had been around enough to know that it was necessary for their survival.

Wild reminded himself of an old saying: "There is nothing so vile that the human form cannot become accustomed to." That was becoming truer and truer as every single day passed in their desperate predicament.

Their situation, however, was not one of options but one of necessity. The combination of the rations the dogs needed to consume each day, the unpredictability of the ice, and the opportunity for rations for the men made a compelling argument for the grim decision. Besides, if the crew were to sail to land, then the dogs could not come with them in the three boats, Wild rationalized.

Three days later, Wild and Worsley bagged a sea leopard and two seals for meat but also for the blubber, which fortified the men against the bitter cold.

Worsley estimated that they were within one hundred miles of land and Elephant Island. In the depths of desperation and near starvation, the men found this to be a glimmer of hope.

17
CANDLES

Easter Sunday
April 23, 1916

WITH THE *ENDURANCE* LOST AND the crew on the ice, and at the other side of the Arctic with the Ross Sea Part stranded, it was Easter Sunday and a time for thoughts of home and those at home. The men entertained thoughts of their loved ones and all that was happening during these extraordinary and unprecedented times.

Eastbourne, Sussex, England

Emily looked out the window of the redbrick home on Milnthorpe Road and down on to the road below her. She looked left and looked right as if her husband might be home any moment from work. But Emily's husband, Ernest Shackleton, wasn't a lawyer like her father, nor did he work in an office or a factory. Her husband was a polar explorer, and periods of absence weren't measured in hours or even days but in months and years.

She took a deep breath and sighed and lit the candle in the downstairs window as always—just in case he needed it to find his way home. She knew in her heart that one day he would come home, and she would patiently wait for that day. She had done this before and suspected that this may not be the last time.

Eversholt, Bedfordshire, England

Mrs. Mary Wild, with two of her boys in the Antarctic, not heard from for months, continued the family tradition in their absence. It was Sunday, Easter Sunday, and she busied herself over the open stove, tending her roast beef and of course her famous Yorkshire puddings.

Her husband, Ben, was in his study reading. Today they would have three of their eight sons for lunch and all three of their daughters. Today they would have a celebration and would toast Frank and Ernest, dearly beloved absent sons and brothers.

Frank was the eldest and had often been on his explorations and therefore absent. Mary looked out the window at the fields of the North Yorkshire Dales, the sun shining down after the morning's showers, and thought of her boys and how they would be that day.

She turned to the table, already set for the feast, and quietly and unceremoniously lit a candle for her boys. "Safe travels and fair winds," she said as a blessing as the wick took light along with the light in her heart.

Annascaul, County Kerry, Ireland

Barry Crean was out in the fields of the Crean family farm as he was finishing his day. He lit a pipe and looked down at the ocean below him. It was Easter Sunday, a day before the resurrection and a big day for the Irish people. He would not be involved, but he knew many who would be. He had his own business to tend to and the family farm, and he would support the cause from afar.

He thought of the men on the fields of battle in Europe, and he thought of his own brother, Tom, fighting his own war in some far-off remote and frozen land.

He reached into his pocket, brought out his hip flask, and took a swig of the finest Irish whisky. "To you, my brother Tom. Fair winds be with you." He toasted the skies, the sea, and distant lands beyond the ocean before him.

Kingston upon Hull, England

Eliza was still called Eliza Sawyer although married to Alfie Cheetham. He had disappeared on his polar adventures, leaving her to cope with their nine children, many of whom barely knew their father thanks to his long periods of absence. The options in Hull and the life of a trawlerman were not the best, but at least trawlermen would get home most nights and get paid, she thought.

Alfie had been away for two years now. The last Eliza had heard from him was a letter he'd written her from Buenos Aires eighteen months ago—not a thing since.

Eliza was a busy mother and didn't have too much time to think. She looked out the window and, in the reflection, saw her unkempt hair. She brushed it to one side. Then she caught sight of her threadbare clothes. With as much resentment as sadness, she wished for her Alfie to come home so they could open that pub they had both once dreamed about.

Lewisham, London, England

Marjorie had gone to Southwest India Docks to see off her love, Lewis Rickinson, as he sailed away on the *Endurance* back in August 1914. Apart from the collection of love letters he had sent her eighteen months previously, she had not heard anything from him since he had left. In fact, no news had come back since the confirmation of their departure from South Georgia.

She sat on the train, on her way home from visiting her friend, another girlfriend of the *Endurance* crew, Lillian Mitchell, in the city and thought about her love and if Lewis would ever return.

As she looked out the window and the London buildings and streets passing by, and as the train neared her station, she thought of her and Lewis's last kiss and his promise that they would marry upon his return "Come home, my love," she whispered out the window.

Stepney, East London, England: Lillian Mitchell said goodbye to her soul mate Marjorie. They were both in the same predicament and badly missed their men. She waited for Alexander to return one day so they both could be married. Marjorie and she had fantasized about having a joint wedding at the famous traditional Saint Mary-le-Bow church and being blessed to the sound of the Bow Bells.

Lillian was a Scottish implant, her parents from Glasgow. They would like that too. Ever the optimist, Lillian had no fear that her love would return someday soon. They would marry and have children. "Hurry up home, Alex Kerr."

Newport, South Wales

Millie Blackborow had last heard from her son, Perce, in a letter he sent from South Georgia informing her that he had stowed away on a polar exploring ship, the *Endurance*, and was off to the South Pole. She'd read the letter to her husband, Edwin. Both churchgoing folks, they had said a prayer for their son, Perce, every Sunday and after lunch at home, or at the local pub. They would come home, and both would light a candle for their beloved son to return.

Bolton, Lancashire, England

Nancy Smith had just finished tidying the house and cleaning the kitchen after their Easter Sunday lunch in their two-up, two-down redbrick house on the cobbled street close to the mill where she and her husband had grown up and where they still lived.

Jimmy, her son, had long gone to the army, in 1909, serving in both India and Egypt. But now he was in the horrors of the Great War.

Soon he would be heading to the Somme. She feared for his life each day, wishing that he had just followed in his father's footsteps and worked in the mill, although that was just a dream. Many young men had been compelled to go and face their enemies in Europe, many never coming back.

Nancy lit a candle in the front window as a symbol for Jimmy to come home safely and in one piece one day. She hoped and prayed.

Konopiště, Benešov, Bohemia

Worlds apart in the four-winged, three-story chateau of Konopiště, thirty miles from Prague, Princess Sophie and her two brothers, Maximillian and Prince Ernst, each lit a candle for both their parents. They did this every night since their mother and father had failed to return from Sarajevo that fateful day. None of them had ever gotten the chance to say goodbye.

The Gorbals, Glasgow, Scotland

Lizzie Littlejohn knew why Harry wanted to get out of Glasgow. She understood. She wanted to get out of Glasgow too. She resented Harry for going alone and, even more, for taking their cat, Mrs. Chippy. "Och, I didnay mind the miserable old fool taking off, but I ask yer, why did he have to take me bloody cat?" she would say to her friends, only half joking.

Lizzie had been down to the Anchor for a few bevvies that afternoon. Her bitterness was welling as she toasted, "To me absent husband and me ship's cat! Cheers!" She saluted all those interested in the bar, adding, "Up yer Donalds."

These were hard times in general. It was a time of austerity accentuated by all that was happening as the wheels of industry turned, the skies got ever darker with pollution and the clouds of war, and people's hearts were saddened by the absence of loved ones so dear.

PART IV

COLD CALM

18
ELEPHANT ISLAND

Day 634
The Weddell Sea

FRANK WILD FELT A SENSE of relief, as he was sure they all did, when the three lifeboats were finally launched into the Weddell Sea. A channel had opened up, and Shackleton decided to take the risk of making a dash to open water, despite the possibility that if the channel rapidly closed in, then they'd all die.

Relief resounded as the channel widened until eventually they were in open ocean, dark blue and sapphire green, icebergs abounding. The sense of being in control of their own destinies for the first time in months brought with it an overwhelming surge of joy, despite the perils of probably the most dangerous waters and ocean on the planet.

They had been flirting with existence for months, dealing with the freezer of Mother Nature's south. Ginormous icebergs jutted out of the ocean like glistening mountains rising from the sea. The *Endurance* crew were floating between the bergs like miniature pieces, feeling safe in the shadow of these beasts, yet the reality was more tenuous than could be imagined.

They had all witnessed the sheer force of the ice as it had crushed the *Endurance* at the snap of a finger, how she had been at the mercy of the untamable power that surrounded her and crushed her beam by beam, from stern to bow, and eventually consumed her within the dark depths.

Wild knew that if the ice were to decide to close around them, they would never be seen again. He was also very aware of the dangers of these gigantic floating beasts of beauty and their ability to crush the men in an instant. The forces around them were unimaginable in terms of absolute weight and power. The crew were just mere men, and their creations were dwarfed as they slipped by these monsters carved of ice.

It was a moment for celebration as the passengers of the *James Caird*, the *Dudley Docker*, and the *Stancomb Wills* broke into song. This was the first time they had been afloat for many months and in control of their own navigation. It felt like an elated form of freedom, although so basic in its form, testament to how down their spirts had been floating on thin ice for so long.

"Row, row, row your boat gently down the stream. Merrily, merrily, merrily, merrily, life is but a dream" came ringing out from the three boats, skimming across the water between them in this surprisingly tranquil and silent yet deadly place.

Although all the crew had their sea legs, it had been some time since they were accustomed to the swell, and in such small crafts many of the men were affected by seasickness as they battled their way across the treacherous ocean toward land.

There were some options, but Elephant Island still looked the most likely given the current and the direction of the wind, but all options were perilous in this great Southern Ocean, treacherous in every aspect, particularly its often gigantic storms, waves, currents, and winds. They were just three little boats at the mercy of this great, most perilous ocean.

With only seal meat and blubber on board for sustenance, thirst was now the biggest demoralizer. The crew were seriously worn, strained, thirsty, and hungry. Hunger had become a constant companion and food an obsession.

Their third night at sea, at around midnight, the *Dudley Docker*, towing the *Stancomb Wills*, lost sight of the *James Caird* in the dark and the swell with both parties anxious about the other all night.

The following morning, they were relieved to spot each other once again, just a few hundred yards away, but in the swell and in the dark, with the wind and the noise of the sea, they may just as well have been a hundred miles apart, though they were all relieved that they were not.

Killer whales, like black torpedoes, were all around the boats, darting through the water and breaching the surface as they hunted their prey. These were giant animals, aggressive, alarming as they appeared out of the deep blue, any one capable of tipping the men into the icy ocean at any time they chose, the crew once again at the mercy of the gods above.

Their existence was so fragile in so many ways, it was hard to keep up. It was hard to stay positive. It was very difficult to stay alive with all the odds stacked against them. Desperation set in. Life became unimportant. Survival became a daily reality, the spirit darkened, and in some cases, doom appeared on the dark horizon.

Wild kept hope and his spirits above water as Worsley guided them closer and closer to the refuge of land, something that he desperately longed for, at least a few notches closer to safety and survival.

After five harrowing nights at sea, with Elephant Island now in their sights, the *James Caird* breached the reef and was within reach of the shore. As they came aground, Shackleton shouted, "Off you go, Blackborow. Be the first to stand on the land, my boy."

At that, Blackborow jumped into the surf and immediately fell. No one had realized the extent of frostbite on the young boy's feet. Wild and Crean jumped in behind him and dragged Blackborow and the *James Caird* ashore.

They had reached land!

Wild observed the condition of the crew. They were in bad shape, the perils of their journey thus far having taken their toll, but at least now they were on solid land. Their clothes were worn and frail, and much of the insulation of their woolen coats and mitts had been eroded by wear and the salt of the ocean.

Blackborow's toes were the worst example. Gangrene had set in. Again, the men hadn't realized the seriousness, and of course Blackborow, always the jester, hadn't made a big play of it, keeping his pain and discomfort to himself.

The other two boats were quickly dragged ashore to the pebble beach, the first time the men had stood on solid land for over 497 days. They were the first human beings ever to step foot onto Elephant Island.

Charlie Green immediately went about setting up the galley in a sheltered spot on the beach. The rest of the men dragged the boats up the beach and pulled what stores remained off the boats. While the milk was being boiled and the seal meat roasted, the men danced on the beach, laughing and cheering. Their dried skin was cracking, but they were momentarily celebrating this milestone and choosing to forget the challenges that remained ahead of them.

They chewed on lumps of ice to quench their craving for fresh water while waiting for the hot milk. Wild pulled out his last bottle of Mackinlay's and splashed a drop into each cup, saving a quarter bottle as his final reserve.

They had achieved an almost impossible feat and made it on to dry land at last.

Shackleton raised a toast to the crew: "Here's to all of you pioneers and explorers, and to McLeod and Cheetham, two good sailors, the former a deep-sea salt and growler and the latter a pirate to his fingertips!"

"Ahoy" was the cheer, as if they were real pirates.

Hurley had lost his mittens during the journey. Seeing the usually jovial and optimistic Australian suffering, Shackleton gave him his own mittens for him to warm up.

The blubber stove now at full fire, the crew gathered around, drawing every degree of warmth they could to warm their bodies, dry their sodden and salty clothes, and refresh their souls.

Wild continued his monitoring of the crew, and it was clear that the men were in various stages of fitness with Blackborow being in the direst circumstance with serious frostbite to his toes. Hudson was suffering from lack of mental strength and was having trouble coping with their predicament in general, but there were men who were clearly the strongest in terms of both physical and mental strength.

Crean was always reliable, consistent, calm, and collected. Nothing ever seemed to faze him. Vincent, a former boxer, wrestler, and Royal Marine, was the fittest and strongest of the crew. McCarthy and Marston had both fared well with Shackleton and the big Kiwi, Worsley, never wavering, like lighthouses, towering tall and casting their guiding light.

Although they were all very grateful to be on dry land, Wild knew that even with this big achievement, there was still a long way to go until this was over. And the beach they had landed on could not be a permanent station for the crew.

Wild and a group of men went to search for a better campground and found a location that offered better protection from rockfalls and from the sea. Shackleton called this Wild Point in honor of his right-hand man. Wild was typically quiet on the subject, but inside he was very proud and thankful of Shackleton's appreciation.

Shackleton had turned to him and declared, "Frank, you are the rock of this crew. You are a true leader, one who leads by example and deed. And, my friend, you are my right-hand man."

Right-Hand Man

Grew up dreaming of faraway shores,
Inspired by few who had gone before.
My great-grandfather Captain Cook.
I once read of all his heroics in a book.

My parents raised a Yorkshireman proud and true:
Put up, get on, never ado.
What's the point of twittering on?
Too late when the opportunity is gone.

Grew up dreaming of being a polar explorer,
Knowing from a young age I would adore her.
The last frontier to be conquered by man.
Will one day do it. I know that we can.

To go where no person has gone before
And set foot and walk through that door.
Excitement, the endeavor, the very pride.
You will always want this man by your side.

Straight, determined, sure, and proud.
No nonsense, smart, matter-of-fact, and a dowd.
Traveled the oceans, mountains, and ice in hand.
I would travel no place but this without my right-hand man.

They moved the boats to their new campground, where
they killed sea elephants and seals for meat and blubber.
Despite their relative newfound safety compared to
recent months, at least on dry ground, the reality set in,

and demoralization quickly spread among the crew upon considering their remaining precarious predicament.

Shackleton had already been working through his plans and next steps.

Day 649
Elephant Island

The *James Caird* was packed and ready to go, heading on to the next stage of their rescue mission and on to South Georgia, an 850-mile journey across the Southern Atlantic Ocean, the most perilous ocean on the planet, in a lifeboat. Thanks to McNish and his carpentry skills, it had been converted into something that had the chance of passing as an oceangoing boat, maybe capable of making the hazardous journey ahead of them.

The ocean temperatures were the coldest in the world, dropping as far as −2° Celsius with intense cyclonic storms, the strongest winds on earth, up to two hundred miles an hour, and waves over thirty feet high—then the icebergs that can be deadly to any vessel daring to enter this unforgiving ocean, never mind the makeshift *James Caird*.

Wild was in charge of the beach party. They had upturned the *Dudley Docker* and *Stancomb Wills* to create a bunk for the twenty-two crew who would remain at Wild Bay, Elephant Island. They had industriously set up a decent camp with shelter, a galley, the two bunks, and a store. Hunting parties led by Wild and Hurley had produced a good stock of meat and blubber, and the last remaining item on the list was to identify the two separate crews. Who would stay and who would go onward to seek rescue support?

Shackleton deeply deliberated his choices before making this very difficult decision, sharing his temporary indecision with Wild. First, he had ruled out attempting to take all three boats and all the men to South Georgia. Many of the men were not physically or mentally fit to continue. All three boats were not as well equipped and suited even to attempt making the journey. So he'd made the choice of taking just the *James Caird*. Now, who would join him on the voyage?

He needed to ensure the right balance. On one hand, he needed the strongest men to take with him on this next and most dangerous leg of their journey, but on the other hand, he needed to ensure the safety and sanity of the men who would remain on Elephant Island.

He knew that he needed Worsley with his navigation skills and knack. He really wanted Crean for his brute and mental strength. He wanted his right-hand man, Wild, to join them, but he worried about leaving the crew with no strong leader. Hurley was also an option, and then there was Vincent, who was probably the fittest of the crew, but he was also potentially the most disruptive. Then there was the potentially mutinous McNish. Although he'd been quiet since the incident on the ice, Shackleton no longer trusted him.

Blackborow and Hudson were staying on the island, in no fit state to go any further.

Shackleton sat with Wild and Worsley and shared his thinking and his decision.

"Frank, I want you to stay here with the crew. You have Hurley, Greenstreet, Cheetham, and Kerr to support you and look after the other men. You need to keep a close eye on Blackborow because of his feet, and Hudson because of his mental state. The others will support you."

Wild nodded in acceptance of the boss's decision.

"We have no idea how long we will be gone. It could be as long as three months before we return. But, Frank, you have to be prepared for the worst."

Shackleton didn't need to expound. All three of them knew what he meant, and they dared not discuss the consequences of failure of the mission. He turned to Worsley.

"Captain, I obviously need your navigation magic on the *Caird*, and to make no bones about it, this is no mean feat. We have to find that speck in the ocean, over eight hundred miles away. If the winds or the currents catch us, then we could miss her beyond a country mile with our souls forever lost at sea."

Worsley already knew the enormity of the expectation, but his omnipresent self-confidence was on display for the three of them to see.

"No pressure." Wild grinned at the big Kiwi.

"So, who are we taking with us, boss?" asked Worsley.

"Me and you, obviously. Frank is the onshore leader here. On the *Caird*, Crean is an obvious choice." Both Worsley and Wild nodded, listening intently. "McCarthy next. He's number four. Then I think Vincent, which makes five."

"He's probably one of the fittest men," observed Wild.

"But he's also feisty, and that guided my decision," added Shackleton. They all agreed.

"And what about the final place?" Wild was keen to know.

"That's where I have had my biggest dilemma." Shackleton looked them both in the eye. "I've decided to take McNish." He was looking for a reaction from his two trusted colleagues.

Wild looked at Worsley and back to Shackleton. "Go on."

"I just think he would be better off with me so I can keep an eye on him. That way I won't have to leave him here to cause any trouble."

Wild piped up, saying, "Come on, boss, Harry ain't that bad. He has a good heart. He was having a bad day on the ice. Who knows. We've all had one of those, right?"

Worsley added to the point, "He was pretty attached to that cat of his. It was a hard day for him."

The prospect of having the ship's carpenter on Elephant Island had some appeal to Wild, but Shackleton's point was also well made. "I'm okay with that, boss, if that's the way you want to go."

Decision made. Shackleton went on to share the news with each of the handpicked individuals on a one-to-one basis. For the most part, the men appeared honored. He left McNish for last, and Wild accompanied him to serve as moral support. The men sat down opposite each other on a pair of rocks.

"Harry, as you know, we are taking the *Caird* and heading on an eight-hundred-mile journey to South Georgia to get a rescue ship to return and pick up the men."

McNish just looked at Shackleton.

"Look, Harry, I am deeply sorry about Mrs. Chippy. It was a necessary decision, Harry, at that time," Shackleton appealed. This was the first time they had talked about it since. A tear came to the carpenter's eye. By no means an emotional man, Harry was a core Glaswegian, and tears didn't come easy. Shackleton went on. "Harry, I want you to join me on the *James Caird*."

"Och. Aye, boss, I'd love to join yer. It'd be an honor," he stuttered.

"You've done some good work, Harry. The *Caird* is a different boat now, surely able to take us all the way to South Georgia." Shackleton smiled back at McNish.

"Aye, boss, that she is."

With heavy hearts and unspoken hope, the twenty-two put their trust in the crew of the *James Caird* to make their mission impossible and return to the others with safe passage back home.

Shackleton and Worsley estimated that they would need one month's rations and supplies for the six men. They worked with Orde-Lees, who coordinated the stocking of the boat. McNish worked on shoring her up for their long and tumultuous journey ahead.

The stores for the boat included thirty boxes of matches, six and a half gallons of paraffin, one tin of methylated spirit, ten boxes of flamers, one box of blue lights, two Primus stoves, one Nansen aluminum cooker, six sleeping bags, a few spare socks, a few candles, and some blubber oil.

In addition, they loaded food rations, including three hundred sledding rations, two hundred nut rations, six hundred biscuits, a case of lump sugar, thirty packets of TruMilk, a tin of Bovril cubes, Cerebos salt, thirty-six gallons of water, and two hundred fifty pounds of ice.

Then they had a sea anchor, binoculars, charts, a prismatic compass, an aneroid, and of course Worsley's sextant.

The Elephant Island crew lined up on the shore as the *James Caird* pushed away into the heavy surf and headed for the reef gateway and the wild ocean beyond.

Frank Wild stood in the middle of the group on shore. The men around him watched as the little lifeboat disappeared out of sight, turning into a speck on the horizon.

"Fair winds, my friends," mouthed Wild, barely audible on the wind.

Blackborow, now in much pain from gangrene, pleaded, "Will they make it, boss?"

"Listen, boy, if anyone can make it, that would be Shackleton. We are in safe hands. Now let's deal with those toes of yours before the gangrene eats you up."

At that, they carried Blackborow into the bunk, where Macklin and McIlroy removed each of Blackborow's gangrenous toes, one by one, with the help of chloroform and a nip of Wild's last remaining Mackinlay's for numbing of the pain and providing some comfort.

Wild's characterization was that life on Elephant Island was a mere existence. He did his best to lift and maintain the spirits of the men in the direst of conditions and in the light of their weighty plight. Their improvised hut provided shelter from the incessant bitter cold winds, rain, and snowstorms. Charlie Green did his best to make do with the monotonous ingredients of predominately seal meat and penguin, rationing their supplies to spruce up the flavors and keep the men's morale up at least with a sense of sustenance.

As each day passed, they talked about Shackleton's return, and each day, Wild and the other men looked out to sea as if it were a certainty that one day the boss would return.

As each day went by, the prospect of rescue diminished in their minds, and the sense of hopelessness of their situation increased.

Wild was a seasoned campaigner, and he knew Shackleton better than anyone. He knew that Shackleton either would be dead, drowned on the *James Caird*, or would do everything humanly possible to return and rescue Wild and the crew. He also knew that if there was one man whom he could trust to achieve that enormous feat, it was Sir Ernest Shackleton. Wild trusted the boss implicitly, but then again, he had no other choice under the circumstances.

Wild kept the men as busy as possible. There was only so much one could do on a bare and barren island. They hunted and explored for any other resources or materials that Elephant Island had to make their existence better. They performed routine cleaning and clearing of their camp and the shelter. The regularity of meals was important, but as the rations depleted, the food became less and less appetizing. Eating for survival and not pleasure had become a chore.

Each night around the blubber fire, or if too stormy in their shelter, they would talk through the various scenarios of the *James Caird*'s progress and potential demise. They talked about alternative options, for example, passing ships. They obsessed over their situation. Their only respite was to think of home and loved ones and the chances of returning someday, their only glimmer of hope.

Shackleton, Worsley, and the four crew of the *James Caird*—Crean, McNish, McCarthy, and Vincent—sailed from Elephant Island and looked back at the shore until the remaining crew on the island had disappeared from sight. They settled in under the protective deck that McNish had built, going into their cramped quarters, leaving Shackleton and Worsley above to take the first watch as they sailed into the night.

Shackleton and Worsley sat atop the *James Caird* as they made their way out of the protection of Elephant Island and into the furious South Atlantic Ocean.

Within just a few hours, they were facing the most severe weather and sea conditions known to humankind as the *James Caird* was tossed around like a child's toy in full gale. The waves rolled in from the east on the heels of the west wind, rising like small mountains in a steady train that seemed endless. Indeed, the winds are a constant in the high latitudes below Cape Horn and the Cape of Good Hope. They set up towering rollers that marched ever onward. A stiff current beset the east as well. Navigation in storm conditions was impossible, so Shackleton had the crew bring the bow to the wind and seas. One of the men deployed the sea anchor, a canvas cone held open with a frame. The crewman dumped the cone into the water. The wind and waves pushed the boat backward, and the cone slowed the movement, keeping the bow more or less moving into the heavy weather.

For Shackleton and Worsley up top, at least they had a sense of purpose: steering the boat through the storm. Shackleton knew for the four men below, lying there, that trying to get some sleep was almost impossible as they were bounced around the ocean, just waiting for that big wave to take them out and spill them into the icy cold depths below.

After that first night, Shackleton was relieved to see the first light of dawn. He enjoyed the sense of calm after the storm as the waters were relatively still with only a mild to moderate swell and a light breeze. Shackleton invited the men above deck to feel the warmth of the sunlight on their bodies and their wet clothes.

As they came up on deck, they looked pale, tired, and exhausted. Shackleton made the point of saying good morning to them as cheerfully as he could muster to help lift their spirits.

"Apologies for the roller-coaster ride, boys," Shackleton said cheerily, making light of how close they had been on several occasions to being consumed by the ocean the night before. McCarthy and Crean nodded with a smile, showing a glimmer of their remaining sense of humor. Vincent and McNish were less receptive, looking the worse for wear of the six.

Crean boiled some water in the kettle and made some tea. They all dipped their biscuits in the tea for breakfast.

This would be the first of many long, dark nights. They trusted the navigation skills of their captain, Frank Worsley, and their leader, Ernest Shackleton. None of the men had any choice. These were their only options. Good options was the consensus.

This was going to be a long, arduous journey.

Shackleton and Worsley went below, exhausted after the night of fighting the storm and hoping to get some rest before the next onslaught, leaving Crean and McCarthy above deck, in charge.

Crean looked up to the sky, the wind, the rain, the sun, and the gods. He spread out his arms and shouted to the heavens, "Come on, yer. Come and get me, big man. I'm right down here. Give me all yer got! Come on!" He bellowed, looking at the sky in defiance, with McCarthy looking on. The others below could hear his big booming voice and his distinct Irish brogue, all of them knowing exactly where big Tom Crean was coming from.

Shackleton smiled as he laid his head on a rolled-up sack. "That's the spirit, big Tom Crean."

Each of the others shared Crean's rage and, to varying different degrees, shared his appetite for the challenge ahead. "Come on. Come and get me!" It was almost a battle cry, worthy of the bagpipes.

"Onward!" whispered Shackleton to himself a personal rally to arms. "Onward always." Shackleton drifted quickly into sleep, and Crean steered the little boat farther north, toward South Georgia and refuge.

19
KING HAAKON BAY

Day 662
The *James Caird*
Off South Georgia

WHEN SHACKLETON AND WORSLEY HAD first met in Burlington Road, Worsley had related his reputation for finding small inches of islands in the Pacific. At the time, this information was lost on Shackleton, who did not relate the warm waters of the Pacific to the icy seas of the south, but now as he looked back, he was eternally grateful for what appeared Worsley's almost magical ability to navigate the seas with almost pinpoint accuracy.

Worsley advised Shackleton that he could not be 100 percent certain of their exact position, but his belief was that they were within ten miles of South Georgia. He went on to warn of the possibility that the fierce winds and currents could take them straight past their intended destination and far out into the South Atlantic Ocean. He expressed the need for diligence over the next twenty-four hours, saying it was paramount. Shackleton already knew this, but it served as a healthy reminder.

The fact that Worsley had gotten them within ten miles of South Georgia, a relative speck in the enormous Southern Atlantic, was a feat in and of itself. The fact that he had gotten them there with only a sextant and dead reckoning, and barely a direct line of sight to the sun, was an absolute miracle.

"Thank God for Captain Frank Worsley," Shackleton announced as they were within striking distance of their destination. Even Shackleton's spirits were lifted by the news. But he was also laser focused on closing that last ten miles and not falling afoul of the great ocean's currents.

The crew stirred at the announcement, heads popping up from below, seeing the daylight and the specter of land in the not so far distance. After nights at sea, and at the mercy of the ocean, they had made it across the 850-mile passage and were within reach of land, safety, and civilization, the return to Elephant Island and their stranded shipmates now being a real possibility.

Once again, Crean looked up to the skies and bellowed, "Not this time, big man. Maybe next. But for now let us be and help us pass through this land to home."

Shackleton and Worsley looked at each other, exhausted and relieved. They smiled, but they both knew they were not to safety yet. They still had to navigate the *James Caird* into the safety of South Georgia, then make land, and then they still had to make an epic journey on foot and get across the previously unattempted mountains of South Georgia and on to Stromness.

But the fact that they had made it to within ten miles of their target and were almost in sight of land was enough to justify the smile and relief between them. At least for now.

With a fair wind and a hold on their luck, they would hit South Georgia by the next morning.

That night another full gale descended upon the small and humble *James Caird*, and they spent the night making zigzag maneuvers as they fought the storm. In the dark, the wet, and the blistering cold, amid the ferocious seas and the unfathomable winds, the *Caird* survived.

The *Caird's* rudder was damaged, and given the diminishing state of Vincent, McNish, and McCarthy and all that they had been through since last on South Georgia, Shackleton decided to change course and head toward land on the uninhabited southwest coast of the island. This was not the initially intended side, not the easiest route by far, but if they were to miss the island altogether, they would be surely doomed and their souls left behind on Elephant Island forever.

Shortly after noon the following day, they caught their first sight of South Georgia, which lifted their spirits to no end, but it would be another two days, including a rising storm, before they made their break and headed into Cave Cove at the entrance of King Haakon Bay.

As they got through the break and into the calmer waters, the entire crew of six sat on top of the *James Caird* as they sailed in. Shackleton noted the faces of wonderment and awe, not only at the miraculous feat they had all just endured but also at the breathtaking mountains that arose above them with the prospect of civilization now only a few miles away.

They made it to shore and stumbled onto the pebbly beach like a group of drunkards walking out of the pub after a Saturday night session. The staggering came from the fact that the human brain adjusts for motion. They needed to get their land legs back.

They quickly pulled the *James Caird* up on the beach and created their camp, which Shackleton named Peggotty Camp.

Vincent and McNish were now in bad shape as the toll of this latest leg had bitten hard. Emaciated and hungry, they were also worn out and thirsty.

Shackleton and Worsley went for a hike to work out their initial ascent to reach the other side of the island. They were also tired and exhausted, but Shackleton couldn't get the image of his crew on Elephant Island out of his mind. He felt he must rescue them at all costs. They were his responsibility, his men, his crew.

By the time the two leaders came back, Crean had cooked up a feast, a contrast from where they had come. He included the abundance of wildlife and shrubs in cooking a very hearty and very welcome meal. The stew of albatross chicken was a real treat and a pick-me-up for all the men, including Shackleton.

"Nicely done, Tom. Very nicely done. You'll be giving Charlie Green a run for his money when we pick the others up," Shackleton commented, complimented, and cajoled.

"Aye, boss, not too bad is she." He smiled back, and the six laughed together, crashing their mugs of tea as if they were back in the Ritz.

As Shackleton was contemplating their next steps, he assessed that McNish was certainly the worse for wear physically and that Vincent, although physically strong, was mentally affected by the ordeal, having lost much of the will to carry on.

McCarthy was in much better shape, but Shackleton decided that he would be left to look after the other two until he and Worsley came back to their rescue.

Looking around him at their new camp, Shackleton said, "You boys will be just fine here at Peggotty Camp, your new home for a while, until we come back in a few days' time." The three agreed silently with nods and appreciative smiles. They also knew they had no appetite to scale the mountain before them.

From there, it would be Shackleton, Worsley, and Crean who would make the final thirty-six-hour march across previously unentered terrain and across the mountains and glaciers to the whaling station of Stromness, which meant civilization, safety, and a means to rescue their crew stranded on Elephant Island.

The Ross Sea Party
Hut Point, McMurdo Sound, Antarctica
May 8, 1916

Mackintosh announced to the group that he and Hayward intended to head across the sea ice to Cape Evans. Both Wild and Joyce looked at him as if he were deranged. The sea ice was far too young and thin, and a big storm was brewing in the south. True, they had been stuck in this dark, smelly, miserable hut for over a year, but they both knew the risks of what their captain was proposing. All the same, Mackintosh was the leader, and it was his choice.

Apart from tying him up to a chair and restraining him, there was little they could do. Mackintosh had Hayward behind him, an apparent volunteer for the suicide march, although he didn't look too convinced that the idea was a good one.

"We're off to Cape Evans to find the hut," Mackintosh said to no one in particular.

"Aye, that would be stark raving," stated Joyce matter-of-factly. "Why in hell's name would you want to do that?" Joyce, the most experienced polar expeditioner among them, added.

"We are shipless, our provisions are running low, and quite frankly I could do with a change of scenery," Mackintosh said, looking down at his feet then lifting his head to stare at Joyce.

Early in the landing, Joyce had tried to influence Mackintosh to no avail.

"Well, it's your choice, boss, but I'm telling you now that despite this smelly place," he said as he looked around the hut, "you'll be much better off in here than you will be out there."

Hayward looked down at his feet and didn't raise his head.

"What do you think, Hayward?" asked Joyce.

Hayward looked up for the first time, opening his mouth as if to speak, but Mackintosh spoke for him. "He's with me. He wants to get out of this hole too." He turned to Hayward. "Don't you, son?"

Hayward just nodded apologetically, apparently in full submission.

Having packed light, the two left the hut and headed into the cold. Two hours later a bitter storm brewed and a blizzard ensued, roaring for two whole days.

Once it was over, Wild and Joyce headed out of the hut, following Mackintosh and Hayward's unbelievably still visible trail, but they found nothing, not even their bodies. They would try again several times in the coming days, but to no avail.

They didn't know for certain that Mackintosh and Hayward had not made it until July 15, 1916. This was the date when they arrived at Cape Evans themselves. They knew that Mackintosh and Hayward's decision was risky, if not suicidal, but they all hoped they had somehow made it against the odds.

They hadn't. Mackintosh and Hayward were gone. Gone forever.

Day 673
Cave Cove
King Haakon Bay, South Georgia

After a restless sleep, Shackleton stirred Worsley and Crean. The three started to ready themselves for the long trek ahead of them. McNish helped them drive salvaged shortened nails from the *James Caird* into their boots to help them grip the inevitable snowy and icy frontiers ahead of them. McCarthy cooked up a breakfast of whitefish he had caught the evening before on hand lines, serving it with some leftover biscuits and hot tea, much appreciated by all—their second almost proper meal in the last twelve hours.

With the full moon glowing above, they took in their breakfast and then said goodbye to Vincent, McNish, and McCarty. One after another, with Shackleton in the lead, they started their traipse, traversing the first glacier that rose from the sea up into the mountains.

After a couple of hours, they were at twenty-five hundred feet above sea level and the snow underfoot was slowing them down. The soft, newly laid snow, ankle-to-knee-deep, made their progress both slow and exhausting.

As daylight came at three thousand feet, Shackleton looked down to see what appeared to be a frozen lake. The footing below was showing signs of fissures and fractures, leading them to take caution with their every step as they trudged forward.

"One sure foot in front of the other," said Shackleton, borrowing an old saying.

"Aye," said Crean. "The road to hell is paved with good intentions." That was another old saying that Crean thought highly amusing given their circumstances. Their hearts were lightened with hope as they made every step forward on their march, no matter how dangerous.

"Onward!" chimed in Worsley, mimicking one among Shackleton's rich repertoire of motivational sayings, chosen and applied at the right moment. The three men shared a moment of humor that only those together in times of extreme adversity can recognize. Worsley sniggered to himself for the next hundred yards.

"I am glad you're amused, Captain Worsley!" Shackleton feigned being hurt, prompting Worsley to snigger even more.

The beauty of the scenery that surrounded them escaped them as they focused on their task at hand, fighting with their exhaustion, the elevation, the lack of equipment, their now threadbare clothing, and the freezing and bitter cold.

As they trudged on, Shackleton turned his thoughts to the men of the Terra Nova Expedition a few years earlier. Robert Falcon Scott had been beaten to his goal of making it to the South Pole by the Norwegian Roald Amundsen by just thirty-four days. Scott and four companions made it to the pole in mid-January 1912, only to discover the Norwegians had beaten them to it. Then Scott's whole party died on the return journey, their bodies, journals, and photographs found by a search party eight months later.

Shackleton looked over at Tom Crean, who had been part of that search party. It was he who had buried the bodies in their frozen and lonely graves.

At this advanced stage of Shackleton's own journey of survival, with his men being in the same predicament, he was as much inspired by the opportunity of life and the fear of death in an icy and inhospitable grave as he was determined not to fail. Failure was simply not an option. He had come too far for that.

The mountain continued to soar before them. The beauty of the glaciers inched their way, aided by gravity, and the snowfields stretched as far as the eye could see.

Throughout that day, the three continued with climb after climb, across glaciers, up escarpments, across snowfields. Seemingly with each one they conquered, another was put in their way.

"He's testing us," announced Crean. "The big man is testing us again," he added, the irritation clear in his voice.

Shackleton and Worsley looked at each other again, rolling their eyes in humor.

"Come on, Big Tom, keep on pushing," suggested Worsley.

"Even the man upstairs cannot keep up with you, Tom," added Shackleton.

"Aye. That might be true, boss, but let me tell yer both right know, he's testing my patience, so he is."

Shackleton could do nothing but smile at himself as they continued to march on, one foot in front of the other. It was nigh on impossible not to admire the sheer grit and determination of a man like Tom Crean, not that there were many men like him. Crean was Shackleton's number one choice to join the *Caird* party on this crazy mission. Shackleton, almost like an apparition, saw the Lord coming down to them from the heavens and reaching down, threatening to take them all away from the side of the mountain, and big Tom Crean standing there in defiance before the Maker himself, arms stretched out before him. "How dare you mess with me!"

As they trudged on in silence, Shackleton glanced across to the big Kiwi Frank Worsley and wondered at the luck of his walking in to Burlington Road that day, apparently as a result of a dream that he'd had, a premonition that he was destined to join the *Endurance*. He remembered Worsley's grand entrance and how he had liked him almost immediately. It was not the right time for praise—it wasn't quite over yet—but Shackleton noted how grateful he was to have him as his captain.

"I bet you're glad you had that dream now, Captain," Shackleton teased.

"Nowhere I'd rather be in the world right now than by your side, trudging over this bloody mountain," Worsley cracked back.

With no tent and no sleeping bags, and now at forty-five hundred feet, the men found the temperatures tough to survive. Their clothing had long lost its quality to insulate and protect and above all its ability to resist water and dampness. They could see grasslands below them, a more likely scenario for surviving the night.

They were so close to their goal, and each man was running on empty as mental strength overrode their bodies. They just kept moving, putting one foot laboriously in front of the other, their spirits lifted by the welcome sight of grass and trees, the sound of birds, and the promise of human company ahead.

At first they cautiously climbed down the slope to the more attractive prospect below them, not knowing if there was a crevasse or a cliff at the bottom, but then, in unison, they unroped and started to slide down the slope on their backs like kids in a winter snow scene, sledding at Christmas.

Crean shouted, "Woo-hoo, let's go, big man," looking over at Worsley, the two of them now side by side at the top of the snow-covered slope.

Shackleton and Worsley were close behind. "After you, big Tom Crean." All three slid down the slope like three little kids together with gay abandon. What more could they face? What more could fate and Mother Nature put in their way? What should they care anymore? *Let's just go for it!* Who dares wins, and they were winning for the first time in a very long time with the finish line almost in sight.

They had descended nearly a thousand feet in just a few fun minutes, and now they were at a safer altitude with more protection from the harsh and bitter wind. There was no intent to sleep as they might never wake up. They would continue to march through the night, but they did feel themselves worthy of a rest, a cup of tea, and some biscuits. Crean obliged with the duties, and they all sat in the silence among friends for a few moments, sharing a pipe of their much-dwindled and threadbare tobacco supply.

It was yet another long and arduous night as the three, almost in a trance, just plodded on, one foot in front of the other, one after another, all night long, like a slow beating rhythm whirring around in the head, almost hallucinogenic, mesmerizing, with delirium setting in.

At 6:00 a.m., they went through a gap. At the other side, sunlight was blessing the scene. Twenty-five hundred feet below, they could see water and the coastline of the other side of South Georgia.

"Boss, it looks too good to be true," Worsley said, his lips cracked and frostbitten.

Crean, now like a drunken sailor, made his own observations: "Is that a bloody mirage he has sent down to us, or is that the east side of South Georgia?"

"I think you are right, Tom. That is our destination. That, my friends, is the mighty fine Stromness."

They three looked at one another, gave each other a bear hug and continued on, knowing they still had a good way left to march, but the worst was over and it was only going to get better from here.

As they pushed on, Shackleton mused on the phenomenon that the last leg is always the hardest when one is within sight of victory, of completion, of finishing the race. He had noted in the past that this is when an athlete, or a soldier, or in their case an explorer is the most vulnerable because of complete exhaustion and the possibility of being careless and making mistakes. This final leg was when one had to concentrate the most, although as Shackleton marched on, he realized how hard it actually was to concentrate when it came down to it.

The next obstacle in their way was a slope of scree and slate that was too steep to walk down, and yet they didn't need climbing equipment either. The three roped up and tackled the five-hundred-foot decline slowly. Two hours later they were down to two thousand feet.

The next was a waterfall that had to be traversed. They set up a rope and crossed in order of heaviest to lightest, first Crean, then Shackleton, and then Worsley. The rope could not be recovered, but now with Stromness in site, they hoped they wouldn't need it.

Shackleton looked down. He could see a ship in the harbor letting out some its steam, their first sight of human life in over 675 days.

"Now that, my fair-weather friends, is a *beauty*," Crean said.

"It sure looks pretty," agreed Worsley

Who could disagree? Certainly not Shackleton.

As they marched downhill that last two thousand feet, their steps were lighter, their hearts were brighter, and each of the men was full of his own sense of pride. They had made it.

Crean broke into song, "Danny Boy." The other two joined in.

Day 675
Stromness Whaling Station, South Georgia

Shackleton, Worsley, and Crean got to the top of the rise and looked upon their first sight of humanity for a very long time. Once they had stumbled down the scree and the snow and the ice, they came to a road that would lead them into the whaling station.

Two Irishmen and a Kiwi. Soldiers together. It was as if the bagpipes of victory were playing in the distance. The pipes of the Celts were in their heads, and the sound of the whistle from the whaling station, in the distance, carried on the wind toward them.

Having suffered one of the greatest ordeals known to humankind, frozen solid, losing the *Endurance*, stranded on the ice, escaping to land, and their miraculous crossing of 850 miles to South Georgia, and now at the end of their virgin trek over the mountains, they looked down below at the most beautiful scene of Stromness with the first sight of civilization in almost two years. There was a steamboat in the bay and a cluster of buildings that made the whaling station.

They ventured on with renewed vigor, at the end of their tether, nothing more to give, yet the sight in front of them and the sound of the pipes in their heads helped them to continue with one sure foot in front of the other. Just one more push and they were there.

Lighthouse

Bravely and truly, boldly and rightly,
The guiding light will be there for you nightly.
As you trudge through your challenge, she will bring you home
Wherever your journey, wherever you should roam.

If you look across the distance, there's a lighthouse above the sea.
Like the North Star, it's there for both you and me.
Its light will be a guide if you've lost your way.
One sure foot in front of the other, you'll get there come what may.

When you are in despair and think that all is lost,
When you must make the finish line at all cost,
The final stretch, the final mile,
You can look up to her and smile.

If you look into the distance, there's a lighthouse above the sea.

She is the North Star. She's there for you and for me.
She'll guide you home if you've lost your way.
One sure foot in front of the other, you'll get there come
what may.

Just look up to the mountains, look up to the stars.
Whether land, sea, or desert, you will see her from afar
Shining down, a guiding light
For all that is pure, good, and right.

If you see into the distance, there's a lighthouse above
the sea.
Believe in her, and she'll save both you and me.
Its light will be a guide if you've lost your way.
One sure foot in front of the other, you'll get home, come
what may.
Welcome home!

Suddenly conscious of their own appearance and about to meet people, they considered their beards, cracked skin, and cracked lips. Their clothes were weathered and beaten. Worsley started to rearrange some of the safety pins holding his clothes together and brushing his beard with his fingers in a vain attempt to look presentable.

About half a mile out, two young boys ran past, looked the three men up and down, and ran in the opposite direction. The men got to the whaling stationmaster's house and presented themselves to a man outside.

Shackleton had explained their plight and said that they had just traversed the mountains that towered above. The man looked at them in disbelief. Mr. Sorlle came to the door to see what was going on.

"These men reckon they just trekked over the mountains from Haakon Bay," the man said unconvincingly.

"Well?" said Mr. Sorlle as he turned to look at these vagabonds, even by whalers' standards.

"Don't you know me?" asked Shackleton.

"I know your voice," Mr. Sorlle said doubtfully.

"My name is Shackleton." Mr. Sorlle's eyes widened as the penny dropped and he recalled the famous Sir Ernest Shackleton.

"Come in. Come on in." He ushered them into the warmth and comfort of his home.

"When was the war over?" was Shackleton's first question.

"The war is not over," Sorlle said in a low tone, shaking his head. "Millions are being killed. Europe is mad. The world has gone mad."

"And what news of the *Aurora* and the Ross Sea party?"

"The *Aurora* broke away from its moorings in McMurdo Sound and drifted back to New Zealand with the Ross Sea party stranded," he replied, watching Shackleton's reaction carefully.

Shackleton's heart sank at the news. Both sides of his expedition were stranded and shipless at opposite ends of Antarctica.

They went in and sipped hot tea with fresh milk and cakes. The warmth of the cabin was like nothing else they could remember. The baths were hot, the razors were sharp, and the new clothing provided each of them felt like it was from Savile Row.

At dinner, they appreciated the mutton stew, beer, and wines. After a pipe and a whisky, their exhaustion kicked in and they went to bed. The comfort of sheets, blanket, and pillows ensured that they slept for the next twelve hours. Shackleton was the first one to stir.

He had worked out a plan.

20
THE BRUCE

Day 676
Stromness Whaling Station, South Georgia

WITH THE HELP OF MR. Sorlle, Shackleton dispatched a boat to King Haakon Bay with Worsley to pick up McNish, Vincent, and McCarthy. Then he immediately set about planning to pick up his men from Elephant Island.

Shackleton, Worsley, and Crean had been enjoying the comforts of Mr. Sorlle's hospitality since they had arrived, as well as the feeling of proximity to civilization after so long absent from it, but they all three knew the need for immediate action to rescue their marooned shipmates. Shackleton was especially mindful of this.

Worsley and the relief ship would pick up the three at Peggotty Camp, where they'd also pick up the *James Caird*, and then head to Grytviken to inform the magistrate of the demise of the *Endurance*, find out any further information about the *Aurora*, and see if there was any mail.

The next morning after breakfast, Mr. Sorlle, Shackleton, and Crean took a motorboat to Husvik, another whaling station, where there might be some more news on the war and the *Aurora*, as well as connections to get a ship to rescue the men.

The three men sat together in the cabin at the back of the boat, looking out at South Georgia as they circumnavigated the peninsula and turned the corner into Husvik Harbor.

Shackleton was hungry for news of the *Aurora*, of the war, and of the world, in that order.

There was little more news that Mr. Sorlle could provide them on the *Aurora*, but Shackleton was especially craving any other news as they had lived as dead men for the past two years with no knowledge of the outside world beyond their sometimes grim fight for survival.

Shackleton listened intently as their host Mr. Sorlle recounted the fast acceleration of war in Europe and conflicts and battles with millions wounded and dead; the locking of vast armies that annihilated each other on the battlefields of France and Belgium and on the Russian front; the devastation in Gallipoli; the sinking of the *Lusitania*, the sister ship of the *Titanic*; the murder of the British nurse Edith Cavell; and Henry Ford making his millionth Model T.

Shackleton lapped up all that Mr. Sorlle could recount.

As they arrived in Husvik, they docked on the long jetty way at the front of the whaling station. Mr. Bernsten, the magistrate, was there to greet them. Shackleton and Bernsten shook hands—they knew each other from past visits—and set about securing the *Southern Sky*, a ship to go rescue the crew on Elephant Island.

Worsley had picked up the three from Peggotty Camp and had gotten them back to Stromness. The warmth and abundance of food had made a great impact on McNish, Vincent, and McCarthy, although the emaciated figures of the men told their own tale of how brutal the past two years had been. Shackleton observed McNish and how he was rakishly thin and weak, the rescue probably coming just in time for him. McCarthy and Vincent were both bigger, fitter men, but the toll was written on them too.

Within a couple of days, once insured by Lloyd's of London and fully crewed with willing whalers and captained by Captain Thom, the *Southern Sky*, a whaling vessel, was made ready and steamed out of the bay, heading south.

Shackleton was lightened and relieved to be heading back to Elephant Island and to his men, but the next day, the ice became too much for the *Southern Sky* and its captain. They were forced to turn around and head to Port Stanley in the Falkland Islands.

Despite the help of the governor, Mr. Douglas Young, there was no available ship in the Falklands suitable for making the crossing to Elephant Island and back through the treacherous ice.

This was the first time that Shackleton had access to contact London. He cabled a message to King George V of the demise of the *Endurance*. The next morning, a message from the king came back:

Rejoice to hear of your safe arrival in the Falkland Islands and trust your comrades on Elephant Island may soon be rescued.

—King George V

The message was a great source of pride for Shackleton as it showed he was reporting directly to the king himself, but as he read and reread it, his sense of responsibility grew even deeper as he focused on the words "and trust your comrades on Elephant Island may soon be rescued."

Shackleton woke up in the middle of the night, in his bed, holding the telegram in his hand, replaying the words over and over again in his head and the implied instruction from the king. "Go rescue your men, Shackleton," he blurted out into the darkness. He thought of his right-hand man and friend Frank Wild and could see the faces of all the crew whom he had left behind. "Go rescue your men," he repeated to himself.

With his thoughts haunting and tormenting him, Shackleton scrambled at every opportunity to find a rescue ship. He contacted various governments to ask for their assistance in loaning him a suitable ship. With the advance of winter, he had to act soon to prevent his crew's suffering and causing them to have to survive another winter in their upturned boats as shelter. The picture of that scene again played on his mind, and his doubts about their survival grew.

The British minister in Montenegro wired confirmation of the availability and dispatch of the *Instituto de Pesca No. 1*. By June 10, Shackleton set off once more to Elephant Island to hit heavy ice. The engines were damaged, so once more he was forced to return to Port Stanley.

As they limped into the harbor, HMS *Glasgow* was in port. The crew cheered their hero Shackleton, much to his annoyance as he was so focused on rescuing his men, feeling far from a hero at that point.

Shackleton, Worsley, and Crean jumped on the British mail boat *Orita* and hitched a ride to Punta Arenas, where they were met by a welcoming crowd at the British Association of Magallanes who had raised £1,500 and secured the charter of a schooner, *Emma*, to make one more attempt at rescue before the winter was upon them.

Emma was a forty-year-old schooner, strong and seaworthy, with an auxiliary oil engine. Shackleton, Worsley, and Crean, along with a crew of ten, headed south once more to get within one hundred miles of Elephant Island, returning to Punta Arenas on August 14.

Pushing his luck and the limitations of the seasons, Shackleton begged the Chilean government to lend him a ship. The little tugboat *Yelcho* was the only available. It was wholly and totally unsuitable for thick sea ice conditions. Shackleton had to promise the Chilean officials that he would not touch ice. On August 25, 1916, he headed south once more, knowing that the plight of his crew was desperate. This could be his last chance to rescue them for at least another six months.

As they left the harbor, Shackleton reminded himself of one of his favorite quotes from Robert the Bruce, spoken in King's Cave on the Scottish island of Arran in 1313 as he watched the spider in the cave attempt to spin a web—and on the third attempt it was successful.

"If at first you don't succeed, then try, try, and try again."

Learning from and inspired by the lesson from the spider, Robert the Bruce and his army, outnumbered ten to one, went on to defeat the English at the famous Battle of Bannockburn.

It was leaders like Bruce whom Shackleton admired. They were able to conquer against all odds, fight to the end no matter how fierce the rival and no matter how long the trial, and move onward by placing one sure foot in front of the other, never, never, ever giving up.

Day 777
Wild Bay
Elephant Island

It was a foggy morning on Elephant Island as Frank Wild roused the crew. It was his duty, passed on by Shackleton, to keep the crew alive as they sat on the desolate and barren island and waited for the boss to return and pick them up.

For the past four months, Wild had tried to keep the men in a routine, keep them disciplined, the basis of which would ensure their survival. Without discipline, the crew would quickly slip into an uncontrollable state with who knows what consequences.

Shackleton had already been gone a month longer than he anticipated, and even for Wild it was nearly impossible to stay optimistic about the odds of their survival. The men were now in bad shape, not only from the cold and the conditions but also from their poor diet and very low morale. At times, paranoia had crept in.

"Why did he leave us behind?"

"We should have gone with him."

"Will he come back?"

These were all common questions that had come up. Wild had tried his best to answer them and placate the men.

The dark, dank living quarters beneath the upturned lifeboats were horrible. The stench of blubber oil, seal meat, sweat, and Blackborow's gangrene was enough to turn any man's stomach. The sheer existence of killing seals and penguins for meat and watching their meager supplemental rations deplete day by day was enough to turn any man insane.

Insanity really bothered Wild. He contemplated the consequences and the likelihood of such an occurrence and dared not think about it too much. There is a point when the human being just gives up, lies down, and accepts his fate, falling asleep never to awake. When conditions are so bad, the act of falling asleep forever is a better option than living.

Wild looked out at the ocean as he often did, almost obsessively, praying to one day see a ship on the horizon, Shackleton, a rescue ship. Any ship would do.

They needed respite, and they needed to get off that godforsaken island, out of that living hell.

Keeping up morale was an almost impossible task, and despite his state, it was Blackborow who kept on cracking jokes and trying to keep the men on the sunny side of life. Charlie Green, the cook, also tried his best to lift the souls of the crew, trying different ways to turn their diet into a more appetizing and appealing prospect. It was an impossible task, but the fact that he kept trying each day was testament to his character and an example to the rest of the crew.

The day you stop trying is the first step to the grave, Wild thought.

Each man dealt with the mental and physical torture differently. Alfie Cheetham kept on with his stories and his fantasies about what he would do once he got home. Some fantasized about food, some reminisced about loved ones at home, and some like Hudson just curled up in a ball and spent most of the day in bed.

Wild appreciated Macklin and Hurley, who tried their very best to support him in his efforts and to keep the mood lighter, but it was very, very, very hard.

Their last attempt for a more formal pick-me-up was now several weeks past. Wild, Hurley, and Macklin had decided to hold a Polar Festival and a feast. They had a magnificent breakfast of hoosh, full strength and well boiled, with hot milk. Lunch consisted of Wild's inventive recipe of a pudding made of stale and moldy nut food and a powdered biscuit. Supper was finely cut seal steaks flavored with sugar.

After supper they had a concert with Hussey playing his indispensable banjo, the last remnant saved from the *Endurance* before she was lost. It was Shackleton who had rescued the instrument from the *Endurance* and had entrusted it to Hussey with just the words "We shall need it." It turned out that Shackleton was right.

The banjo would prove to be a lifesaver with Hussey often serenading the men at night while listening to the wind, the rain, and the snow outside. The banjo drowned out the torturous sound of the Antarctic.

For fun, and considering their obsession with hunger and a more varied diet, they ran a poll on what food they would eat at that moment with suet pudding, or as sailors knew it, "the duff," coming in at number one, Macklin repeated requests for scrambled egg on buttered toast with several voting for the prodigious Devonshire pudding—a traditional

English dessert of apricot jam topped with apples and custard, thickened with cake crumbs and with meringue on top.

One night as they were dozing, Cheetham asked of McIlroy, "Do you like doughnuts?"

"Rather!" he said, his enthusiasm obvious.

"Very easily made too. I like them cold with a little jam," Cheetham teased.

"Not bad, but how about a huge omelet?"

McIlroy responded with a deep sigh, "Fine!"

This food fantasy helped, but Hudson and Rickinson were deeply affected and had trouble rising each day, preferring to lie in their sleeping bags much of the time. Orde-Lees became more detached and insular as each day slogged by.

At around 11:40 a.m. one day, it was Marston who muttered as he stared through the rising fog, "Is that a bloody ship out there, boys?"

Although he had only barely spoken the phrase in an audible way, it was a phrase that each of the twenty-two men had dreamed of hearing for the last four months.

"Is that a mirage, or is that really a bloody ship out there or what?" mumbled Marston. They were quiet words, but Wild heard him. Like he had a spark inside him, he looked up and scanned the horizon, his heart beating almost through his chest as he spotted a shape in the distance.

"Well, bugger me," Wild stuttered slowly, the words barely audible above the morning breeze.

Slowly, one by one, the crew gathered on the shore, staring out to the ocean, in their personal thoughts, not quiet knowing if what they were seeing was real. It wasn't the first time that they had a false alarm. On one occasion what they thought was a ship was in fact a whale breaching, and on another it was an errant iceberg they'd seen, but Wild suspected that this was different.

As his mind raced, he thought that this might not be Shackleton but could be any random ship, although not many existed in these remote parts of the world. But even so …

"Boys, we have one last tin of petrol. Break it out, take it to the top of Penguin Hill, and set her alight for all to see," Wild instructed, failing to hide the excitement in his voice. Charlie Green scrambled and packed gasoline-soaked mitts, coats, and socks. Once he got to the top of the hill, he pierced the can with a pickax and lit the beacon.

The smoke from the self-made beacon plumed up into the sky, the wind chasing it in the direction of the object in the distance. As the object came near to them, it slowly became evident that this was no whale or iceberg. "It is! It's a bloody ship!"

As the ship continued to advance, the mood among the crew reached a crescendo. As the ship became clearer in their view, some of the crew just stood and stared. Others started bouncing up and down, linking arms like in some sort of highland fling, and some just stood silent with tears rolling down their cold, cracked faces.

Wild could now clearly see the *Yelcho*, about half a mile out, a fine-built steamer from the shipyards of Glasgow. Wild recognized the familiar figure of Shackleton, his friend, the boss, as he scaled down the ladder to the shore boat. Macklin shared his thoughts for all to hear: "Thank God the boss is safe." It was if Shackleton's safety was more important than their own. Wild was taken aback by the sheer loyalty that this man invoked in the people whom he touched.

"The boss is back!" Wild shouted, trying to hold the tears of excitement, relief, and intense pride in his hero Sir Ernest Shackleton.

The men were jumping and dancing, hollering and hooting, as they watched Shackleton and the shore boat near the beach. As the landing crew made their way to the beach, the men just stood there waving, cheering, and dancing on the beach. Their salvation was here! Shackleton had returned as he had solemnly promised.

The emotions were a mixed bag. Some men danced, some of the men cried, some of the men just stared in disbelief. They had been through a great deal, and they had waited a long time. They'd grappled with the uncertainty: *What if the James Caird didn't make it? Will Shackleton come back for us?* All these emotions played heavily on their hearts and minds. But with their very own eyes they were witnessing his return and their salvation.

As he neared the shore, Shackleton threw packets of cigarettes onto the beach. He knew that much-beloved draw would have run out many weeks ago. The crew lit up, even those who didn't smoke.

As if visiting an old aunt he hadn't seen in a while, Shackleton shouted to the shore, "Are you all well?"

Frank Wild bellowed back, "Better for seeing you, boss! We are all present and correct, sir!"

"Thank God," came the familiar boom of Shackleton.

"What kept you? We were expecting you a month ago!" Wild shouted with typical explorer's humor.

"Not even the great Southern Atlantic would get in the way of a drink with you, my friend. Besides, it's your round, Mr. Wild!"

"I think I might owe you one or two," Wild said.

"I wouldn't miss that for the world!"

Shackleton stepped onto the beach, and the crew let out three cheers: "Hip hip hooray! Hip hip hooray! Hip hip hooray!"

Wild looked at Shackleton and quietly uttered, "Welcome home, boss," with a big grin on his face.

None of the men there that day would ever forget that moment for as long as they all lived. Of that Wild was certain.

Shackleton didn't want to hang about, fearful of the ice and the ocean behind him. Without taking a moment to inspect the camp or move the remaining provisions and rations, they turned tail immediately, returning to the *Yelcho*.

On the *Yelcho*, their first normal meal for months was a shock to many of the men's systems, but the warm bunks were a pleasure, and the throb of the engines was a delight to listen to—cold comfort given from where they had just come.

The *Yelcho* steamed back up to Punta Arenas in short time so that Shackleton could pay his attention to his Ross Sea party and return them to safety and comfort.

2I
EMPIRE

Day 782
The *Yelcho*
Punta Arenas, Chile

SHACKLETON AND HIS WHOLE TWENTY-EIGHT-MAN crew stood on the decks of the *Yelcho* as they sailed into the harbor at Punta Arenas. A collection of multicolored houses and buildings—yellow, blue, orange, and red—with the snow-covered mountains behind was like a sight of heaven for the men who had not seen civilization for nearly two years.

Shackleton stood proud with Worsley on one side and Wild on the other. His men were lined up on each side, looking out toward the shore in wonder and awe. Their ordeal was so recent, yet so far away, but Shackleton knew it wouldn't be over until he rescued the remainder of his men from McMurdo Sound.

He wondered what might have become of them. Knowing that they were a weaker team of men, he had planned their task to be the more routine job of setting up the depots. Apart from Joyce and Wild the younger, there were several inexperienced members of the crew, including the captain of the *Aurora*, Aeneas Mackintosh.

Once they landed, Shackleton would leave as early as he could to find a ship and get to McMurdo Sound. Wild took him back to Punta Arenas. "She's a sight to behold, boss," he said, looking out across the city before them.

"She certainly is, Frank," Shackleton agreed. "We need a quick turnaround as we head to Wellington and the *Aurora* and south to pick up Mackintosh and his men."

"Yep. I hope that they were as lucky as we were," Worsley chimed in.

"They have the benefit of plentiful supplies," noted Macklin with a tone of authority on the matter.

"Let the boys have a run ashore while we provision the ship and head to New Zealand," said Shackleton.

"I think they'll just be happy to touch the mainland," commented Wild. Shackleton wasn't sure if he was speaking for himself, the men, or both.

"You did a sterling job back there, Frank," Shackleton said, looking him in the eye and raising his hand to his shoulder.

Wild just looked back at him with a glint of a smile. "You didn't do too bad yourself, boss." He winked.

"Now let's go save our boys in McMurdo," Shackleton repeated, and they all agreed.

They pulled up to the port and moored the *Yelcho*, gangplanks down. The men, with Crean in the lead, headed down to portside in the general direction of the city center with the restaurants and, of course, the bars.

"No fighting this time!" boomed Shackleton.

"Yes, boss," was their response in harmony. Blackborow was on Crean's back as the latter carried him for purposes of speed given the now absence of toes on his left foot.

"Make sure you do, boys. I won't be bailing you out again," Worsley shouted.

Crean trotted into the distance as though he had never been away and as spritely as he had when they'd done the same thing in Buenos Aires two years previously, even with Blackborow on his back.

"That Tom Crean. I'll tell you, hell of a man," Shackleton observed. The other two wholeheartedly agreed.

The officers headed to the British Club for a very long lunch and libations. It was a good reason for celebration for them all, although the rescue of the men from McMurdo Sound weighed heavy on Shackleton's mind. He could not rest until he rescued them.

And so it was with that overarching desire to rescue the men of the Ross Sea party that Shackleton made his way with the others into the British Club. The pomp and festivities got under way almost immediately. The lunch entailed welcomes and speeches and Shackleton's own summation of their trials and tribulations since leaving Grytviken nearly two years prior.

The British Association of Magallanes, founded May 3, 1899, more commonly known as the British Club, was originally named after Ferdinand Magellan, who was a Portuguese explorer who arranged the 1519–1522 expedition of circumnavigating the globe for the first time.

Located on the upper floor of the Bank of Tarapaca and London, the club was situated immediately adjacent to the plaza. It welcomed gentlemen of the time to its plush interior, including bar, library, and billiard tables, and was patronized by local businessmen, ranch owners, and visiting explorers just like Shackleton and his crew.

He and Worsley, both accomplished public speakers, briefed the eager audience before them. Although so close to the Great White Continent, few in attendance had ever been. Only the brave, the crazy, or the insane made such ventures to the south.

As the story unfolded, the audience were captivated. The explorers' presentation was enough for the British Club's appetite for knowledge. They gladly footed the bill.

After the speeches and merriment were over, they arranged for photographs of the *Endurance* crew, including a portrait of Shackleton and Worsley. For Shackleton, the publicity meant he might have better prospects in future fundraising efforts, because everyone liked a hero.

"Come on, old man," Shackleton said, clapping Worsley on the back, "let's retire to the bar for a relaxing drink."

"Good idea, boss. Good idea."

Shackleton felt tired, oh so tired, after all he'd been through. He eased onto a barstool. "Two Plymouth gin and tonics," he said to the bartender.

When the drinks arrived, Shackleton swiveled around to face his friend and colleague and lifted his glass.

"To the *Endurance*," Shackleton toasted.

"The *Endurance*," Worsley repeated together with Shackleton.

"And to you, Captain Worsley," Shackleton toasted.

"And to you, Sir Ernest Shackleton, boss."

"You know, there were times on that last march when I wasn't sure that we would make it."

"Yep, I know that. Is that why you wouldn't let us rest for more than five minutes?" They clinked their glasses.

"I feared if I let you sleep, you would never wake up."

"Well, that was an option, I will give you that." Worsley smiled.

"And what about Crean? What an amazing man," said Shackleton, nodding his head, with Worsley in agreement.

"He was a mountain," agreed Worsley.

"Do you remember the look on those children's faces when they saw us for the first time?"

"Bloody hilarious!"

"And you smartening yourself and rearranging your safety pins to keep your clothes from falling apart."

"Well, you never know, there might have been a harem of Norwegian belles waiting for us. I wasn't sure if we had hit Grytviken or reached Valhalla. I really wasn't that clear at that point."

They smiled at each other and shook their heads in unison.

"Then the look from Mr. Sorlle when he didn't know who these men were, dressed like tramps and claiming they had scaled the mountains from the other side."

"Absolutely bloody hilarious!" Worsley repeated.

"Then the warmth, the food, the beer, the bed ..."

"At that point, I really did think I was in the Great Hall."

"Captain Worsley, what we have been through together no man can understand, and I am eternally grateful to you and for all that you have done. You have shown to me the greatness of the New Zealand people and the bravery of a nation vested in one man. I am forever in your debt."

"Likewise, Shackleton. Likewise."

"Now let's go and pick up our men from McMurdo Sound."

The Great War
River Somme, Western Front, France

Privates Jimmy Smith and Richie Blundell hunkered in their trench, a long way from Bolton. They had been here just a week, and the daily onslaught and manslaughter was beyond the belief of any man. The rattle of machine guns and the artillery fire was deafening, both outbound and in. The sheer devastation—shocking. Body parts, the screams, and the death all around was more than enough for anyone to witness, never mind absorb or comprehend.

They hung in there, did their bit, and survived, until one day Smith was on duty on the front line and an incoming shell landed in the trench beside him and detonated, creating devastation all around. There was the blood, the guts dripping off his face, the deafening reverberation all around, the minutes of silence amid chaos that delayed the senses and the realization that he was wounded, the shrapnel, the lacerations, and the loss of blood. But at least his wounds were not fatal.

The pair were separated as Jimmy was sent back to England, to a hospital, for treatment and recovery for an eventual return to the front, assuming the boys didn't finish off the job beforehand.

Courage

As Napoleon Bonaparte once uttered,
It takes more courage to suffer than die.
As the machine guns in the distance stuttered,
Was it my mother's turn to cry?

I sit in my trench and think about war,
The men in their thoughts as they contemplate death.
I think to myself what all this is for
And my sweet girl at home, my sweet little Beth.

The shout comes out for us to get up and charge.
I leave my love letters for her in the wall.
My comrades and I, shoulder to shoulder we barge
As the sergeant major repeats his terrifying call.

Up we go above our shelter.
The noise comes down all around.
A bunch of bees swarming, bodies fall helter-skelter.
On to the enemy we all abound.

I take one more step toward the west.
A big German bomb goes off. Am I dead?

The disorientation puts my mind to the test.
I lie in the mud, covering my head.

I realize there's a great hole in my chest,
But one that seems to have no pain.
They pull me out and put me back behind the rest
Through the mud and the pouring rain.

They sent me back to England, thank God,
To recover in my hospital bed.
Four months later I was back in the mud.
I would be better off dead.

Day 874
The Ross Sea Party
Wellington, New Zealand
December 6, 1916

Meeting an old friend, Captain John King Davis, was a bittersweet reunion for Shackleton and Worsley. The British and Australian governments had jointly appointed Davis as the new captain of the *Aurora*, whose mission was to set sail without delay to relieve the beleaguered men of the Ross Sea party. Shackleton had wanted to be in charge and to have Joseph Stenhouse as captain, but this was not to be.

By the time of Shackleton's arrival in Wellington, the *Aurora* had already been repaired and was fully provisioned, including a boatload of coal, to steam down to McMurdo Sound and pick up the last of his men.

On December 20, 1916, the *Aurora* set sail once again from Port Chalmers south on the last rescue mission of the expedition. After a quick passage through the pack ice, she entered the Ross Sea on January 7, 1917, and pulled along the ice edge off Cape Royds on the morning of January 10.

As they approached, Shackleton was on deck scouring the landscape ashore to see if he could detect any signs of life and his Ross Sea party. He continued to scan, seeing nothing, up to the point of boarding the shore boat.

Shackleton led the landing party, in search of the hut he had himself erected during his 1907–1909 visit. They quickly found the hut, and inside there was a note indicating that the Ross Sea party was housed at Cape Evans.

"Bloody hell. They could still be alive," exclaimed Shackleton, not wanting to reveal his surprise overly. He had always been publicly confident that they were all alive and well, but deep within he feared otherwise.

"With a stroke of luck and God on our side," Wild blessed. After all, one of the men was his own brother.

Shackleton sensed something in the distance, and as he looked out toward the bleary horizon, he spotted a pack of dogs, a sled, and seven men behind. As they grew nearer, Shackleton recognized Ernest Joyce and Wild's brother, Ernest Wild, among those men.

"Never a doubt," Shackleton declared with a fair amount of relief. "Never a doubt." He beamed to himself in delight upon seeing the men approach.

"Where the bloody hell have you been?" shouted Joyce as they got closer.

"Yeah, what took yer so long?" added Wild the younger.

Shackleton looked back over at the rescue crew and saw the beaming on their faces upon seeing the men alive.

Now although having men missing, shipless on opposite ends of the Antarctic, certainly wasn't something that Shackleton would ever repeat, the sense of elation and relief at being the rescuer was as powerful as any drug—a drug that Shackleton guessed would be highly addictive if it were available at the local pharmacy.

As the dogs and the sleds pulled up, the men embraced and hugged, both sets relieved to be rescued and to be at the rescue.

Shackleton shared tobacco with the men. He pulled out a bottle of his favored Mackinlay's Whisky, and they retreated to the hut, where they smoked over a dram and caught up.

News of the demise of Mackintosh, Hayward, and Spencer-Smith was received with much sadness. For Shackleton to lose men was like losing a part of himself and marked a personal and very deep failure.

Much to their relief, Shackleton instructed the seven to board the shore boat and get aboard the *Aurora*, get warm, get some food, bathe, and sleep. "Maybe we'll have a libation this evening, boys?" Shackleton winked. The men were excited, to say the least.

Shackleton and the shore party set about searching for the bodies of the dead, to no avail.

As the day drew to a close, the landing party boarded the launch and returned to the *Aurora*.

The seven were in heaven. When Shackleton got to the *Aurora*, he found them cleaned, bathed, and shaven, in the galley finishing their evening meal. They cheered as

Shackleton walked in, and they broke out the resurrected treasure chest with a vast array of the libations that Shackleton had referred to earlier. They drank, they toasted, and they drank again as together they recounted their stories of the past two years and their hardships, which were already being transformed into their adventures, the stories of legend.

Three of the seven had made their excuses and gone to their bunks for a peaceful rest. Two were asleep in the galley at the table. That left Wild, Joyce, and Shackleton.

Joyce, the old character that he was, declared a toast: "To our wives and sweethearts!"

Then they all chorused together, "And may they never meet!"

Over the next eight weeks, the *Aurora* moored at numerous points off the Antarctic coast to access the various huts and depots that either had existed previously or that the Ross Sea party had laid, trying to recover the bodies of the three lost souls.

Eventually, their search became obviously futile, and they decided with heavy hearts to give up. The men erected a cross in memory of the three lost souls. By February 4 they set sail for New Zealand.

Day 939
Wellington, New Zealand
February 9, 1917

The *Aurora* pulled up to Wellington port and moored. Wild stood beside Shackleton on *Aurora's* aft deck as the ship entered Wellington Harbor. He glanced over at his friend and saw the relief on his face.

"Well, we finally made it back," Wild said. "Didn't think it would happen, but it did, despite the stiff odds."

Shackleton sighed. "The crew is in good spirits. At least there's that to be thankful for. I have to say, Frank, that the loss of three men continues to eat away at me. I can't help but blame myself."

The captain of the ship eased off the engines. As the vessel slowed and then stopped, a tug came alongside to nudge her into the dock.

"You're not to blame, boss. What happened was a tragic twist of fate, nothing more."

"I tell myself that, but I'm not convinced."

Wild said nothing. He realized that his friend was troubled. Although joyous at arriving back in New Zealand and joyous about having found seven of the ten men who were stranded in McMurdo Sound, he also showed a depth of sadness and fatigue when Wild looked him intently in the eye.

Soon the ship was secured at the quay. New Zealanders, including a large contingent of indigenous Maori, crowded along the waterfront. Shackleton and the entire crew of the *Aurora* were on the upper deck viewing the Maori welcome, the haka, a traditional ceremonial dance of the Maori culture involving vigorous movements, stamping of feet in unison, and slapping of forearms, chests, and thighs. Originally it was a dance to welcome distinguished guests to their land, although it could have been easily interpreted as the opposite.

"Ka mate, ka mate! Ka ora, ka ora! Tenei te tangata pu'ru-huru. Na'a nei tiki mai whaka-whiti te. Ra! Upane! Ka upane! A upane! Ka upane! Whiti t era! Hi!"

Wild the younger turned to his brother, Joyce, and Worsley. "What the bloody hell does all that mean? Are they going to eat us?"

Wild the elder responded, "No, no, they're only messing. They're big puddings really."

"Aye, bloody big puddings by the looks of it!"

"What they are actually saying is," Worsley went on, wanting to share his humorous insights as always, "'We're going to die. We are at war. We're going to live, but now there is peace. We are going to die, we're going to die. We're going to live, we're going to live, but now we are safe.'"

Shackleton looked at Worsley. "Pretty impressive," he said, admiring his knowledge and translation, and bemused again that there was yet another side of this man that he liked and respected.

Frank Worsley continued, a smug smile on his face: "'This man is so hairy because our leader is so strong. He fetched us and made us shine. He unified us and brought back the sun. Sun, sun, together, peace, side by side. Together, all together. In unison like the hairs on our boss's legs. To sunny days and our prolonged days of peace. *Hey!*'" Worsley accentuated the last word for theatrical effect.

"Bloody hell! Is that true, boss?" Frank Wild turned to Shackleton with a big grin, looking down at his legs.

Shackleton mirrored the look.

Wild the younger asked, "How the bloody hell do you know that stuff?" Pausing a moment, he said, "Did yer just make that up?"

They all burst into laughter without wanting to upset the somewhat scary-looking locals before them.

As the crew disembarked the *Aurora*, the locals performed the haka once again, but this time it was clearly a different version from the last. "Do yer think they're ganning on about hairy legs again?" Wild the younger inquired. The crew stood there silently, intently, showing their respect, and the Maori did the same.

Wild accompanied his younger brother, Worsley, and Joyce to the Thistle Inn with its white exterior perched above the road and its big double wooden doors leading into the wooden bar where a fire was lit. Shackleton would join them in a little while. He had some administrative details to attend to.

The returning explorers were welcomed by all with pints of Hancock's Bitter, a big pot of boiled mutton, mince, and onions, and a pot of mashed tatties.

"Welcome home, boys," came the shout from the landlord.

"Welcome home, Frank Worsley!" he said to their brethren and captain.

There were lots of cheers, songs, and merriment, and plenty of beer consumed, as the boys celebrated their survival and commemorated their dead.

"There are good ships, there are wood ships, and there are ships that sail the sea, but the best ships are friendships, and may they ever be."

They all toasted together and broke out into song, singing "God Save the King."

The Wild brothers and Joyce were playing darts, then flipping beer mats, then arm wrestling as the beer swilled around and spilled. The singing grew louder and the merriment increased. It was like they had just come from the rugby field and were victorious together, the English, the Irish, the Scots, the Australians, and of course the Kiwis. The result didn't matter. The fact that they were, for the most part, still alive and together did.

It was a great day for celebration. The ordeal was over.

Shackleton entered the Thistle Inn and saw that it was packed with men celebrating the rescue of *Aurora*'s stranded crew. The fatigue weighed heavily on him. He recalled how startled he'd been when he looked in the mirror as he was getting ready to arrive in port. He looked ten years older than when he'd first begun the expedition. Not wanting to join the crew, he found himself a quiet corner in the Thistle. He ordered a bottle of the landlord's prized Balblair Whisky, lit his pipe, sat by the fire, and watched the festivities in the pub. He reflected on the journey and the trial they had just survived, at least most of them. Captain Davis joined him. "My old friend," he said, greeting Davis with a weary look and sadness as he ordered another glass and poured a dram for each of them.

As they settled down to their whisky and their pipes, Shackleton asked Davis, "So, what of the war?"

"It's pretty grim. It's pretty damn grim," Davis said. "Millions of men have lost their lives. Millions more wounded. The whole of Europe is at war with each other. After you left, it was like a domino effect, almost every week one country declaring war against the other."

Shackleton shook his head slowly. It was beyond comprehension what had changed in the past three and a half years, what they had been through, the rivers of blood across Europe—and then his own personal war in the icy frontiers of the south.

Different enemies but equally deadly, he thought, but then he reflected, *Maybe that isn't quite true.* Already some of his crew were straight into the thrusts of war, and he himself would soon follow.

"Where, when, how, will it end?" Shackleton asked, knowing his old friend had no answers. Nobody did.

"The Germans started strong, on the rampage across Europe, taking Belgium and France but getting bogged down, probably taking on too many fronts, including the Russians."

"Ah, the Russians, as hard as nails. They're enough for any war machine," commented Shackleton.

"We'll see, Shackleton. We'll see," Davis said.

"And what of Ireland?" Shackleton was hungry for news, including news of his homeland.

"The Germans even tried to get involved with the Easter Rising. They sent a ship over with twenty thousand rifles to arm the Republicans." Shackleton shot him a look. "The Royal Navy sank it before it made shore," Davis said.

Davis took a long sip of his drink, set the glass down, and said, "The Bolshevik revolution in Russia and the uprisings there. The Gallipoli disaster, the *Titanic's* sister, the unsinkable twins. The world's gone mad since you've been away, Shackleton. You missed a lot." Davis drew on his pipe and blew out a cloud of blue-gray smoke.

"Sounds like it! I knew you would miss me." Shackleton raised his glass of Balblair and said, "Cheers."

"Good to have you back, old boy. Certain to clear up these little matters in front of us," Davis said with a grin.

"Cheers! Let's drink to that!"

The Thistle broke into song once more with a raucous rendition of "Jerusalem"—"And did those feet, in ancient times, walk upon England's pastures green"—a song for the empire and of explorers or expeditioners like them.

Davis made his excuses and left. Shackleton was left alone by the fire with his pipe and his old friend whisky in the form of Balblair.

His thoughts turned to Emily and the children at home. He had sent her a telegram from South Georgia letting her know he was alive, but he had yet to hear back from her, and he wasn't quite sure what that meant.

He regretted the visibility of his dalliances before he had left. He kicked himself for his lack of self-discipline and his lack of planning to avoid discovery, yet he also wondered if his lack of discretion was partly due to his subconscious, his almost wanting to be exposed. After all, he was a chancer, a gambler, a risk-taker. He enjoyed the thrill of the unknown, the exposure to new lands. He was a pioneer, an explorer, a polar explorer, one of a kind, and part of a small club, and he liked that.

But with risk comes the phantom of failure. As he puffed his pipe, he reflected on that.

If it weren't for Emily's family wealth, his returns from polar expeditions and business ventures would simply not have been enough to sustain them. He relied heavily on investors to fund his ventures, and rarely had they come up with sufficient commercialization to pay them back, never mind put money into his bank account. He wondered what would become of this failed mission—a lost ship, three of his men dead, and little or no profit from the plans he had once drawn.

He poured himself another whisky and looked around at the boys arm wrestling. Ernest Joyce was winning, his pipe still in its usual place in his mouth, teeth gritted. Wild the Younger was his opponent, his knuckles crashing against the wooden table as the beers went flying and spilled.

Shackleton reflected how very proud he was of all his men, but Frank Wild stood out as his right-hand man. Worsley had overcome his initial doubt and had been there right through to the end, through thick and thin. Tom Crean was a rock, always quiet, a man of few words, never a complaint, just got on with the job no matter how big, no matter how daunting, no matter how impossible.

Shackleton had forgiven Vincent and Hudson for their weakness, and even McNish and his cat. They had all been through a terrible journey, and who was he to criticize anyway?

He felt for Mackintosh and his loss. He felt responsible, accountable, for some of the decisions he had made, especially in regard to the Ross Sea party. He had discounted what should have been a relatively straightforward part of the expedition and had hired accordingly, with a lack of experience that proved to work against them.

He thought about the impossibility of the Weddell Sea and the demise of the *Endurance*, remembering the cracks and the pops as she buckled beneath the ice, then the roar and the thunder of the ice grinding below, just like the plates of the earth as they bumped and grinded.

He held the thought for a moment, introducing no new recollections to allow the gravity of those tortuous moments to sink in, testing his fiber, his soul, and his sanity.

God knows what it did to the men's souls.

He poured another three fingers from the bottle of Balblair, took a sip, and savored the smooth liquid in his mouth before allowing it to trickle down his throat. He clenched his jaw as the whisky went down and then took another puff on his pipe, blowing smoke rings in the air by the fire, a proper polar explorer.

Polar explorers spend a lot of time on their own, in their own thoughts. It is a solitary life, so solitude is part of the job, the vocation of choice for Shackleton.

He thought about the demise of Spencer-Smith and perhaps the naivete, maybe as a result of his having hired him in the first place. He regretted that and thought about his brothers and sister, and his last words according to Wild Junior and Joyce.

"Mind if I join you, boss?" asked Ernest Joyce, shaking Shackleton from his thoughts.

"Yes, yes, of course. What's going on? Win all your arm wrestles? Don't think about asking me." Shackleton smiled.

"How are you doing, boss?"

Shackleton returned the look. "You know, Ernest, for all I have seen you drink, I don't think that I have seen you drunk," he declared.

"Plenty of practice, boss."

"No doubt." They both laughed. Shackleton poured him a three-finger shot of Balblair.

"You're a bloody legend, boss," Joyce announced, raising his glass for a toast.

For a moment, Shackleton almost blushed. This was a true compliment from a true warrior, a legend in his own right.

"Nowhere near the legendary status of Ernest Joyce," Shackleton said, clinking glasses.

Joyce lit his own pipe. For a moment they enjoyed the silence between friends, the comfortable silence that only two comrades, two warriors, could share as they both looked into the fire, enjoying the warmth and the crackle as the men in the Thistle started to dwindle and go to their cozy bunks for the night. Now there were just a handful left, including Shackleton and Joyce by the fire, together. This wasn't the first time, and Shackleton hoped it would not be the last.

Shackleton broke the silence. "We didn't conquer the Antarctic, Ernest, but what we did do, through our failure, was that we found success in our efforts and achievements."

Joyce looked down into his whisky, nodding, perhaps with a slight hint of inebriation.

"Every man is a hero, each one facing up to adversity. Each man, apart from three, have come out of this alive and hopefully are better men as a result." Joyce continued to nod as he sat back in his chair.

"It is the bravery of such men like you, Joyce and Frank Wild, Worsley, Crean, Macklin, Cheetham, Charlie Green, and even the stowaway Blackborow who will make this story the story of legends, legends like you, Joyce, like Wild the younger, like Mackintosh. This day is for you, Joyce, not me. This is for all the Weddell Sea and Ross Sea party crews to celebrate their achievements and heroic efforts of survival and conquering against all the odds."

Shackleton heard the snoring then looked at Joyce, realizing that he had passed out with two of the three fingers he had poured of the Balblair remaining.

Shackleton stayed there for a while by the fire with his friend, who was asleep, and his bottle of Balblair, which gave comfort to his thoughts and his demons.

Whisky

Oh my wee little dram,
Where do you come from, Glasgee, Oban?
With yer little wee cutie hat and yer tam,
When you thinkin' marriage, I am yer man.

Over the glen and far away,
Across the lochs just for a day.
Hither there and hither here,
Take a trip to here, ma dear.

Sipping nips by the fire,
Thinking of you and where we can go.
Sitting here and the conversations flow.
What next? Where will we go next?

We should stay here for a while.
Venturing off, can take a break.
It's not bad, after all, our wee whisky pile
Sitting here for a while. After all it is just great.

Yee shouldnay think too in depth
As the wee one will put yer mind to rest.
Remember, Irish whisky is different from Scottish whisky, and you oughta
Never mix the former with anything other than ice or water.

22
HOME

The Great War
Passchendaele, Belgium
1917
The Crew of the *Endurance*

THE THIRD BATTLE OF YPRES started again in earnest. Jimmy and Richie were back together and in the breach once more for the control of the ridges south and east of the Belgian city of Ypres.

After two major assaults and recognition for his contribution, Jimmy's wounds still stung and reminded him of the horrors of war. He was no longer a willing participant.

He often wondered of the exploits of the *Endurance* and about the dark places, the danger, and the rewards of notoriety and recognition the men were pursuing.

Although still very dangerous, it had to be better than this as he cowered with his hands over his head, rocking, listening to the onslaughts all around him.

Jimmy

A bunch of boys straight from the fields,
Young men from school and the mines,
Given a uniform, a tin hat, and a gun.
We're off to Europe for a bit of fun.

Though the training was elementary,
And the wooly, itchy uniforms complimentary,
Many couldn't even hit a barn door.
But this they knew, I think, what they were fighting for.

The reality came with such abundance.
Blood and guts, brains and innards.
Men screaming for their mothers,
Reaching out to their sisters and brothers.

For those who had sweethearts back at home
Or for those with children, nightmares of being alone.
Hanging up their dog tags on the trench's wall,
Thinking, *We're doing this for you all.*

When the terrible moments come and go
With the realization that you are still alive
And that many didn't make the cut,
It's enough to make you stay put.

Stay put, never to fight again.
Three battles and thousands of dead is enough for
any man,
Especially me, Jimmy, from Bolton, a Wanderers fan.

His refusal to participate twice got him in hot water. He was brought up on charges, put on orders, and humiliated. He had had enough and left the unit, only to be found in the local town and dragged back for court-martial. He did not speak, did not represent himself, just listened to the verdict and the punishment doled out by the officers in their regalia and their handlebar mustaches.

The sentence was death by firing squad, and Jimmy didn't care. When the day came, he faced it with stoic resignation. The soldiers tied him to a chair backed up against a wall. They blindfolded him and placed a white disc over his heart to serve as a target for the twelve men whose duty it was to kill him.

In the distance, the sound of the pipers danced on the wind, deceiving the ear with regard to their distance, somehow sounding as they were moving closer, piping their distinctive sound of defiance, of bravery, of being able to stand up to anything in adversity. They were piping even for this brave soldier who was weary from battle, who had taken more than most men could stand and who was now at his inevitable end.

Jimmy was not the soldier he once had been in Egypt and India. The Somme had seen to that. Gallipoli was enough, and now with the prospect of facing Passchendaele—he simply couldn't face anymore. He had already seen too much.

He didn't utter a word at his trial, and he didn't say anything now either. He just closed his eyes beneath his blindfold and listened to the pipes in the distance, thinking of his mother sitting at home in the cobbled streets of Bolton in their redbrick house and thinking about the *Endurance* as she had sailed off from Plymouth docks all those years ago. How he wished he had gone on that trip instead of this.

Then he heard the commander order the squad to ready and aim.

"Fire!"

Jimmy gritted his teeth, expecting death. Instead of death, searing pain shot through him as several bullets struck him.

Why aren't I dead? he wondered, coughing and gagging on his own blood.

Then, unbelievably, he heard the officer order Richie to finish the job or face a firing squad himself. The cruelty of it all amazed Jimmy, despite his pain, despite his abject terror at what was happening to him.

"I'm so sorry, mate," Richie said.

"Just do it," Jimmy said, barely able to speak because of the pain. "Don't blame yourself. This is what I want."

"Private Blundell!" shouted the commander. "Fire!"

Suddenly Jimmy felt a blinding flash of pain, and then everything went black.

EPILOGUE

Glasgow
1930

BACK IN HIS TENEMENT IN the Gorbals with his bride, Maggie, a year after meeting Harry McNish in Wellington, Walter Mitchell saw the announcement in the *London Times* marking the passing of his friend Mr. Harry "Chippy" McNish.

London Times, Issue 21379, September 25, 1930

Death of Mr. McNish. Went twice to Antarctica (per Press Association). WELLINGTON, this day. One of the few who have taken part in two expeditions to the Antarctic, Mr. Harry McNish, died in Wellington last night, aged sixty-four years.

Walter's thoughts had often ventured to his encounter with the ship's carpenter, his fellow Glaswegian, the polar explorer. When Walter had met the legendary Frank Wild in Cape Town on his passage back home, Wild, the right-hand man, had filled in some of the blanks and added to the stories McNish had shared.

Harry had wanted Walter to share his book *Dramming* with Wild, which he did. Harry wanted Wild's blessing, his acknowledgment, desperately seeking the acknowledgment he deserved.

Frank Wild was a humble yet confident man, a legend, yet modest, a rock, yet quietly spoken and mild-mannered. He was grateful for the connection, and he was also happy to tell his own tales related to this greatest ordeal.

He spoke of his sadness at Shackleton's unexpected passing in South Georgia on his ship the *Quest* in the early hours of the morning. He spoke of how Shackleton, complaining of back pain, had summoned the surgeon and the ship's doctor, Macklin, to his cabin for an examination.

"You've been overdoing things, boss. You need to lead a more normal life," Macklin had advised.

"You're always wanting me to give up things. What is it I ought to give up?" Shackleton asked.

"Chiefly whisky, boss," was the response as he looked over at the near-empty bottle of Mackinlay's on the cabin table.

A few moments later, at 2:50 a.m., on January 5, 1922, Shackleton suffered a fatal heart attack and died.

Walter's mind went back to the announcement in the *London Times*:

McNish was a member of the expeditions to the Antarctic led by Captain Scott and Sir Ernest Shackleton.

Born in Port Glasgow, 11 September 1874, McNish served his time in a shipbuilding yard in Glasgow. The first ship in which he went to sea was the *Barlillan*, a three-masted square-rigged craft of 2,508 tons.

He joined the navy and was a ship's carpenter for twenty-three years.

Frank Wild's fortunes had changed as well, or was it that his fortunes were always the same, with exploration being simply an escape from reality. In any event, Walter did notice the almost visible effects of Wild's life, which apparently had taken its toll.

Wild had been flitting from one job to the next, having moved to South Africa with his new bride. Times were hard, work was hard to come by, and life married to a polar explorer was not easy, Wild had explained, as if Walter's meeting with Harry, and now his connection to Wild, was some sort of acceptance into the Polar Club.

"Problem with Harry was that the boss never did quite take to him, you know." Wild went on to explain how he had been Harry's sponsor to get him on the crew in the first place, on the basis of his experience and legendary carpentry skills. "He was as experienced as they come, and I wanted him on board," explained Frank Wild during their long supper in Cape Town. "He wasn't a bad lad at all. In fact, I liked the old boy," Wild had told Walter.

Remembering the meeting, Walter knew that Harry would have liked that, and he hoped that Harry had received his letters telling him just that and also that he'd had the chance to read them before he died.

> He then went to Dundee and worked on the building of the *Discovery*, which was to go south with Captain Scott. Mr. McNish joined her as carpenter, the trip lasting two years and three months from Port Chalmers. Captain Scott got only as far as the Beardmore Glacier on that occasion.

Walter's thoughts turned to all the crew members of the *Endurance* and the *Aurora* and how, through his reading, his research, and Harry's book, poems, and drawings, he had discovered an amazing story of heroic leadership, extreme bravery in the face of adversity and desperation, survival, and celebration and sadness too.

He thought of the cataclysmic events in Sarajevo and the children left behind, orphaned. He recalled the losses of Mackintosh, Hayward, and Spencer-Smith—all perished—and the tragic tale of a war hero, Jimmy Smith, who, after having experienced too much for any man to face, was finally put out of his misery by his best friend, Richie Blundell, a horror that the latter would take to his grave.

He thought of Shackleton, of Worsley, and of Wild and their amazing demonstrations of leadership. He thought of Emily in Eastbourne with her children and of big Tom Crean.

Walter turned back to the *London Times* and read the final passages of the obituary:

> After Shackleton's 1914 Imperial Trans-Antarctic Expedition, McNish went to sea with the New Zealand Shipping Co. and finally worked his passage to New Zealand with the intention of settling there.
>
> McNish later became an inmate of Ohiro Home, Wellington. He died at Wellington Hospital.

Walter Mitchell went to his cabinet, pulled out a bottle of Balblair, poured a generous nip, raised his glass, and saluted. "To Mrs. Chippy!" He looked down at his desk and patted the manuscript that included McNish's previously unseen poems, *Dramming*. He would one day soon get it published as he had promised to McNish in Wellington.

A statue of Mrs. Chippy would be a later and welcome addition to McNish's last resting home, by his graveside near Wellington, New Zealand.

After Shackleton's death in South Georgia, he was buried in Grytviken with the king's flag he had been given all those years previous.

Later, after Frank Wild's death, Wild's ashes would be laid to rest in South Georgia with his great friend the boss, Shackleton—on his right-hand side of course.

To my comrades
who fell in the white warfare
of the south and on the
red fields of France
and Flanders.

—Sir Ernest Shackleton

Imperial Trans-Antarctic Expedition

SY Endurance and Her Crew

The SY *Endurance* (formerly *Polaris*)

Launched: December 17, 1912
Shipbuilder: Christian Jacobsen
Place of origin: Framnæs Shipyard, Sandefjord, Norway
Type: Barkentine
Tonnage: 348 gross registered tonnage (GRT)
Length: 144 feet
Beam: 25 feet

Probably the strongest wooden boat existing at that time. Every joint and fitting double braced, double the number of frames as other ships. Keel made of solid oak, and the bow made from single solid oak trees for maximum strength.

A barkentine or schooner barque is a sailing vessel with three or more masts: a square-rigged foremast, fore-and-aft-rigged mainmast and mizzenmast, and any other masts.

Sir Ernest Shackleton

DOB: February 15, 1874
Place of origin: County Kildare, Ireland
Position: Expedition leader

Shackleton, one of the pioneers of polar exploration, studied at Dulwich College, South London, and had a love for reading, the written word, and poetry. At sixteen he went to sea on the North-Western Shipping Company's *Hoghton Tower*. In 1898 he was certified as a master mariner, qualifying him to command a British ship anywhere in the world.

After the expedition, Shackleton volunteered for the army and insisted that he see active service. A heart condition and a burgeoning drinking problem stopped that, and he was sent first to Buenos Aires to boost pro-British propaganda and then went back to Europe and Spitzbergen to establish a British presence under the guise of a mining operation. From there, it was on to north Russia and the British involvement with the civil war.

On September 24, 1921, Shackleton left England on what would be his last expedition, aboard the *Quest*, headed to South Georgia, where he died of heart failure and was laid to rest.

Shackleton was married to Emily and was father to their three children, Raymond, Cecily, and Edward.

Expeditions: Discovery (1901–1904), Nimrod (1907–1909), Imperial Trans-Antarctic (1914–1917), Shackleton–Rowett (1921)

John Robert Francis "Frank" Wild
DOB: April 10, 1873
Place of origin: North Riding, Yorkshire, England
Position: Second-in-command

Frank Wild was an explorer and went on five expeditions to Antarctica, for which he was awarded the Polar Medal with four bars, one of only two men to be so honored.

Born in Skelton, close to Marton, the birthplace of Captain James Cook, Wild's maternal grandfather was Robert Cook, allegedly the grandson of the great explorer.

He joined the merchant navy at the age of sixteen, rising to the rank of second officer before joining the Royal Navy at age twenty-six and serving on HMS *Edinburgh*.

Wild was considered Shackleton's right-hand man. The two had a very high level of mutual respect as they served with each other on various polar expeditions.

He died on August 19, 1939, in Klerksdorp, South Africa, aged sixty-six.

Wild's widow had his ashes sent to South Georgia to rest at the right-hand side of the resting place of his boss, Ernest Shackleton.

Expeditions: Discovery (1901–1903), Nimrod (1907–1909), Aurora (1911), Imperial Trans-Antarctic (1914–1917), Shackleton–Rowett (1921–1922)

Frank Worsley

DOB: February 22, 1872
Country of origin: New Zealand
Position: Captain

Worsley was a New Zealand sailor and explorer who became a good friend of Shackleton over the years, serving on the *Endurance* and the *Quest*. Beyond their initial impromptu meeting, he marched shoulder to shoulder with Shackleton from Elephant Island, on the *James Caird*, navigating their way eight thousand miles across the Southern Ocean to South Georgia. He also made the thirty-six-hour march to Stromness to return and rescue the crew of the *Endurance*.

Upon his return from Antarctica, he joined the war effort and captained the Q-ship PC-61 and was responsible for sinking the German U-boat UC-33 on September 26, 1917.

He joined Shackleton on *Quest*, and even into his sixties he was still adventuring, this time treasure hunting for pirate treasure on Cocos Island.

He was married to Jean. The couple had no children.

Worsley died on February 1, 1943, of lung cancer in Claygate, England, at the age of seventy.

There is a bust of Worsley in his hometown of Akaroa, New Zealand.

Lionel Greenstreet

DOB: March 20, 1889
Country of origin: New Zealand
Position: First officer

Greenstreet, a Kiwi, at the age of fifteen became a sea cadet, joining the New Zealand Shipping Company. He gained his master's certificate in 1911 and, as a ship's young officer, wrote to Frank Worsley, captain of the *Endurance*. As it happened, Worsley's previous appointee had decided to accept his papers to join World War I, opening the position for Greenstreet. The *Endurance* had already sailed to Plymouth, where Worsley and Greenstreet met and the latter was given the job of first officer.

On his return, Greenstreet accepted a commission with the Royal Engineers on the barges on the Tigris in Mesopotamia.

He married Millie, who died in 1955. Greenstreet passed away on January 13, 1979, at the age of ninety.

Tom Crean

DOB: July 20, 1887
Place of origin: County Kerry, Ireland
Position: Second officer

Tom Crean was an Irish explorer and a member of three major expeditions during what is known as the heroic age of Antarctic exploration.

He left the family farm to enlist in the Royal Navy at the age of fifteen, lying about his age as the enlistment age was sixteen.

Crean was one of the six-man crew of the *James Caird*.

He was married to Ellen Herlihy and had three children, Mary, Kate, and Eileen.

In 1938, Crean became ill with a burst appendix and was taken to the nearest hospital in Tralee, but no surgeon was available. Because of the delay, an infection developed. He died a week later on July 27, 1938, at the age of fifty-one.

There is a statue of Crean holding a pair of hiking poles in one hand and two of his beloved sled dog pups in the other.

Alfred "Alfie" Cheetham

DOB: May 6, 1866
Place of origin: Liverpool, England
Position: Third officer

Cheetham was born in Liverpool with his family moving to Hull. He went to sea as a teenager, working on the fishing fleets of the North Sea.

He married Eliza Sawyer, and they had eleven children together.

After the Imperial Trans-Antarctic Expedition, Cheetham enlisted in the mercantile marine, serving as second officer on SS *Prunelle*. On August 22, 1918, the ship was torpedoed by a German U-boat and sank in the North Sea.

Hubert "Buddha" Tor Hudson

DOB: September 17, 1886
Country of origin: England
Position: Navigator

Hubert Hudson was a navigating officer of the Royal Navy before he joined the *Endurance*. He was known for his ability to catch penguins for meat as they were surviving being trapped on the ice. He suffered a severe mental breakdown on the expedition. Despite the crew members' concerns about the chance of his survival, he recovered to health.

Upon his return in 1917, he took part in World War I, serving on mystery ships.

In World War II, as a Royal Navy Reserve convoy commodore, he died after the German U-boat U-552 torpedoed his ship the *Pelayo* on June 15, 1942.

Lewis Raphael Rickinson

DOB: April 21, 1883
Place of origin: London, England
Position: Engineer

Lewis Rickinson was an English marine engineer. Born in Lewisham, England, he joined the *Endurance* as chief engineer.

Upon his return from the expedition, he joined the Royal Navy.

In 1918 he married Marjorie Snell, and they had two children, son Lewis and daughter Betty. After the war he became a consulting engineer.

With the coming of World War II, he joined HMS *Pembroke* and rose to the rank of engineer naval commander, in which position he served until he was diagnosed with lung cancer.

He died at a hospice in Berkshire on April 16, 1945, at the age of sixty-one.

Alexander Kerr

DOB: December 2, 1892
Place of origin: London, England
Position: Engineer

Born in East Ham, Kerr was a Londoner and an English marine engineer serving as second engineer, reporting to Lewis Rickinson aboard the *Endurance*.

Upon return from the Imperial Trans-Antarctic Expedition in 1917, Kerr joined the Royal Navy and, with his polar experience, went to the North Russia intervention to support the nonczarist and noncommunist forces of revolutionary Russia.

In 1917, Kerr married Lillian Mitchell, and they had two children, Jack and Eileen Kerr.

In later life he built a business as a wholesaler to small shops, selling confections, tobacco, and newspapers.

Kerr died in Stepney Hospital, East London, on December 4, 1964, aged seventy-two.

Alexander Hepburne Macklin

DOB: 1889
Country of origin: India
Position: Surgeon

Macklin was born in India, where his father was a doctor. Later he grew up in the Isles of Scilly, where he found a love of boats and the sea. He went on to Plymouth College and the University of London and then to Victoria University, Manchester, where he qualified as a doctor.

Shortly after qualifying, he applied to join the *Endurance* and was accepted.

Upon his return from the expedition, he earned a commission with the Royal Army Medical Corps and served in France, Russia, and Italy and was awarded the Military Cross for bravery as he tended the wounded under fire in Italy.

He rejoined Shackleton on the Shackleton–Rowett Expedition. On January 5, he confirmed that Shackleton was dead of heart failure and prepared his body for burial.

In 1926 he established a medical practice in Dundee, where he stayed until the start of World War II, when he returned to the Medical Corps as a major and served in East Africa. He retired from the army in 1948 as an honorary colonel.

He married Jean in 1948. They had two sons, Alexander and Richard. Macklin died on March 21, 1967, at the age of seventy-eight.

James McIlroy

DOB: November 3, 1879
Place of origin: Ulster, Ireland
Position: Surgeon

Earning his medical degree at Birmingham University, McIlroy worked at the Queen Elizabeth Hospital in Birmingham as a surgeon before heading off to Egypt and Japan to practice medicine, after which time he joined cruise ships in and around the East Indies.

After the Imperial Trans-Antarctic Expedition, McIlroy was badly wounded at Ypres.

In 1921, he joined Shackleton again. Unfortunately, Shackleton died aboard with Frank Wild completing the expedition on his behalf and in his memory.

In World War II, McIlroy's ship the SS *Oronsay* was torpedoed off the west coast of Africa. McIlroy spent five days in a lifeboat before being rescued.

He died on July 27, 1968, in Surrey, at the age of eighty-nine.

Sir James Wordie

DOB: April 26, 1889
Place of origin: Glasgow, Scotland
Position: Geologist

A Scottish polar explorer and geologist, Wordie, a Glaswegian, was the son of a carting contractor who studied at the Glasgow Academy and obtained a BSc in geology from the University of Glasgow. He graduated from St. John's College, Cambridge, in 1912.

Wordie sailed on nine polar expeditions in total and later became a prominent oracle on all things polar. He became chairman of the Scott Polar Research Institute and president of the Royal Geographical Society. During his term, he helped plan the first successful ascent of Mount Everest by Edmund Hillary.

He died in Cambridge on January 16, 1962, at age seventy-three.

Leonard Hussey

DOB: May 6, 1894
Place of origin: London, England
Position: Meteorologist

Hussey was an English meteorologist born in Leytonstone, England. He entered the University of London in 1909, taking a course in psychology, and went on to King's College London to gain degrees in meteorology and anthropology.

At an archeological dig in Sudan, he read Shackleton's advertisement in the *London Times* and wrote to him asking for a position on his expedition.

Shackleton sifted the letter from the almost five thousand responses and invited Hussey to meet with him, later agreeing to appoint him on the basis that, according to Shackleton, he "looked funny."

After the expedition, Hussey was commissioned in the Royal Artillery, serving in France. Later he transferred to operations in Murmansk, in northern Russia.

In World War II, Hussey joined the Royal Air Force, becoming a squadron leader before his retirement in 1954.

Hussey died on February 25, 1964, in London at the age of seventy-two.

Reginald James

DOB: January 9, 1891
Place of origin: London, England
Position: Physicist

After displaying adolescent skills as a math prodigy, James was awarded a stipend to pursue studies at St. John's College, Cambridge. He joined the *Endurance* as a naturalist.

On his return, James joined the Royal Engineers, rising to the rank of captain. He performed tasks of artillery spotting on the western front. He returned to the University of Manchester as a lecturer and again rose through the ranks, specializing in problems of x-ray crystallography.

In 1936 he married Annie Watson, and in 1937 he moved to South Africa, becoming a professor at the University of Cape Town.

James died on July 7, 1964, at the age of seventy-three, leaving behind three children, John, David, and Margaret.

Robert Clark

DOB: September 11, 1882
Place of origin: Aberdeen, Scotland
Position: Biologist

Clark was a Scottish marine biologist hailing from Aberdeen in the north of Scotland. Through Aberdeen University he became a zoologist for the Scottish Oceanographical Laboratory in Edinburgh.

Clark was a keen golfer and angler and was elected to play cricket for Scotland in 1912.

After *Endurance*, he returned to Scotland, served with the Royal Navy Volunteer Reserve of minesweepers, and married Christine Ferguson.

In 1924, Clark was once again recalled to play cricket for Scotland.

In 1935 he was elected a fellow of the Royal Society of Edinburgh. He retired in 1948 and died two years later at his home in Murtle, Aberdeenshire. He had no children.

James Francis "Frank" Hurley

DOB: October 15, 1885
Place of origin: Sydney, Australia
Position: Photographer

Hurley, an Australian photographer and adventurer, was born in Glebe, Sydney, Australia. At the age of thirteen, he ran away from home to work at the Lithgow steel mill, retuning two years later.

He bought his first camera at the age of seventeen and taught himself his art, setting up a postcard business where he gained a reputation for taking dangerous shots and stunning images never seen before.

Soon after returning from Douglas Mawson's Australasian Antarctic Expedition of 1911, he was snapped up by Shackleton as much for his expertise as for the rivalry that existed between Mawson and Shackleton.

On Hurley's return from Antarctica in 1917, he joined the Australian Imperial Force (AIF) as an honorary captain to film scenes of the Third Battle of Ypres.

Hurley married Antoinette Rosalind Leighton on April 11, 1918. The couple had four children, identical twin daughters

Adelie and Toni; a son, Frank; and their youngest daughter, Yvonne.

Hurley died in Sydney, Australia, on January 16, 1962, at the age of seventy-six.

George Edward Marston

DOB: March 19, 1882
Place of origin: Hampshire, England
Position: Artist

George Marston was an English artist born in Southsea, England. He studied art at Regent Street Polytechnic. He joined Shackleton on the Nimrod Expedition (1907–1909) and served as expedition artist on the Imperial Trans-Antarctic Expedition and the *Endurance*.

Marston died on November 22, 1940, at age fifty-eight.

Thomas Orde-Lees

DOB: May 23, 1877
Place of birth: Rhine, Germany
Position: Motor repairman and storekeeper

Orde-Lees was a pioneer in the field of parachuting and was one of the first non-Japanese men known to have scaled Mount Fuji during winter.

The illegitimate son of a former barrister and chief constable of Northampton and the daughter of the headmaster of Boston Grammar School, he was born in Aachen, where his pregnant mother had been sent to give birth in privacy.

His family were well-off. He enjoyed private schooling at the prestigious Marlborough College and then went on to the Royal Navy Academy and Royal Military College Sandhurst, afterward joining the Royal Marines.

He served in China during the Boxer Rebellion.

Orde-Lees was released from his military duties to join the *Endurance* as a representative of the Royal Navy.

After the expedition, he recommissioned and went to the war.

He continued to be a pioneer in parachuting, at one point jumping off Tower Bridge in London as a publicity stunt.

As Japan entered into World War II, Orde-Lees was forced to move. He headed to New Zealand.

On December 1, 1958, he died in a mental hospital, having suffered from dementia, at the age of eighty-one. He is buried in Karori Cemetery, Wellington, close to his fellow *Endurance* crew member Harry McNish.

Harry "Chippy" McNish

DOB: September 11, 1874
Place of origin: Port Glasgow, Scotland
Position: Carpenter

Harry McNish, referred to as Harry or by his nickname, Chippy, was a career carpenter, having worked on the *Clyde* and having served in the merchant navy. He was married three times, to Jessie Smith, who died in 1898; Ellen Timothy, who died in 1904; and Lizzie Littlejohn. McNish (sometimes spelled "McNeish") was the owner of the *Endurance* ship's cat, Mrs. Chippy.

McNish moved to Wellington, New Zealand, and became homeless, living in the port and supported by many of the sailors there until his death in 1930. He was buried in Karori Cemetery with a statue of his cat, Mrs. Chippy, beside him.

Charles "Charlie" Green

DOB: November 24, 1888
Place of origin: Surrey, England
Position: Cook

Charlie Green was born in Richmond, Surrey, England. He was a British ship cook, learning his trade from his father, who was a master baker. He left home at the age of twenty-two to join the merchant navy. In October 1914, on the crew of the *Andes*, he heard word that the *Endurance* was seeking a cook, and he jumped ships in Buenos Aires.

After the expedition, he joined the Royal Navy and served as a cook on the destroyer HMS *Wakeful*. He was wounded in August 1918.

He then went on to join the Shackleton–Rowett Expedition, and upon his return he once again joined the merchant navy before retiring in 1931.

Green was one of the last surviving crew at the fiftieth anniversary in 1964.

Walter Ernest How

DOB: December 25, 1885
Place of origin: London, England
Position: Able seaman

Born in Bermondsey, London, Walter How became a sailor at the age of twelve. He married Helen Varey in 1913, and his first daughter was born just six weeks before his departure on the *Endurance*.

Upon return to England in 1917, How joined the merchant navy and the war effort.

He died of cancer on August 5, 1972, at age eighty-six.

William Bakewell

DOB: November 26, 1888
Place of origin: Joliet, Illinois, USA
Position: Able seaman

Bakewell was the only American on the crew. He joined the *Endurance* in Buenos Aires as an able seaman. Born in Joliet, Illinois, he returned home and married Merle in 1925, and they had a daughter, Elizabeth.

In August 1945 he purchased a farm in Michigan.

Bakewell died on May 21, 1969, in Dukes, Michigan.

Timothy "Tim" McCarthy

DOB: July 15, 1888
Place of origin: Kinsale, Ireland
Position: Able seaman

Tim McCarthy, an Irishman from Kinsale, was an impressive member of the team. His skill and aptitude during their journey were both recognized by Shackleton and appreciated by the rest of the crew.

He was part of the six-man team on board the *James Caird*. The journey had taken its toll. He was one of the three who stayed in Cave Cove beneath the upturned boat for shelter.

Upon his return to Britain, McCarthy joined the Royal Navy Reserve as a leading seaman. He was a gunman on SS *Narragansett*, an oil tanker, which on March 16, 1917, was torpedoed and sunk. McCarthy, at twenty-eight, was the first of the *Endurance* team to die.

Thomas Frank McLeod

DOB: April 3, 1873
Place of origin: Glasgow, Scotland
Position: Able seaman

A Scottish sailor from Glasgow, McLeod went to sea at the age of fourteen. In 1910, he joined the Terra Nova Expedition led by Captain Robert Falcon Scott. He was an able seaman.

After this expedition, McLeod joined Shackleton on the Shackleton–Rowett Expedition.

In 1923, McLeod immigrated to Canada, working as a fisherman and later as a school caretaker. He later moved to a retirement home in Kingston, Ontario, and died on December 16, 1960, at age eighty-seven.

John William Vincent

DOB: January 24, 1884
Place of origin: Birmingham, England
Position: Boatswain

John Vincent was a sailor and one of the five men who accompanied Shackleton from Elephant Island to South Georgia on the *James Caird*. He became a sailor at the age of thirteen and later became a trawlerman in the North Sea.

Vincent, a keen amateur boxer and wrestler, was a tough man in one of the toughest trades known to humankind at that time. He was recognized as probably the fittest man on the Imperial Trans-Antarctic Expedition of 1914.

On the journey from Plymouth to Buenos Aires, Vincent got into arguments with the crew, including Thomas Orde-Lees. After Shackleton joined them, he demoted Vincent to the status of able seaman.

After the expedition, Vincent joined the crew of a vessel chartered by the foreign office that was torpedoed while in the Mediterranean. During World War II, he served in the Royal Navy Reserve and was given the command of the armed trawler HM Trawler *Alfredian*. While on board he developed pneumonia. On January 19, 1941, he died at the naval hospital in Grimsby, England.

Albert Ernest Holness
DOB: December 7, 1892
Place of origin: Hull, England
Position: Stoker

Born in Hull, Yorkshire, England, Holness was the stoker for the *Endurance*. Despite the fact that she was a rigged barkentine, she had a coal-burning engine and spent much of her time under steam. Holness reported directly to the chief engineer, Rickinson, and second engineer, Kerr.

After the expedition, he worked on the trawlers of the North Sea. At the age of thirty-one he was washed overboard, never to be found.

William "Steve" Stephenson
DOB: April 19, 1889
Place of origin: Hull, England
Position: Stoker

Stephenson was born in Kingston upon Hull and was a veteran of the Royal Marines prior to joining *Endurance*.

After the expedition he worked on the fishing trawlers in the North Sea before retirement.

Stephenson died in Hull Hospital on August 19, 1953, at age sixty-four.

Perce Blackborow

DOB: 1896
Place of origin: Newport, Wales
Position: Steward (after having been found as a stowaway on board)

Born in Monmouthshire, Wales, Blackborow was a Welsh sailor.

He and his friend William Bakewell traveled from England to Buenos Aires to find work. Bakewell was appointed to the *Endurance* as an able seaman. Blackborow was not offered a position and was taken aboard the ship as a stowaway by Bakewell and Walter How. Upon his discovery, and much to the wrath of Shackleton, he was given the position of steward.

Blackborow returned to live in Newport, South Wales. He died of chronic bronchitis and a heart problem in 1949 at the age of fifty-three.

Imperial Trans-Antarctic Expedition

The SY *Aurora* and the Ross Sea Party

The SY *Aurora*
Launched: 1876
Shipbuilder: Alexander Stephen and Sons
Place of origin: Dundee, Scotland
Type: Barque rigged steam yacht
Tonnage: 380 gross registered tonnage (GRT)
Length: 165 feet
Beam: 30 feet

Built for the Dundee Seal and Whale Fishing Company, the *Aurora* was a solid oak ship reinforced with steel plate. Between 1911 and 1917, the *Aurora* made five voyages to the Antarctic region for both exploration and rescue missions.

Aurora was last seen in 1917 when she departed Newcastle, New South Wales, Australia, bound for Iquique, Chile, with a cargo of coal. She disappeared at sea, presumed to be the victim of a German mine.

Aeneas Lionel Acton Mackintosh
DOB: July 1, 1879
Place of origin: Tirhut, British India
Position: Commander, Ross Sea party

Aeneas Mackintosh was a merchant navy officer and explorer. He commanded the Ross Sea party contingent of Shackleton's Imperial Trans-Antarctic Expedition of 1914.

Mackintosh's competence, experience, and leadership were all called into question as the disastrous Ross Sea party expedition unfolded with the drift of the *Aurora* and with ten men, including Mackintosh, stranded on the Antarctic.

On May 8, 1916, Mackintosh and Hayward marched off to Cape Evans and shortly afterward were caught in a severe blizzard. Neither of the men were ever seen again.

Richard W. Richards
DOB: November 14, 1893
Place of origin: Bendigo, Victoria, Australia
Position: Physicist

Dick Richards was an Australian science teacher, and at just twenty years old he joined the *Aurora* as physicist, having just completed his studies at the University of Melbourne.

Upon his return, he received £70 for his efforts, despite having signed up for the expedition with no agreement on pay.

He went on to become the principal of Ballarat College. He outlived all the members of the expedition, dying at the age of ninety-one.

Victor Hayward
DOB: October 23, 1887
Place of origin: London, England
Position: General assistant

Victor Hayward, a London-born accounts clerk, joined the expedition after previously spending some time working on a ranch in northern Canada. This experience, along with his so-called can-do attitude, earned him a place on the team.

Hayward disappeared with Mackintosh as they ill-advisedly left the shelter of their hut to walk across the ice in an attempt to reach Cape Evans.

Reverend Arnold Spencer-Smith

DOB: March 17, 1883
Place of origin: Streatham, Surrey, England
Position: Chaplain and photographer

Spencer-Smith was a clergyman and amateur photographer. He joined the Imperial Trans-Antarctic Expedition as chaplain and photographer.

He shared the same birthdate as Captain Lawrence Oates, who famously said before his own disappearance in the Antarctic, "I am stepping outside. I may be some time," never to be seen again.

Spencer-Smith was educated at Westminster City School, King's College London, and Queens' College, Cambridge. He was ordained into the Scottish Episcopal Church in 1910.

Suffering from exhaustion, scurvy, and frostbite, Spencer-Smith collapsed on the Beardmore Glacier while on a mission to lay the depots. Ernest Wild pulled him along on his sled. Spencer-Smith, uncomplaining, often delirious, died on the barrier on March 9, 2016, aged thirty-two years.

Spencer-Smith dedicated his final diary entry to his father, mother, brothers, and sister. His wallet would be found some eighty-four years later with three photos of a camping expedition with his brothers at home.

Joseph Stenhouse
DOB: November 15, 1887
Place of origin: Dumbarton, Scotland
Position: First officer (subsequently captain)

Stenhouse received a last-minute appointment as first officer of SY *Aurora* and sailed for Sydney on the SS *Ionic* on September 18, 1914, to join her as she was being refitted and restocked.

Stenhouse was the temporary commander of the *Aurora* when she was attached to a large ice floe and was blown out of McMurdo Sound into the Ross Sea. With no means to raise steam, and with trying weather conditions, the *Aurora* eventually broke with the ice and drifted back to New Zealand.

Upon arrival, Stenhouse immediately went about the repairs to the ship, readying her for return to McMurdo Sound and the rescue of the stranded crew.

Stenhouse was killed in action during World War II in the Red Sea. His ship exploded and sank after being struck by a mine.

Ernest Wild
DOB: August 10, 1879
Place of origin: North Riding of Yorkshire, England
Position: Storekeeper

The younger brother of Frank Wild, Ernest made just a single trip to the Antarctic as a member of the Ross Sea party. Despite this, he was an experienced mariner, having grown up with the ocean in his blood, a descendant of Captain

James Cook with nearly twenty years of experience at sea under his belt.

Wild always saw the lighter side of life and, like his older brother, appeared to have a way of facing and tackling almost any level of adversity.

He was a critic of Mackintosh and his leadership.

After the expedition, Wild joined the Royal Navy, joining HMS *Pembroke* then HMS *Biarritz*, serving in the Mediterranean. He died in the Royal Navy Hospital, Malta, on March 10, 1918, from typhoid.

Ernest Joyce

DOB: December 22, 1875
Place of origin: Feltham, Sussex, England
Position: Manager of sledding equipment and dogs

Joyce went to the Greenwich Royal Hospital School for Navy Orphans as a child, where he received vocational training for a position in the lower decks of the Royal Navy. He had blue eyes and a fair complexion as a child, similar to Peter Pan. Later a tattoo on his left forearm and a scar on his right cheek gave him the look of a sailor and a polar explorer. In 1891, at the age of sixteen, he joined the Royal Navy as a boy seaman.

At only 5'7" in height, Joyce was equally known for his abrasive manner and his value and experience as a crew member.

Expeditions: Discovery (1901–1904), Nimrod (1907–1909), Australasian Antarctic Expedition (1911), Imperial Trans-Antarctic (1914–1917)

John Lachlan Cope
DOB: 1893
Place of origin: London, England
Position: Biologist and surgeon

Alexander Stephens
DOB: 1886
Country of origin: Scotland
Position: Chief scientist

Andrew Keith Jack
DOB: 1885
Country of origin: Australia
Position: Physicist

Irvine Gaze
DOB: 1890
Country of origin: Australia
Position: General assistant

Aubrey Howard Ninnis
Position: Motor tractor specialist

Lionel Hooke
Position: Wireless telegraph operator

Leslie Thompson
Position: Second officer

Alfred Larkman
Position: Chief engineer

Adrian Donnelly
Position: Second engineer

James Paton
Position: Boatswain

Clarence Maugher
Position: Carpenter

Sydney Atkin
Position: Able seaman

Arthur Downing
Position: Able seaman

William Kavanagh
Position: Able seaman

Shorty Warren
Position: Able seaman

Charles Glidden
Position: Ordinary seaman
Sean Grady
Position: Fireman

William Mugridge
Position: Fireman

Harold Shaw
Position: Fireman

Edwin Thomas Wise
Position: Cook

Emile d'Anglade
Position: Steward

Time Line

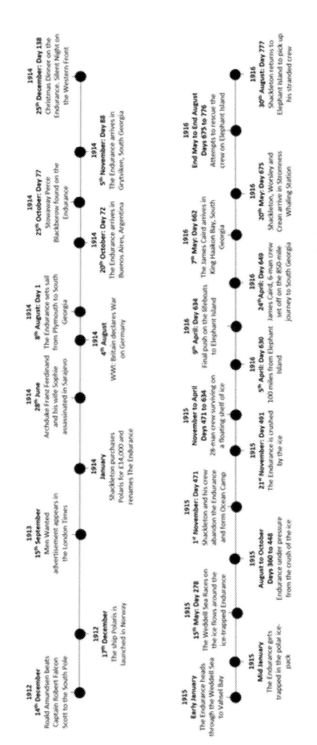

1912
14th December
Roald Amundsen beats Captain Robert Falcon Scott to the South Pole

1913
15th September
Men Wanted advertisement appears in the London Times

1912
17th December
The ship Polaris is launched in Norway

1914
28th June
Archduke Franz Ferdinand and his wife Sophie assassinated in Sarajevo

1914
January
Shackleton purchases Polaris for £14,000 and renames it The Endurance

1914
4th August
WWI. Britain declares War on Germany

1914
8th August: Day 1
The Endurance sets sail from Plymouth to South Georgia

1914
20th October: Day 72
The Endurance arrives in Buenos Aires, Argentina

1914
25th October: Day 77
Stowaway Pierce Blackborow found on the Endurance

1914
5th November: Day 88
The Endurance arrives in Grytviken, South Georgia

1914
25th December: Day 138
Christmas Dinner on the Endurance. Silent Night on the Western Front

1915
Early January
The Endurance heads through the Weddell Sea to Vahsel Bay

1915
Mid January
The Endurance gets trapped in the polar ice-pack

1915
15th May: Day 278
The Weddell Sea Races on the ice flows around the ice-trapped Endurance

1915
August to October
Days 360 to 448
Endurance under pressure from the crush of the ice

1915
1st November: Day 471
Shackleton and his crew abandon the Endurance and form Ocean Camp

1915
November to April
Days 471 to 634
28-man crew surviving on a floating shelf of ice

1915
21st November: Day 481
The Endurance is crushed by the ice

1916
9th April: Day 634
Final push on the lifeboats to Elephant Island

1916
5th April: Day 630
100 miles from Elephant Island

1916
24th April: Day 649
James Caird, 6-man crew set off on the 850-mile journey to South Georgia

1916
7th May: Day 662
The James Caird arrives in King Haakon Bay, South Georgia

1916
20th May: Day 675
Shackleton, Worsley and Crean arrive in Stromness Whaling Station

1916
End May to End August
Days 675 to 776
Attempts to rescue the crew on Elephant Island

1916
30th August: Day 777
Shackleton returns to Elephant Island to pick up his stranded crew

After a short respite in Punta Arenas, Chile, Shackleton then went on to Wellington, New Zealand, to the Aurora and on to McMurdo Sound where he picked up the survivors of the Ross Sea Party. Despite having men stranded at each side of the Antarctic, The Imperial Trans-Antarctic Expedition only suffered one casualty, Blackborow and his first bitten toes, and three fatalities – the Captain of the Aurora, Mackintosh, Hayward and Spencer-Smith.

Night Watches

On a ship, there are scheduled watches during the night. Each watch is four hours in duration. The watches include the following:

Monkey Watch (from 16:00 to 20:00)
Considered an easier shift as most of the crew are likely active aboard the ship.

Donkey Watch (from 20:00 to midnight)
The crew going to bed. Not a bad watch; still some reasonable opportunity for sleep and routine.

Rat Watch (from midnight to 4:00 a.m.)
Crew asleep. Nothing much more to watch than the ship's rats.

Dog Watch (4:00 a.m. to 8:00 a.m.)
Considered the most difficult watch with cleaning in readiness for the morning, and the danger associated with waking up the crew and getting bitten.

Sea Ice Nomenclature, from J. M. Wordie's Observations

slush or sludge: The initial stages in the freezing of seawater, when its consistency becomes gluey or soupy.

pancake ice: Small circular floes with raised rims; the result of the breakup in a gently ruffled sea of the newly formed ice into pieces that strike against each other and form turned-up edges.

young ice: Applied to all unhummocked ice up to about a foot in thickness. Owing to the fibrous or platy structure, the floes crack easily, and where the ice is not overly thick, a ship under steam cuts a passage without much difficulty.

land floes: Heavy but not necessarily hummocked ice with generally a deep snow covering, which has been held up in the position of growth by the enclosing nature of some feature of the coast or by grounded bergs throughout the summer season, when most of the ice breaks out. Its thickness is, therefore, above average.

floe: An area of ice, level or hummocked, whose limits are within sight. Includes all sizes between brash on the one hand and fields on the other. "Light floes" are between one and two feet in thickness (anything thinner being "young ice"). Those floes exceeding two feet in thickness are termed "heavy floes," being generally hummocked.

field: A sheet of ice of such extent that its limits cannot be seen from the masthead.

hummocking: Includes all the processes of pressure formation whereby level young ice becomes broken up and built up.

hummocky floes: In contrast to young ice, the structure is no longer fibrous but becomes spotted or bubbly. A certain percentage of salt drains away, and the ice becomes almost translucent.

the pack: This is a term very often used in a wide sense to include any area of sea ice, no matter what form it takes or how disposed.

pack ice: A more restricted use than the foregoing, to include hummocky floes or close areas of young ice and light floes. Pack ice is "close" or "tight" if the floes constituting it are in contact; it is "open" if, for the most part, they do not touch. In both cases it hinders, but does not necessarily check, navigation.

drift ice: Loose open ice where the area of water exceeds that of the ice. Generally, drift ice is within reach of the swell, and is a stage in the breaking down of pack ice, the size of the floes being much smaller than in the latter.

brash: Small fragments and roundish nodules; the wreck of other kinds of ice.

bergy bits: Pieces, about the size of a cottage, of glacier ice or of hummocky pack washed clear of snow.

crack: Any sort of fracture or rift in the sea ice covering.

growlers: Still smaller pieces of sea ice than the above, greenish in color and barely showing above water level.

lead or lane: Where a crack opens out to such a width as to be navigable. In the Antarctic it is customary to speak of these as leads, even when frozen over to constitute areas of young ice.

pools: Any enclosed water areas in the pack, where length and breadth are about equal.

Whisky

Mackinlay's Rare Old Highland Malt Whisky: During Shackleton's Nimrod Expedition, to bolster team spirit, he personally ordered twenty-five cases of Mackinlay's Rare Old Highland Malt Whisky.

A century later, three cases of the whisky were found, perfectly preserved, frozen into the ice beneath Shackleton's base camp at Cape Royds.

Later, world-renowned master blender Richard Paterson recreated the antique whisky, now known as the Shackleton.

Dead Reckoning

This is the process of calculating one's current position by using a previously determined position, or fix, and advancing that position based upon known or estimated speeds over an elapsed time and course.

Reference to the art of dead reckoning appeared in the *Oxford English Dictionary* as early as 1613. It is considered as much as a science as a dark art.

Yorkshire Puddings (Yorkie Puds)

A traditional favorite that has spanned far beyond the boundaries of the English county of Yorkshire.

Yorkshire pudding is traditionally served as an accompaniment to roast beef and roast meats, extended to sausages, stew, and even just meat gravy to soak up as a delicious staple.

Legendary in its trickiness to perfect, Yorkshire pudding requires the right recipe, the right consistency, and, critically, the right amount of oven heat for baking.

The recipe is as follows: four eggs, one cup of milk, one cup of flour, and a pinch of salt for the batter. Then two tablespoons of lard (or, even better, beef drippings) to line the baking tray. Heat the tray with the lard (or drippings) in the oven so it is scorching hot, although not so hot that it burns. Pour in the batter and bake for twenty minutes or until golden brown.

Getting the correct heat for the drippings and the proper airiness of the batter, and not opening the oven door too often, are tips for making this wonderful dish to accompany almost any meal.

Extraordinary Times

There was probably more happening in the world during the early twentieth century than at any other period of history. There were the mind-blowing feats of engineering, inventors inventing, industrialists building, and entrepreneurs creating, and the entire continent of Europe was involved in the Great War. And then, at the very bottom of the globe, what is considered to be the last great expedition of the golden age of Antarctic exploration was taking place with Shackleton, Worsley, Wild, the other men, the *Endurance*, and the *Aurora*.

These were without a doubt extraordinary times. Below you will find a compilation of key events organized by year from 1912 to 1918.

1912

December 14: Roald Amundsen wins the race to the South Pole.

January 1: Sun Yat-sen forms the Republic of China.

January 17: Captain Robert Scott's expedition arrives at the South Pole, one month after Roald Amundsen.

February 14: Arizona is admitted to the Union as the forty-eighth state.

April 10: RMS *Titanic* sets sail from Southampton for her maiden (and final) voyage.

April 14: RMS *Titanic* hits an iceberg at 11:40 p.m. off Newfoundland.

April 15: At 2:27 a.m., RMS *Titanic* sinks off Newfoundland as the band plays on.

April 18: Cunard Liner RMS *Carpathia* brings 705 survivors from the RMS *Titanic* to New York City.

May 5: Fifth Olympic Games open in Stockholm, Sweden.

May 8: Paramount Pictures is founded.

June 8: Universal Pictures is founded.

August 24: Alaska becomes an organized incorporated territory of the United States.

September 15: Conflict between Turkey and Montenegro breaks out in Albania.

October 2: Mahatma Gandhi arrives in South Africa on a twenty-six-day tour.

October 8: Montenegro declares war on Turkey, beginning the First Balkan War.

November 5: Woodrow Wilson is elected twenty-eighth president of the United States.

November 12: British explorer Robert Scott's diary and body are found in Antarctica.

November 24: Conflict in the Balkans grows into an acute international crisis with major powers supporting either Austria or Serbia.

November 25: Socialist International rejects that world war is coming.

December 8: German emperor and king Wilhelm II of Prussia calls a "war council."

1913

January 16: British House of Commons accepts home rule for Ireland (but the Great War gets in the way of that).

May 30: Treaty of London is signed by the Great Powers, the Ottoman Empire, and the victorious Balkan League (Serbia, Greece, Kingdom of Bulgaria, and Montenegro), bringing an end to the First Balkan War.

July 12: One hundred fifty thousand Ulstermen gather and resolve to resist Irish home rule by force of arms; since the British liberals have promised the Irish nationalists home rule, civil war appears imminent.

November 6: Mahatma Gandhi is arrested for leading Indian miners' march in South Africa.

December 1: Ford Motor Company institutes the world's first moving assembly line for the Model T Ford.

December 11: *Mona Lisa* is recovered two years after it was stolen from the Louvre Museum, Paris.

1914

February 7: Charlie Chaplin debuts the silent film character the Tramp in *Kid Auto Races at Venice*.

April 22: Babe Ruth plays his first professional game as a pitcher: Six-hit, 6–0 win.

June 6: First flight that constitutes *out of sight of land* from Scotland to Norway.

June 28: Franz Ferdinand, archduke of Austria, and his wife, Sophie, are assassinated in Sarajevo by young Serb nationalist Gavrilo Princip.

June 29: Jina Guseva attempts to assassinate Grigori Rasputin in his hometown in Siberia.

July 29: Armed resistance begins against British rule in Ulster.

July 28: Austria-Hungary decides against mediation and declares war on Serbia, the first declaration of World War I.

August 3: First seaworthy ship passes through the Panama Canal.

August 3: Germany invades Belgium and declares war on France, beginning World War I.

August 4: Britain declares war on Germany.

August 4: The United States declares neutrality with regard to the outbreak of World War I.

August 7: Famous Lord Kitchener poster "Your Country Needs You" is launched across the United Kingdom.

August 11: John Bray patents animation.

August 15: Lieutenant Charles de Gaulle is injured as German bombs destroy Dinant, Belgium.

August 20: German Army captures Brussels.

August 22: First encounter between British and German troops in Belgium.

August 30: First German bombing raids on Paris.

September 6: World War I. First Battle of the Marne begins; French and British forces prevent German advance on Paris (till September 12).

September 8: HMS (formerly RMS) *Oceanic*, sister ship of RMS *Titanic*, sinks off Scotland.

September 22: German submarine sinks three British ironclads; 1,459 die.

October 19: US Post Office uses first motorized vehicle for mail collection and delivery.

October 31: Great Britain and France declare war on Turkey.

December 21: First feature-length silent comedy film released—*Tillie's Punctured Romance*, starring Marie Dressler, Mabel Normand, and Charlie Chaplin.

December 25: Legendary "Christmas truce" takes place on the battlefields of World War I between British and German troops. Instead of fighting, soldiers exchange gifts and play football.

1915

January 25: Alexander Graham Bell in New York calls Thomas Watson in San Francisco on the new Transcontinental Telephone Service.

January 30: German submarine attack on Le Havre.

February 12: Adolf Hitler receives the Iron Cross (Second Class) for bravery in World War I.

February 17: Battle of Gallipoli commences.

February 18: Germany begins a blockade of Britain.

February 20: Panama–Pacific International Exposition (World's Fair) opens in San Francisco.

February 21: Russian Twentieth Army Corps surrenders to the German Tenth Army after being surrounded.

April 22: First military use of poison gas (chlorine, by Germany) in World War I.

May 25: Second Battle of Ypres ends with 105,000 casualties.

June 1: First zeppelin air raid over England.

September 29: First transcontinental radio telephone message is sent.

October 12: Henry Ford manufactures its one millionth automobile at the River Rouge plant in Detroit.

October 16: Great Britain declares war on Bulgaria.

October 19: US bankers arrange a $500 million loan to the British and French.

October 23: Twenty-five thousand suffragettes march on Fifth Avenue in New York City, for women's rights.

December 14: Jack Johnson is the first black world heavyweight boxing champion.

1916

February 10: Britain Military Service Act is enforced, introducing conscription to military service.

March 1: Germany starts attacking ships in the Atlantic.

March 28: First performance of "Jerusalem" by George Parry, set to words by William Blake, at the Queen's Hall, London.

April 9: SS *Libau* sets sail from Germany with a cargo of twenty thousand rifles to assist Irish Republicans. The captain changes the ship name to *Aud* to avoid British detection.

April 18: The United States warns Germany that unless it stops attacking unarmed ships in the Atlantic, it will break diplomatic relations.

April 21: Ulster Protestant and Irish nationalist Sir Roger Casement lands at Tralee Bay, Ireland, from a German submarine; he is later discovered at McKenna's Fort and arrested by the Royal Irish Constabulary.

April 22: Captain Karl Spindler scuttles the *Aud* near Daunt's Rock to prevent its cargo of twenty thousand rifles, destined for Irish Republicans, from falling into enemy hands.

April 24: Easter Rising of Irish Republicans against British occupation begins in Dublin.

May 31: The Battle of Jutland, the largest naval battle of World War I, between the British Grand Fleet and the German High Seas Fleet, begins. A total of 8,645 Germans die in the British victory. This is the last the German Fleet is seen in World War I.

June 15: William Boeing, the aviation pioneer, launches the Boeing Model 1, a seaplane, the first Boeing product. It flies for the first time.

June 24: Mary Pickford becomes the first movie star to receive a contract for $1 million.

June 30: General Douglas Haig reports, "The men are in splendid spirits," the day before the Battle of the Somme begins.

July 1: First day of the Battle of the Somme: the British Army suffers its worst day, losing 19,240 men.

September 6: First supermarket, the Piggy Wiggly, opens in Memphis, Tennessee.

September 15: First use of tanks in warfare, "Little Willies" at Battle of Flers-Courcelette, part of the Battle of the Somme.

September 17: Manfred von Richtofen, the Red Baron, wins his first aerial combat near Cambrai, France.

September 29: American oil tycoon John D. Rockefeller becomes the world's first billionaire.

November 7: Jeanette Rankin is elected to US Congress as the first female representative, a Republican for the state of Montana.

November 18: General Douglas Haig finally calls off the First Battle of the Somme with over one million killed or wounded.

November 19: Samuel Goldwyn and Edgar Selwyn establish Goldwyn Pictures.

December 7: David Lloyd George replaces H. H. Asquith as British prime minister.

December 15: French defeat Germans in World War I Battle of Verdun.

1917

January 1: T. E. Lawrence, Lawrence of Arabia, joins forces with Sheik Feisal al-Husayn, beginning his Arabian adventures.

February 13: Dutch erotic dancer Mata Hari is arrested in Paris on suspicion of being a German spy.

February 26: Czar Nicholas II orders the army to quell civil unrest in Petrograd (Saint Petersburg). The Russian army mutinies.

March 8: Russian "February Revolution" begins in earnest. Protests break out across Europe in celebration of International Women's Day. Riots begin in Saint Petersburg over food rations and the conduct of the war.

March 11: British forces occupy Baghdad, the capital of Mesopotamia, after Turkish forces are evacuated.

March 12: A German submarine sinks an unarmed US merchant ship, the *Algonquin*, on the same day that US president Woodrow Wilson gives executive order to arm US merchant ships.

March 15: The last Russian czar, Nicholas II, abdicates and nominates his brother Grand Duke Michael to succeed him.

March 16: Russian Grand Duke Michael, brother of Czar Nicholas II, declines the Russian throne.

March 20: After the sinking of three more US merchant ships, US president Woodrow Wilson meets with his cabinet, who agree that war is inevitable.

April 6: The United States declares war on Germany.

April 16: Vladimir Lenin issues his radical *April Theses* calling for Soviets to take power during the Russian Revolution.

May 18: First units of the American Expeditionary Force, commanded by General John J. Pershing, are ordered to France.

June 5: Ten million US men begin registering for the draft in World War I.

June 13: The deadliest German air raid on London during World War I is carried out by Gotha G.V bombers and results in 162 deaths, including 46 children, and 432 injuries.

June 16: First All-Russian Congress of the Soviets convenes in Petrograd, Russia.

June 19: The British royal family, which has had strong German ties since George I, renounce their German names and titles and adopt the name of Windsor.

July 28: Silent Parade, organized by James Weldon Johnson, of ten thousand African Americans march on Fifth Avenue, New York, to protest lynching.

October 6: Battle of Passchendaele. Canadian troops capture the village of Passchendaele in the Third Battle of Ypres with 250,000 casualties on both sides.

October 8: Leon Trotsky is named chairman of the Petrograd Soviets as the Bolsheviks take control.

October 15: Dutch exotic dancer Mata Hari is executed by firing squad for spying for Germany, allegedly having sent up to fifty thousand to their deaths.

October 21: First Americans to see action on front lines, US at Sommervillier, under French command.

November 6: Bolshevik revolution begins with bombardment of the Winter Palace in Petrograd during the Russian October Revolution—Red October.

November 7: October Revolution in Russia. Lenin and the Bolsheviks seize power, capture the Winter Palace, and overthrow the provisional government.

December 7: The United States becomes the thirteenth country to declare war on Austria during World War I.

1918

January 16: Austria and Germany are disrupted by strikes as people express impatience with their leaders continuing the war.

January 25: Russia is declared a republic of Soviets.

January 27: *Tarzan of the Apes*, the first Tarzan film, premieres at Broadway Theater.

February 10: Trotsky declares that Russia is leaving the war.

February 18: Germany renews its offensive against the Russians, making dramatic gains against disorganized and dispirited Russian troops.

February 22: Germany claims the Baltic states Finland and Ukraine, taking them from Russia.

March 11: Moscow becomes the capital of revolutionary Russia.

April 1: The Royal Air Force is created from the Royal Naval Air Service and the Royal Flying Corps.

April 20: The Red Baron, Manfred von Richtofen, shoots down his eightieth victim before his death the following day. Canadian pilot Arthur Roy Brown is credited with the kill.

May 21: US House of Representatives passes amendment granting women the right to vote.

July 17: The Romanov royal family are executed by a Bolshevik firing squad in the basement of Ipatiev House, Yekaterinburg, Siberia.

July 18: US and French forces launch the Aisne-Marne offensive. The following day, the German Army retreats.

August 4: Adolf Hitler receives the Iron Cross First Class for bravery at the recommendation of his Jewish superior Lieutenant Hugo Gutmann.

August 8: The Allies launch the Hundred Days Offensive, beginning with the Battle of Amiens, where five hundred tanks and ten Allied divisions attack German lines.

August 12: Allies defeat Germans at the Battle of Amiens, the last great battle on the western front.

August 13: Bayerische Motoren Werke AG (BMW) is established as a public company in Germany.

August 20: Britain opens an offensive on the western front.

September 3: Allies force Germans back across Hindenburg Line.

September 12: US forces launch an attack on German-occupied Saint-Mihiel.

September 14: Austria-Hungary sends a note to the Allies requesting peace discussions, but the Allies reject the offer.

September 26: Beginning of the Meuse-Argonne Offensive with more than one million American soldiers in the largest and most costly offensive of World War I.

September 29: Allied forces score a decisive breakthrough of the Hindenburg Line.

October 4: The musical *Sometime* with actress Mae West premieres in New York.

October 21: Germany agrees to further concessions to end World War I, which involved over seventy million military personnel, nine million military deaths, and seven million civilians.

October 31: Meanwhile, Spanish influenza is a worldwide pandemic and kills fifty million to one hundred million people worldwide. In this single week, it kills over twenty-one thousand people in the United States alone.

November 11: Armistice signed by the Allies and Germany comes into effect, and World War I hostilities end at 11:00 a.m., the eleventh hour of the eleventh day of the eleventh month.

ABOUT THE AUTHOR

WILLY MITCHELL WAS BORN IN Glasgow, Scotland. He spent a lot of time in bars as a kid growing up, in his youth, and into adulthood. He always appreciated the stories, some of which were true, some of which were the products of imagination, and some of which were delusional. But the stories Mitchel writes are true, based on true events, balancing fact and fiction.

A shipyard worker, he headed down from Scotland to Yorkshire with his family to work in the steel mills. He retired and turned to writing some of the tales that he had listened to all those years, focusing on bringing those stories to life.

Operation Argus

Operation Argus is fast paced, thoughtful, and personal. It is an insightful story that touches the mind and the heart and creates a sense of intrigue in the search for the truth.

While sitting in the Rhu Inn in Scotland one wintry night, Willy Mitchell stumbles across a group of men in civilian clothes, full of adrenaline, like a group of performers coming off a stage, wherever that stage may have been that night. To the watchful eye, it was clear that these men were no civilians. Close-knit, they engaged in banter and drank beer, yet they were completely alert as each of them checked out Mitchell, looking at his eyes and into his soul. Willy Mitchell would learn in time that this group would be referred to as call sign Bravo2Zero.

Operation Argus is a story of fiction based on true events as five former and one serving Special Air Service soldiers converge on San Francisco for a funeral of their good friend, only to find that his apparent heart attack was not as it seemed. A similar concoction of polonium-210 was used to assassinate Litvinenko in London years previous.

Bikini Bravo

Bikini Bravo continues to follow the adventures of Mitch, his daughter Bella, and the team of Mac, Bob, and Sam as they uncover what seems to be an unthinkably complex web of unlikely collaborators, but for a seemingly obvious common good—power, greed, and money.

Many years ago, Mitchell stumbles across a bar in Malindi, Kenya, West Africa, and overhears the makings of a coup in an oil-rich nation of West Africa. Could it be true that a similar plan is being hatched today?

Lord Beecham puts together the pieces of the puzzle and concludes that the Russians, along with the Mexican drug cartels and a power-hungry group of Equatorial Guineans, have put together an ingenious plot to take over Africa's sixth-largest oil-producing nation in an attempt to win influence in Africa. Also involved is the cartels' desire for turning dirty money into good and the Africans' desire to win power and influence.

Bikini Bravo is another book of fiction by Mitchell that masterfully flirts with fiction and real-life events spanning the globe and touching on some real global political issues.

Mitch's daughter, Bella, is the emerging heroine in this, the second book of the Argus series.

Cold Courage

Cold Courage starts with Willy Mitchell's grandfather meeting with Harry McNish in Wellington, New Zealand, in 1929. In exchange for a hot meal and a pint or two, McNish tells his story of the *Endurance* and the Imperial Trans-Antarctic Expedition of 1914.

According to legend, in 1913 Sir Ernest Shackleton posted a classified advertisement in the *London Times* reading, "Men wanted: For hazardous journey, small wages, bitter cold, long months of complete darkness, and constant danger. Safe return doubtful. Honor and recognition in case of success." According to Shackleton, that advertisement attracted over five thousand applicants, surely a sign of the times.

Following the assassination of Archduke Ferdinand earlier that year, at the beginning of August, the First World War was being declared across Europe, and with the blessing of the king and the approval to proceed from the first sea lord, the *Endurance* set sail from Plymouth, England, on its way to Buenos Aires, Argentina, to meet with the entire twenty-eight-man crew and sail south.

Shackleton was keen to win back the polar exploration crown for the empire and to be the first to transit the Antarctic from one side to the other.

The *Endurance* and her sister ship, the *Aurora*, both suffered defeat, resulting in thirty-seven of Shackleton's men being stranded at opposite ends of the continent, shipless, cold, hungry, and fighting Mother Nature herself for their survival.

This is a tale of the great age of exploration and the extraordinary journey that these men endured, not only in Antarctica but also upon their return to England amid the Great War.

This is the story of the *Endurance*, the Imperial Trans-Antarctic Expedition of 1914, and all that was happening in those extraordinary times.

REVIEWS

Cold Courage, Willy Mitchell

This is an enthralling story that successfully weaves together narratives from around the globe during the time of the Great War. The author brings out the courage, heroism, determination, and leadership of Sir Ernest Shackleton and his crew on the Imperial Trans-Antarctic Expedition from 1914 to 1917.

The official history of the British Antarctic Survey (BAS) describes this as "one of the most dramatic polar adventures." Shackleton planned to make the first crossing of the Antarctic continent, but before he reached the proposed landing point in the Weddell Sea, his ship *Endurance* was beset and crushed by sea ice. The crew finally escaped in small boats to Elephant Island, where they survived a dreadful winter living under their upturned boats.

Shackleton decided that the only way to ensure rescue was to attempt to reach South Georgia. He made the voyage with five companions across some of the roughest seas in the world in a small open lifeboat, the *James Caird*. Landing in South Georgia, he and two others had to cross the mountainous island before seeking help from the whaling station.

The Chilean government generously loaned Shackleton a small tug called *Yelcho*, in which he was able to rescue all twenty-two comrades from Elephant Island, no easy undertaking. That the entire party survived is testament to his remarkable leadership.

Your reviewer was delighted to read more about the sacrifice and steadfastness of Perce Blackborow. Perce, a young sailor from Newport Monmouthshire, South Wales, is the only person to have stowed away on an Antarctic expedition. On his discovery, he was subject to a fearful interrogation by Shackleton, who eventually allowed Perce to remain on board, working as a steward and helping the carpenter Harry McNish look after the ship's cat, Mrs. Chippy.

On reaching Elephant Island, Blackborow, the youngest of the crew, was given the honor of being first ashore.

As explained by Andrew Hemmings in his book *Secret Newport*, Perce was suffering from frostbite and had to be carried by his fellow crew members. Perce subsequently contracted gangrene, and the expedition's surgeon Macklin, assisted by McIlroy, carried out the necessary amputations.

Perce Blackborow did recover after this makeshift surgery. After spending three months in a hospital in Punta Arenas, Chile, he returned to Wales to a hero's homecoming. Perce was such a modest man that he avoided the welcome party at Newport railway station by going across the tracks and walking out the other side. He soon volunteered to join the Royal Navy but was turned down because of the lack of toes on his left foot. He was, however, accepted into the mercantile marine, where he served until 1919. He went on to become a dock boatman at the Alexandra docks, Newport, while the merchant marine was renamed the merchant navy.

It is fair to say that Perce, who received the Bronze Polar Medal, is one of Newport's heroes. He was much loved but undercelebrated in the city of his birth.

It is gratifying that Willy Mitchell in this book, *Cold Courage,* does full justice to the story of Shackleton and his crew in a vivid and readable style.

Andrew Hemmings BA (Hons), FCILT, is an author and researcher.

Powerful storytelling, which paints the epic Trans-Antarctic Expedition in context of historic milestones. This is a page-turner of note!

Alta Wehmeyer is a writing teacher, coach, and educator using her passion of all things Antarctica as the focus.

Willy Mitchell's *Cold Courage* goes beyond the bleak commentary of history and into the fascinating fantasy of human interaction.

Here we have a parallel universe of characters having their own world war, including engaging in a pub brawl with the Germans in South Georgia and playing soccer on the ice. At the same time, we glimpse loved ones back at home going about their more ordinary lives on Easter Sunday, April 1916.

I enjoyed reading this blending of fact and fiction. Any attempt by a writer to examine and illuminate the extraordinary world of polar exploration during the heroic age is to be commended.

Stephen Scott-Fawcett, FRICS, MA (Catab), is fellow of the Royal Geographical Society, a committee member of the James Caird Society (London), and editor of its academic journal. His book *The Shackleton Centenary Book* was published in 2014 by Sutherland House. He has published many articles on polar history and arranges polar conferences in the UK and elsewhere in Europe. Stephen also administers a large Facebook group, Sir Ernest H. Shackleton Appreciation Society, with 3,850 members, including many polar professionals, adventurers, and heroic age progenies.